Praise

MW00830405

"Extraordinary...Once again, the authors color-fully integrate authentic archaeological and anthropological details with a captivating story replete with romance, intrigue, mayhem, and a nail-biting climax."

— Library Journal

"It is fascinating to see how much like us these early tribesmen, and that the more things change, the more they stay the same."

— Romantic Times

People of the Owl

Also by W. Michael Gear and Kathleen O'Neal Gear

People of the Owl

The Earliest Americans
Book 1

W. Michael Gear

Kathleen O'Neal Gear

WOLFPACK
PUBLISHING
— EST 2013 —

People of the Owl
Paperback Edition
Copyright © 2024 (As Revised) W. Michael Gear and
Kathleen O'Neal Gear

Wolfpack Publishing
1707 E. Diana Street
Tampa, Florida 33609

wolfpackpublishing.com

Illustrations by Ellisa Mitchel.

Paperback ISBN 978-1-63977-685-6
eBook ISBN 978-1-63977-684-9

With special thanks to the Chamberlin Inn in Cody, Wyoming, for providing us a refuge every time we need a quiet, beautiful place to discuss the plot and characters of our next literary project.

Acknowledgments

This book was inspired by Dennis Labatt during our visits to the Poverty Point site. Every North American archaeological site should have such a dedicated and enthusiastic supervisor. We would like to thank Robert Connolly, Lisa Wright, Linda York, and Kay Corley for their assistance during our visits and for their cooperation in providing Poverty Point Objects—cooking clays —for our ongoing research in prehistoric starch, phytolith, and pollen analysis at Poverty Point.

We would especially like to acknowledge the work of Dr. Jon L. Gibson, who has dedicated so much of his life to the interpretation of Poverty Point's archaeology.

Once more, we would like to thank our longtime friend and colleague, Dr. Linda Scott Cummings, for her endless enthusiasm and pioneering ethnobotanical research. Working with us, she has recovered the first starches, pollens, and phytoliths from Poverty Point cooking clays. Now, when we say they were cooking foods like yellow lotus and little barley in the earth ovens, we can prove it. Thanks, Linda.

Nonfiction Foreword

Ask any American to name the oldest city in the United States and he might tell you St. Augustine, Florida (A. D. 1565). Among an enlightened few, the name Old Oraibi (A. D. 1240), in the Hopi Mesas, might pop up. But, with apologies to both of these places, we wish to point out that North America's oldest city was not located in Florida—or even in the Southwest—nor was it built around St. Louis, or in the fertile valleys of Ohio. Rather, to find it, you must journey to northeastern Louisiana, just outside of the small town of Epps. There, under the superb management of the state of Louisiana, you can still walk the stunning earthworks of Poverty Point, North America's first true city.

While earthen mound construction begins over six thousand years ago in North America, Poverty Point was inhabited between 3,750 and 3,350 years before present. From radiocarbon dates, most of Poverty Point's incredible earthworks were created during the last century of occupation. At its height, a permanent population of several thousand people lived on Poverty

Point's curving ridges. They traded for goods as far north as Wisconsin and Ohio. Materials were imported to Poverty Point across nearly fifteen hundred miles of Archaic wilderness.

The site itself is huge. From Lower Jackson Mound on the south to Motley Mound on the north is a little over five miles. The main earthworks cover more than four hundred acres and may contain as much as *one million cubic yards* of earth that was dug out of the ground and packed on human backs to build this leviathan. In sheer size, it would remain unmatched for another fifteen hundred years.

We agree with Jon Gibson that Poverty Point is a grand-scale projection of the human mind onto the landscape. Its form was not accidental or random, but a reflection of a shared vision of their physical as well as spiritual world, their kinship systems, and creation mythology.

A note on kinship: Non-Western societies organize their social structure in many different ways. What we see reflected in Poverty Point's architecture suggests two moieties, or social divisions, that contain three clans each. We have utilized a matrilineal matrilocal kinship system since that was present throughout the south.

Our reconstruction of prehistoric cosmology in *People of the Owl* must remain tentative, but we have looked for constants in South and Central Eastern Woodland mythology and oral tradition. We discarded elements that reflect later Mississippian—*People of the River*—agricultural traits. What is left is a shared tripartite belief in the surface of the earth, the sky above, and the underworld.

We have used real places as a setting for the story.

Poverty Point is Sun Town. The Panther's Bones is set at the Caney Mounds (site 16CT5) in Catahoula County. When Saw Back is exiled, it is to the Jaketown site in Mississippi. Twin Circles references the Clairborae Site near the mouth of the Pearl River in southern Mississippi. While we did not extensively explore distant Poverty Point settlements in *People of the Owl,* sites containing Poverty Point's distinctive artifacts have been found as far away as the Florida Gulf Coast.

So, what explains this spectacular thirty-five-hundred-year-old cultural fluorescence? These people were hunter-gatherers. Intensive corn agriculture wouldn't catch on for another two thousand years. The answer seems to lie in the richness of the Lower Mississippi Valley and its yearly floods. The people at Poverty Point ate everything that walked, crawled, swam, burrowed, and grew in their benevolent food-rich environment. In short, the Lower Mississippi Valley provided the surplus in resources that allowed remarkable cultural achievements.

In the coming years, we hope to learn a great deal more. As of this writing, one-half of one percent of the site has been excavated. In our own research with Linda Scott Cummings on Poverty Point Objects—PPOs—or cooking clays, we have recovered the first starches, phytoliths, and pollen residue from the food they cooked in their earth ovens thirty-five hundred years ago. As more research is tackled, our view of this complex site is going to change substantially. It will be important research. We believe that Poverty Point was to North America what the Fertile Crescent was to Europe: *the place that generated and disseminated cultural concepts that would influence subsequent cultures across the eastern woodlands.*

Information on the site is as close as your computer: povertypoint@crt.la.us. Jon Gibson's excellent read, *The Ancient Mounds of Poverty Point,* is available from the University Press of Florida. For an overview of the whole of North American archaeology, we recommend Brian Fagan's *Ancient North America* published by Thames and Hudson. At the end of *People of the Owl* you will find a selected bibliography. Finally, we urge you to visit the Poverty Point State Commemorative Area in person. Until you experience the wonder of it yourself, you will never fully understand the magic.

Preface

Arnold Beauregard liked to think of himself as a modern-day cowboy. His family had first come to Louisiana in the 1720s. To this day, his mother insisted to anyone who would listen that, yes, Beauregard was French, but that their ancestry was Creole. True French aristocracy rather than that Johnny-come-lately Cajun riffraff that had begun trickling into Louisiana in the 1760s.

Fact was, the clinging fingers of the past still pulled at old Louisiana families. But for Arnold, the lure was the Old West, not antebellum plantation life. In his dreams, he was a cattle baron, not a cotton king.

The SUV, a Toyota Land Cruiser, could be seen waiting just past the gate as he turned into the farm lane off Route 577. He pulled up and stopped his brand-new white Chevy one-ton behind the Toyota before shutting off its big diesel engine.

Picking up his cell, he punched the office number, and at the secretary's voice, said, "Julie, I'm at the

Hoferberg place. Those archaeologists are already here. I'll have my cell on if anything comes up."

A genuine straw Stetson was perched atop his black crew cut. The left breast pocket of his Wrangler snap shirt outlined an obligatory can of Copenhagen. A tooled-leather belt snugged his waist while six-hundred-buck Lucchese razor-tips peeked out from under his creased boot-cut jeans.

Yep. One hundred percent cowboy.

The irony, of course, was that his business was farming, not ranching. Not the actual sweating-in-the-sun-and-driving-the-tractor kind of farming, mind you, but administration.

He stepped out of the Chevy and walked toward the people climbing out of the Toyota. His first thought was to glance at his watch. If this didn't take too long, he could check on fertilization and field prep over at the Badger Unit this side of Alsatia and be back to Delphi in time for lunch.

"Mr. Beauregard?" a tall, thin man called from the Toyota's driver's side. He wore bifocals and looked about fifty, with a neatly trimmed beard and brown cotton pants. To his right stood a blond woman, medium height, perhaps thirty, in jeans, long-sleeved shift, and hiking boots. She had a pensive expression— and eyes way too intelligent to be in a face that pretty. Next to her was a grungy-looking kid, maybe twenty-five, with long, bushy brown hair pulled back in a frizzy ponytail. He had on a checked shirt, baggy pants, and running shoes that had to have been stolen off a bum on Bourbon Street.

"Call me Arnold," he answered, extending a hand. "You're from the university, right?"

"Dr. Emmet Anson," the bearded man said as he shook.

"I'm Patty Umbaugh," the pretty blonde said. "I'm with the state. Department of Culture, Recreation, and Tourism."

He smiled thinly. The state? What the hell did they have to do with this?

"Rick Penzler," the longhair told him, giving him a cool, somewhat arrogant look.

"My pleasure," Arnold answered evenly, turning this attention to Anson. "Dr. Anson, you asked for a meeting concerning the Hoferberg property. Said it had something to do with some dead Indians?"

Anson nodded. "That's right. A couple of years back we did some work on the mounds out back there." He pointed down past the house and barn toward the bayou. "Mrs. Hoferberg had talked about taking steps to protect and preserve the site. She had mentioned that when the time came to sell the property, that we might be able to come to some sort of agreement."

Arnold stuck his thumbs in his belt, saying, "I see." That bought him time while he considered. "Well, I don't know anything about any site here. The thing is, the bank foreclosed on the Hoferberg farm, Dr. Anson. Our dealings have all been through the bank when we acquired title to this property. Any questions relating to that would have to be directed to Otis, our attorney."

"Yes, we know," Patty Umbaugh said seriously. "The reason we called this meeting was to see if we could come to some agreement—with your corporation, of course—concerning the archaeology."

Arnold gave her his winning cowboy smile. "Well,

that would depend, I suppose. We'll be happy to hear what you have to say."

From the look Penzler was giving him, you would have thought Arnold had wrapped tape sticky-side-out on his fingers when the collection plate went by of a Sunday morning.

"Why don't we drive down and show you what we're talking about," Anson suggested. "It's kind of boggy down there." He glanced at the shining Chevrolet. "Want a ride?"

"This won't take long, will it?"

"Half an hour?" Anson asked, raising a hopeful eyebrow.

"Let me get my cell phone."

He stepped back to his truck, unplugged his cell, and stuffed it into his shirt pocket. By the time he walked up to the passenger door, Umbaugh and Penzler had climbed into the back. Anson was at the wheel and turned the key as Arnold slammed the passenger door.

"What do you do, Mr. Beauregard? For *BARB*, I mean?" Anson asked as they started down the tree-lined lane.

"I'm the operations supervisor. That means I drive from farm to farm, seeing to it that the local managers are doing their jobs and that everything is running smoothly. I act as the corporation's eyes and ears in the field. Rambling troubleshooter and problem solver." He chuckled as he pulled out his Copenhagen and took a dip. "I guess you'd say that I'm the feller that makes the machine run."

"What does *BARB* stand for?" Prenzler asked flatly. "What does it do?"

At the tone in Prenzler's voice, Arnold fought the urge to crane his neck and spit snoose on the kid's filthy shoes. "It's short for Brasseaux, Anderson, Roberts, and Beauregard. We're the board. We buy up bankrupt family farms in northern Louisiana and southern Arkansas, recondition the soil, and make them pay. Our equipment is stored and serviced at our shop several miles east of Monroe. In all, BARB runs more than six hundred thousand acres of agricultural property."

He smiled down, admiring his expensive boots. If truth be told, neither BARB nor Arnold even owned a cow. Still, he never missed a rodeo, and his daughter, Mindy, had a beautiful barrel horse that she kept in the stable at their elegant house north of Monroe.

"Take this place." Arnold flipped his index finger around in a circle. "We'll have a crew in here next week to take out these trees." He waved expansively at the lines of stately oaks that shaded the lane.

"Take out the trees?" Penzler asked incredulously.

"And these buildings." Arnold nodded at the white-frame house and shabby-looking barn as they drove into the yard. They stood empty now, looking forlorn. "Our crew will salvage what we can from the structures, anything we can sell for scrap. Then we'll bulldoze the rest."

"Why?" Umbaugh asked, concern in her voice. She was looking longingly at the old red barn, its huge door open to expose an empty gloom.

"Miss, uh, Patty did you say? You gotta understand. This house and barn, these trees, shucks, even this lane we're driving on, isn't in production. The margin in American agriculture is about as thin as a skeeter's peter. It's because in this country we have the cheapest and best food in the whole world. At the same time, urban sprawl and development is taking millions of acres a year out of production. At BARB we grow food, and we're good enough at it that we can still make money."

"Six hundred *thousand* acres?" Penzler asked hostilely as Anson passed the barn and followed a two-track between two large fallow fields. A quarter mile ahead, trees rose in a gray thicket, barely starting to bud in the late-March warmth.

Arnold couldn't stand it. He turned, letting his gaze bore into the squirrely kid's cold blue eyes. "You might ask Mrs. Hoferberg how much she made on this place these last few years. This farm has just over a thousand acres of good land under cultivation. Mrs. Hoferberg was sixth-generation—going clear back to the civil war. Hell, her great-great-great-granddad waved to U. S. goddamned Grant when he went by on his way to Vicksburg. The family farm just can't cut it in a global economy."

"So you plow it all up?" Penzler asked.

"Productivity drives the country," Anson said easily. "Myself, I'm not so sure I wouldn't rather just go back to the good old days. Fish, hunt, raise a few cows, and grow a garden. Life would be so much simpler."

"Suits me," Anson said easily as he skirted the fallow field.

"You hunt, huh?" Arnold glanced at the bookish-looking Anson.

The professor smiled. "Hey, I grew up in Melville, down on the Atchafalaya. When I wasn't running a trotline, I was after ducks or rabbits with my old 20-

gauge. Went to Harvard on scholarship, so I had to lose the accent."

Arnold nodded. "What got you into archaeology?"

"Hunting and fishing," Anson said with amusement. "I wanted to know how people made food before John Deere and Cargill."

Anson followed an overgrown track into the trees, dropped down through a marshy area, and up over a hump of dirt. Pulling to a stop, he looked around and shut off the engine. "This is it."

Arnold opened the door and stepped out. Overhead, branches wove a gray maze against the cloud-speckled March sky. Irregular humps in the land could be seen. It reminded him of a brown, leaf-covered golf course. "What am I supposed to be seeing here?"

Umbaugh stepped up beside him, pointing to the contours of land. "This is a Poverty Point period mound site. It dates to about thirty-five hundred years ago."

"Poverty Point?" Arnold cocked his head and spit some of the Copenhagen floaters onto the damp leaves. "Like the state park down the road a piece?"

"That's right. Have you been there? Seen the museum and earthworks?"

"Naw. I just drive through. It's old Indian stuff, isn't it? You seen one pile of dirt, you've seen them all. I mean, hey, they ain't coming back."

He could sense Penzler's blood beginning to foam.

Anson walked around the front of the Toyota. "Personally, I wish they would. I've got a half a lifetime's full of questions to ask."

"Like what?" Arnold followed Anson up onto the low embankment of earth and looked around. For all the world, it appeared to him like old levees and meander bottoms.

Anson had a curious gleam behind his bifocals. "The pyramids were new when these people built the first city in North America. You're in agriculture, you can understand the problem, Mr. Beauregard. How do you build a city like Poverty Point, organize the labor to move over one million cubic yards of earth, and do it without agriculture?"

"What do you mean, without agriculture? You gotta have agriculture. Tell me how you're gonna be Bill Gates and invent computers when you're out for half a day hunting and fishing for each meal."

"Tell me indeed," Anson agreed. "But they did it. Right here in northern Louisiana, they created a miracle." He turned, waving his arm in a circle. "Everything started here. It's Egypt and Babylon. Moses and Ramses. I can feel it in my bones."

"God, here he goes again," Penzler muttered, walking off a stone's throw to study the low mounds.

When he was out of earshot, Arnold asked, "Why is he here?"

Anson's lips bent in amusement. "He's finishing his Ph.D. on Poverty Point trade relationships. He's got this idea of interlocking clan territories regulated by the redistribution of resources." Seeing Arnold's look of incomprehension, he added. "Like groups of relatives that trade back and forth to keep the family together. That sort of thing, but on a larger scale."

"What was that bit about Egypt and Moses? What's that got to do with Louisiana?"

"It's the same period of time." Anson pointed at the low earthworks. "Sure, these people didn't build huge cities of stone. They didn't leave us records of their leaders or their laws. But they did something that the Egyptians, the Babylonians, the Hittites, and all of their Old World contemporaries didn't."

"What was that?"

"Back before the first Pharaoh even thought of a pyramid, the people at Poverty Point put together a cross-continental trading system. But their most important gift to the future was an idea."

"Or so you think," Patty Umbaugh chided. Glancing at Arnold, she said. "We've barely scratched the surface here. We haven't even investigated a tenth of a percent of the archaeological sites in Louisiana. If Dr. Anson is right, we're sitting on a wealth of revelations about these people."

Arnold cocked his jaw, considered, and asked point-blank. "What is your interest in our farm? So far as I know, this site is on private property."

Umbaugh nodded. "Yes, Mr. Beauregard, it is. Louisiana has over seven hundred mound sites that we know about. Hundreds more that we don't. Perhaps thousands have been destroyed by field leveling, and others have been hauled away over the years for highway fill, causeways, and levees. We would like to work with you in the preservation of this site. We have programs—"

"Yeah, yeah, I know about government *programs*. It sounds so good. 'We're from the government, we're here to help you.' Next time you turn around, you're in noncompliance with some damn thing. That, or some EPA or OSHA asshole is poking his nose up your bohungus to certify your fertilizer, or check the green cards on the hired help, or the frogs are being born with too many legs, or some damned thing."

"I know, but our program—"

"With all due respect, Ms. Umbaugh"—he gave her the ingratiating smile again—"we would like to politely refuse your help."

"Well," she said with a sigh, "thank you for at least letting me come and see the site. I'll leave you a card, and if you ever have any questions—"

"Yeah, right, I'll call."

Anson turned, head tilted. "Mr. Beauregard, I can sure understand your attitude about the government."

"You can?"

Anson nodded. "Out of fear of the government, some of the most important mounds in the state have been bulldozed by worried landowners."

"They must have snapped those guys' butts right into court before they could grab their hats."

"It was private property," Anson replied laconically. "Just like your farm here. I'd hope that we've all learned our lesson. You see, the reason we're here is that you are the legal owner of this site. We want to let you know what you have here, and why it is important."

"What's it worth?" he asked absently, squinting at the mounds of dirt. Just at rough guess, he figured it at about ten thousand cubic yards.

"Worth?" Anson shrugged. "In dollars, not much. But when it comes to information—to the questions we can answer—it's priceless. This is a satellite site, an outlier tied to the Poverty Point site a little ways up Bayou Macon." He pointed to the thicket of trees that dropped off toward the muddy bayou no more than fifty yards beyond the brush.

Patty Umbaugh said, "We have a registry of sites—"

"Nope!" Arnold shook his head categorically. "First you register it, then every tourist in the damned world wants to trespass on your property to see it, and some government bureaucrat wants to tell you how to run it." He waved a finger. "The answer is no. Period."

She looked pissed, but he had to hand it to her, she did a good job of covering.

Anson rubbed his jaw. "If you don't want to work with the state to preserve the site, that's fine. Would you mind, however, if we brought field school students up from time to time to dig here? Everything that we find belongs to you, of course. You can keep the artifacts here, or at your corporate headquarters, or we would be happy to curate them at the university."

Arnold rolled his lip over his chew and slowly shook his head. "I don't think so, Dr. Anson. First off, there's liability to think about. What if one of your students fell and broke his neck, or some such thing? Or they snuck in at night to dig for arrowheads? And third, sure, BARB might own this site free and clear now, but who's to say what's gonna happen in the future? I heard tell of folks got taken to court over down by Lake Charles by some Injun group over a burial ground. We don't need those kinds of headaches."

Anson looked as if he were about to throw up. "But you will preserve the site, right?"

Arnold smiled. Hell, cowboys and Indians never did get along together. "Yeah, well, we'll take it under consideration. Like I said, either we're efficient, or well, just like your Indians. Extinct."

Arnold squinted in the midday sun. The soft Gulf breeze blew up from the southwest. It sent puffy clouds sailing across the sky and brought the promise of afternoon rains. The big yellow Caterpillar growled and roared as it dropped the rippers and rolled a sweetgum stump out of the damp black soil. The roots popped and snapped like firecrackers.

The Hoferberg farm was unrecognizable now. The old oak trees that had shaded the lane had been cut down and sold for lumber. The house and barn, the foundation, the cisterns, and outbuildings had been flattened or plucked up with the backhoe and trucked off. Where the trees had somberly guarded the archaeological site, now an unrestricted view of the Bayou Macon could be seen. Only the canebrakes under the slope of Macon Ridge remained standing.

Arnold had made a special effort to be here for the leveling. He'd never seen an archaeological site until Dr. Anson brought him here. And he sure as hell had never seen one scraped flat before. So he was curious. As the Cat cut great swaths through the mounds, he walked along with his cup of black coffee—because real cowboys drank it that way—in his hand. He spat his Copenhagen every now and then, and looked at the black dirt.

Most of Macon Ridge was a tan-brown loess, a silt blown clear down from the last glaciers up north. But the dirt in and around the mounds was crankcase-dripping black. Every now and again, he had picked up one of the oddly shaped clay balls—finding them the perfect weight to fling out into the bayou—and wondered what the Indians had used them for.

Little flat flakes of stone came up, and yes, he had even found a gray-stone arrowhead a while back. He had wanted to find an arrowhead just as much as he wanted to see Indian bones come rolling out of the ground, but the rich, loamy soil seemed against him on that one. All in all, there wasn't much exciting to see. So how, then, could that Dr. Anson have spouted all that nonsense about ideas, and trade, and all the rest?

Out by the highway, the big John Deere 9000s, brought in on flatbeds, were already starting their runs. By noon tomorrow, the whole of Hoferberg farm would be disked, harrowed, fertilized, and ready for the trucks bringing the seed drills.

Arnold shook his head, disappointed at the bulldozing. He had expected something a bit more entertaining than featureless black dirt rolling under the blade. He looked again at the gray-stone arrowhead—a big thing, as long as his finger—and slipped it into his pocket as he turned to walk back to his truck. Glancing at his watch, he could still meet Harvey Snodgrass at the Delphi café and show off his arrowhead.

He was watching his razor-toed cowboy boots as they pressed into the damp black earth. The light brown polish looked so clean and fresh against the dirt. That's when the gleam caught his eye. He bent, reaching down past some of the endless, oddly shaped clay balls, and picked up a little red stone.

With his thumb, he cleaned the clinging dirt away and stared in surprise. It was a carving. A little red potbellied stone owl. Something about it reminded him of a barred owl.

Arnold was more than a little intimate with barred owls, having shot his first one when he was fifteen. Not content just to leave it lay, he'd dragged it home to show off to his friends. Someone called the warden. But for quick work with a shovel, they'd have caught him with that owl. It had been closer than a skeeter's peter.

Turning the little red owl, he could almost believe that the craftsman who'd made it had carved a mask on the face. A masked owl? What did that mean?

Thing was, he couldn't call up that Dr. Anson and ask. It wasn't as if they'd parted on good company.

"Sorry," he told the little owl. "Reckon your home had to go. Trees got to go down and crops got to go in. People can't live without farming. It's the future, little guy."

He opened the door on his shiny new pickup, and paused, studying the little owl one last time before he put it in his pocket. "It's not like your Indians are coming back."

Thunder roared so close it was deafening. Arnold jerked his head up to stare at the sky.

The lightning bolt flashed white-blue, the *clap-bang!* startling the soul half out of Jose Rodriguez's body where he sat at the Caterpillar's controls.

"Madre de dios!"

With the afterimage of the flash still burning behind his eyes, Jose leaped from his idling Cat, and ran. He reached Arnold within moments. Rolling him over, Josh got his second fright for the day. The lightning bolt had done horrible things to Arnold's head.

"Blessed Mother," he whispered and backed away.

Jose glanced at the tiny red owl that lay in the soil inches from Arnold's fingers. It glinted in the storm light like a glaring eye.

Jose crossed himself, then he stumbled for the open driver's door of Arnold's pickup. The cell phone was fried. He had to get to a phone. Fast! As he cranked the wheel and sped away, the rear tires pressed the little red owl back into the rich black soil.

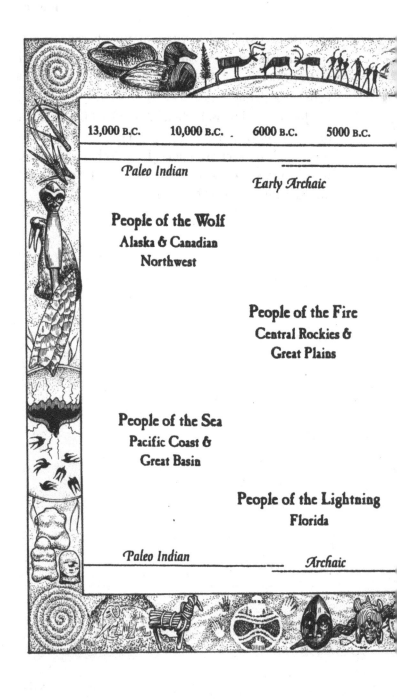

13,000 B.C.	10,000 B.C.	6000 B.C.	5000 B.C.

Paleo Indian

Early Archaic

People of the Wolf
Alaska & Canadian
Northwest

People of the Fire
Central Rockies &
Great Plains

People of the Sea
Pacific Coast &
Great Basin

People of the Lightning
Florida

Paleo Indian

Archaic

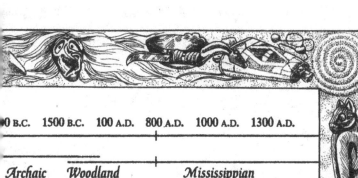

0 B.C.	1500 B.C.	100 A.D.	800 A.D.	1000 A.D.	1300 A.D.

Archaic   *Woodland*   *Mississippian*

People of the Earth   **People of the Mist**
  Northern Plains   Chesapeake Bay
    & Basins

                          People of the River
                            Mississippi Valley

              People of the Masks
                  Ontario &
              Upstate New York

              People of the Lakes
              East Central Woodlands
                  & Great Lakes

                          People of the Silence
  People of the Owl   Southwest Anasazi
  Lower Mississippi
      Valley

        Basketmaker
                          Pueblo

W

S

N

NORTH

E

to Ground Cherry Camp

Dying Sun Mound

Raised Causeway

Rattlesnake Clan

Eagle Clan

Snapping Turtle Clan

Southern Moiety

Pine Drops House

Men's House

Morning Lake

Turtle's Back

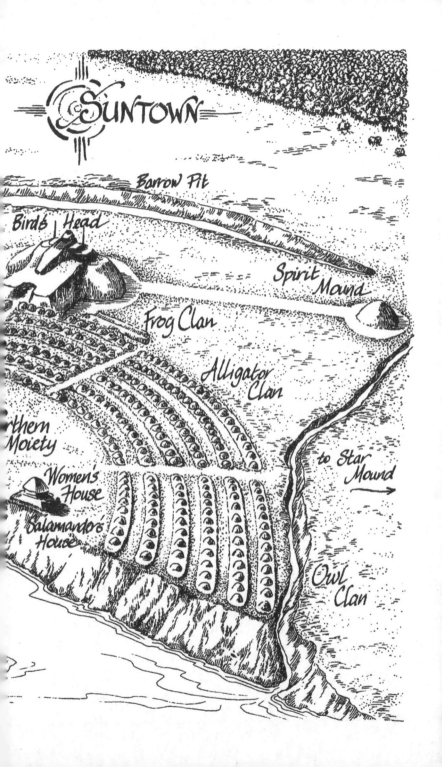

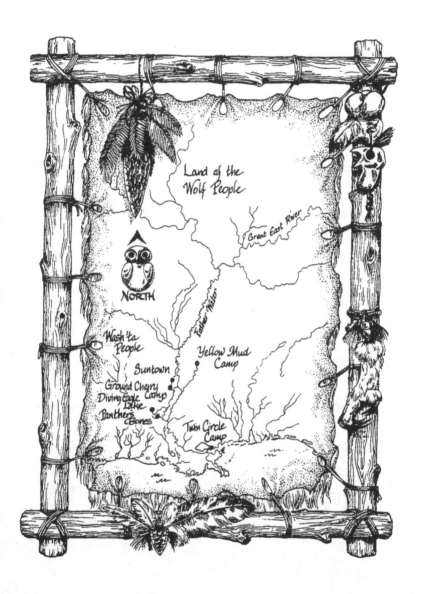

Land of the
Wolf People

Great East River

NORTH

Father Water

Wash'ta
People

Yellow Mud
Camp

Suntown

Ground Cherry
Camp
Diving Eagle
Lake
Panther's
Bones

Twin Circle
Camp

People of the Owl

Prologue

From the shadowed mouth of her cave, old Heron stared out past the Tree of Life. Another in the endless cycles passed as the winter broke and the old Dance started again.

In the far north, the strengthening spring sun released moisture from the winter-banked snows. At the same time, warm winds blew glistening silver bands of rain up from the gulf to fall on the awakening forests. Freshets added their contribution to the flood as it swelled, rippling like flexed muscles along the great rivers that fed the Father Water.

The waters flowed, draining the continent, swirling and breaching the banks, cutting crevasses through the levees. In places it rerouted the wide span, changing its course, dissecting backswamps and meanders. Where it rushed, soils were scoured, and old glacial gravels were lifted and carried along, pattering like hail down the worn channel. In other places, the water slowed, dropping its load of fine silt. It was ancient—this dance of *movement and renewal—the majestic pumping heartbeat of the continent.*

As it neared the gulf, the great river slowed and spread its bounty over the wide, tree-choked floodplain. There, hemmed by a ridge of glacial dust on the west and ancient eroded hills to the east, the waters disgorged their final rich bounty of silt and sand before filtering down to the crystal blue gulf.

Limpid brown water inundated the backswamps, rising around the trees. Silt settled slowly. It swirled when churned by silver-sided chad, suckers, and long gar; aquatic insects burrowed through its brown blanket. Crawfish hunted those still depths, picking through the muck with delicate claws—alert for the ever-prowling catfish, heron, or bass. Cypress and tupelo swelled, their leaves lush, while prop roots sucked nutrients from the renewed mud. The flood was life, rebirth.

The old woman sharpened her gaze. She tilted her head, hearing the faint voice rising and falling. "Yes, I hear you. Where are you, boy?"

Extending her hand, she could feel tendrils of Power being gathered, manipulated.

"The Brothers," she whispered. "They're at it again. Always fighting."

They were old adversaries, those two. Day and night, order and chaos, they remained inextricably bound yet opposed, creations from the dawn of time. In this place, for this latest duel, they had taken the form of birds: one white, a silent hunter of the night breezes, the other black, a raucous creature of the sun-drenched sky.

She could feel the tension between them rolling out of the future. A lonely boy's voice called out, caught at the point where their lines of Power collided.

Another of their endless contests was approaching, borne across the still evening waters on four slim canoes. How would it end this time?

Chapter One

Dark clouds slipped soundlessly across the sky as night fell. The faintest glow could be made out in the periodic breaks between the flooded trees. The lead canoe sailed silently forward, driven by the fatigued strokes of two young men. Unease reflected in the youths' dark eyes. Behind them, brown water rippled in the expanding V of their wake. It licked at the trunks of bitter pecan and water oak, then lapped against pioneer stands of sweetgum, hackberry, and ash that rose above the backswamp.

In the dusky shadows, three more slim vessels followed, the occupants silently paddling their craft. On occasion, they glanced warily about at the hanging beards of moss, at the silvered webs spun by hand-sized yellow spiders, and at the clinging mass of vines. Occasionally a copperhead draped from a water-crested branch.

"White Bird, are you sure you know where you are going?" a young paddler called from the second boat.

He spoke in the language of the river—a Trade pidgin that had grown over generations.

"I know these backswamps as surely as you know the twists and turns of your forests back home, Hazel Fire. Trust me." White Bird blinked his eyes where he sat in the rear of the lead canoe with his back pressed hard against the matting that cushioned the concave stern. He had hoped to be home by nightfall. Ahead of him, Yellow Spider's paddle moved mechanically, his arms as tired and loose-jointed as White Bird's own.

"I don't blame them for being nervous." Yellow Spider scratched at a chigger bite on his calf. "It is a frightening thing, being cast loose in so much water, never knowing which way you are going. Remember how we felt in their country?"

Twelve long moons had passed since they had struck north, following the winding course of the Father Water, keeping to the backwaters, avoiding the river's current as they battled their way upstream. By the fall equinox, they had landed their canoe in the far northern country of the Wolf People.

Trade was old, but it was mostly conducted between peoples, or by solitary Traders in canoes who traveled the rivers. The key was the river system that linked the huge continental interior. Copper from the great northern lakes, special chert from Flint Ridge in the northeast, soapstone from the eastern mountains, and hematite from the northwest were but a few of the exotic Trade items prized by the Sun People. But goods moved slowly and in a trickle. The farther a person traveled from the source, the more valuable the Trade was. The farther a Trader traveled, the less likely he would have the items he started with. The

Power of Trade was that items be Traded at each stop.

White Bird and Yellow Spider had tried a different tack. They had carefully avoided the River Peoples, often traveling by night, on their journey northward. Upon their arrival, with their Trade intact, they elected to spend the winter. That meant freezing and shivering in the Wolf People's thatch-sided huts while snow twirled out of the cold gray skies, and frigid winds moaned through the naked trees. In that time they had traded judiciously, offering their beautifully dyed textiles, their basswood rope and cordage, small sections of alligator hide, and necklaces made of the beast's teeth and claws. They had pitched in with the hunting, packing firewood, and generally making themselves useful. Both had struggled to learn as much of the language as they could. As honored guests, each had been provided with a young woman, and by the time of their departure, their wives had begun to swell with children.

"These women," the chief had told them, "they do not wish to go south and live with strangers. Their families, clans, and people are here. They will be here when you come back."

Their Trade had been wildly successful. So much so that the piles of goods stacked in their small hut would have overflowed their single canoe. In the end, it had taken all of White Bird's guile, the promise of immense wealth, and the gift of half of his profits, to talk three additional canoes into accompanying them south.

With the breaking of the river ice, White Bird, Yellow Spider, and the Wolf Traders had loaded their canoes and slipped them into the frigid current. The descent of the river had taken but two moons, a third the time needed to paddle upstream. Nor had the journey been as dangerous, their travel time through potentially hostile country being shorter, their numbers larger and more threatening to potential raiders.

As they neared the end of the long voyage, their narrow craft were stacked gunwale high with fabric sacks that contained the winter's Trade: chipped stone blanks, copper beads, thin sections of ground slate, polished greenstone celts, and adzes. In addition, they had large winter hides from buffalo, elk, and a highly prized hide from the great silver bear. Smaller prime hides came from beaver, northern bobcat, mink, and marten. One hide, traded from the far north, came from something called a carcajou—an animal they had never seen—but the fur was black, lustrous, and soft. Other pouches contained herbs and medicinal plants: wild licorice for sore throats, alum root for diarrhea, gay-feather for heart and urinary problems, puccoon for wounds, menstrual problems, and to stay awake, mint for tea, the relief of gas, and stomach problems, yucca root for joint soreness and a laxative, and coneflower for toothaches.

But in White Bird's mind, the most important thing he carried was the fabric sack of goosefoot seeds that rested between his feet. That was the journey's greatest prize. And for that, he would gamble everything. What would the People do for a man who offered them the future?

"I thought we would be there by now," Yellow Spider muttered, banking his paddle long enough to roll his muscular shoulders.

"The cut across from the crevasse is longer than you remember." White Bird smiled. "Besides, if you will recall, we were fresh and excited when we left here last spring."

"And the backswamp is deeper," Yellow Spider added. "Look at this." He gestured at the high water ringing the trees. "Fishing must be more difficult this spring with such deep water. People will be adding on to their nets. We should have gone northwest for ironstone. Given the depth of the water and the size of the nets needed to fish these currents, net sinkers will be in demand."

"We did fine." White Bird tapped the sack of goose-foot seed with his foot. "Besides, had we gone northwest, the mountain people wouldn't have provided their women. Not like those Wolf People." He paused thoughtfully as he stroked with his paddle. "I, for one, will miss Lark. She kept the robes more than warm."

As Yellow Spider picked up his paddle, White Bird rested his across the gunwales and rolled his weary shoulders. Fatigue ran from his fingers, up his arms, and into the middle of his back. His belly had run empty long ago, as though nothing but hunger lay behind the corded muscles. An image of Lark flashed in his head. He remembered the sparkle in her eyes that first night when she had crawled into his bed. If he closed his eyes, he could almost feel her hands tracing the swell of his chest and the ripple of muscle that led down past his navel. Her gasp of delight as she reached down to grip his manhood lingered in his ears.

"Yes," he whispered into the stillness of the swamp, "I shall miss you, Lark." In his nineteen turning of seasons, he had never had a full-time woman before.

The notion that she had been waiting every time he returned to their cozy home had grown on him. She was a strange one, true, raised as she was by a different people with different gods and peculiar beliefs, but she had been pretty, devoted to him, and always there. Rot take it, a man could get used to living like that.

"I wouldn't worry," Yellow Spider said smugly as he ducked a clump of hanging moss. "Your mother probably has a whole string of women lined up for you. Not only are you worthy—as our return will prove—but you're in line to replace your uncle." He hesitated tactfully. "If you haven't already."

"Uncle Cloud Heron will be fine. Owl help me if he isn't."

Yellow Spider laughed. "Oh, stop it. You'll be a better Speaker for the clan than anyone I know. You have a way about you, White Bird. A calm assurance that no one else has. People can't help but like you. Look at how we did up north. Look at the return we got. How are you going to explain that you gave half of your Trade to these barbarians?"

"Watch your tongue." White Bird shot a quick look back over his shoulder. "You never know if any of them have been learning our language. Lark and Robin were learning it quickly enough."

"I was just thinking how much I miss that Robin." Yellow Spider sighed. "Somehow, I think the clan is going to marry me off quick as a snap. Who knows whom they'll pick for me." He paused. "Unlike you. Or are you sorry that Lark isn't in your canoe instead of me?"

"Come on, Cousin. Think! Lark and Robin belong up there. That's where their families are. They'd be strangers here, cast loose without kin of any kind. And you're right. The clan will have you married to at least one other woman, perhaps two, within the turning of seasons."

Yellow Spider lowered his voice. "Do you think Spring Cypress is a woman yet?"

White Bird shrugged. "If she is, she may be married already." Did his voice cloak the sudden sense of worry? She'd begun her fourteenth summer when he and Yellow Spider had left for the north. But for a late menstruation, she'd have been married—most girls were by that age.

"I talked to Spring Cypress before I left. It was a risk we had to take. Even if she passed her moon, her uncle, Speaker Clay Fat, could have been persuaded to wait."

"Or not, as the case may be."

"Are you always so gloomy?"

"No, I'm just connected to this world. You, my cousin, live in another. Take those seeds you're so enamored of. Goosefoot is goosefoot. We have our own. Why invest in someone else's?"

"Because these seeds are twice as big as ours."

"If they'll even grow here." Yellow Spider smashed a mosquito that managed to penetrate the grease he'd smeared on his skin. "The dirt's different."

"Dirt's dirt."

"Shows what you know. And the seasons are different. It doesn't get as cold here. Maybe those seeds are just like ours and...and it's the cold that makes them get that big."

"Trust me."

Yellow Spider nodded in the shadowy half-light

that penetrated the canopy of trees and filtered through the hanging moss and vines. "To be sure, Cousin. I've trusted you this far, and look where it has gotten me. I am coming home with the most successful Trading venture ever. Not just a canoeful of goods, but four! We own the world, Cousin!"

White Bird smiled into the increasing darkness. They did indeed own the world. No matter that the Wolf Traders considered half of their canoes' contents to be theirs, the fact was that it would all end up being spread among the clans. The credit would be his. People would listen to him. His influence would maintain his clan's position, and if anything, add to Owl Clan's prestige. The seeds at his feet were the next step in changing the people, making them greater than they had ever been.

Suffused with the glow of success, he barely heard the whisper of wings in the darkness as an owl circled above, charting their progress.

Chapter Two

Jaguar Hide had come to his name from the spotted yellow hide he continually wore. He had been but a spare youth, running for his life, when he'd fled to the south. In a leaky canoe, he had traveled along the coast, avoiding the grease-smeared tribesmen who lurked in the salt marshes. After being plagued by mosquitoes and salt-cracked skin for several moons he had found safety in the tropical forests. There, attached to a small band of tribesmen—refugees like himself—he had lived for four long turning of seasons, learning their various languages and living hand to mouth.

The day he had tracked the great spotted cat had changed his Power, changed his life. That morning he'd followed the cat's tracks, seeing where the paws pressed so delicately into the mud. The forest had swallowed him as though to digest him in a universe of green. Water had dripped from the palmetto and mahogany.

He and the jaguar had seen each other at the same moment. In that instant of locked eyes, he had seen his death—and refused to meet it. As he extended his arm to cast, the jaguar leaped. The dart nocked in his atlatl might have been an extension of his Dream Soul, so straight did it fly. He was still staring into those hard yellow eyes as the fletched dart drove half of its length into the great cat.

The animal's flying impact sent him rolling across the forest litter, but the cat's attention had centered on the stinging length of wood protruding from the base of its throat. The first swipe of its paws had snapped the shaft. Thereafter, the frantic clawing did nothing more than tear the splintered shaft sideways in the wound. Great gouts of blood pumped with each of the cat's heartbeats.

When the jaguar finally flopped onto its side in the trail, their gazes remained joined. The cat's strength drained with each bloody exhalation. To the end, the claws extended and retracted, as though in the cat's brain, it was rending the man's flesh. He watched the pupils enlarge as the cat's raspy breathing slowed. He was still staring, partially panicked by fear, when the animal's Dream Soul was exhaled through those blood-caked nostrils, and having nowhere else to go, entered his own body.

Later that night, in a rain-drenched camp, he had squatted under a palmetto lean-to and eaten the cat's meat. He could remember the blue haze of rain-slashed smoke. He could still smell it and taste the sweet meat in his mouth. Jaguar's Power had penetrated his heart and wound its way around his souls.

The frightened youth he had been was eaten that night—consumed by the jaguar's Power. The next morning, he had stridden forth a different man, and begun the long journey north, alternately canoeing and portaging the sandbars that blocked the salt marshes. He had returned to his people, and with the Power of the jaguar in his blood, he had destroyed his old enemies, taken five wives, and closed his fingers around his people until they all fit within his grasp.

That had been tens of seasons ago. No longer young, he looked up at the soot-stained roof of the cramped house he now crouched in. Spiderwebs, like bits of moss, wavered in the heat waves rising from the low-banked fire. Before him, on a cane mat, lay his nephew, young Bowfin, wounded and dying as evil spirits ate his guts out. The boy's sister, Anhinga, crouched beside him, and the mother, Jaguar Hide's sister, Yellow Dye, balanced on her feet, her chin on her knees as she sobbed softly.

In his mind's eye, Jaguar Hide could see himself: Gray hair had been pulled into a tight bun on the back of his head and pinned with a stingray spine. His old jaguar hide, once so bright yellow, now lay hairless over his shoulder, the smeared skin tattered in places, shiny from wear in others. The turning of seasons had treated the hide no better than they had him.

A fabric loincloth sported the design of a spotted cat on the front and rear flaps where they hung from the waist thong. His brown skin, weathered from sun, cold, and storm, was puckered here and there with scars. It had lost its supple elasticity and turned flaky, grainy with age and loose on his wiry muscles. He still had his bones, big and blocky, a frame that had once given him a rare strength among men. The muscles, however, had faded with the turning of seasons until now he was but a gnarly shadow of himself.

He knotted his bony fist. If he were young again, he would show them. He would pay them back for this.

"Elder?" the young man on the mat croaked. Dried blood mottled his sweat-shiny skin. He raised a trembling hand. Jaguar Hide took it in his own, feeling how cold it was, how weak. He forced himself to ignore the rising stench that came from the wound and curled around his head.

"Save your breath, Bowfin. You need to regain your strength, then we will go back and teach that filth a thing or two about invading our territory."

The young man swallowed hard, his eyes shining in the firelight. Jaguar Hide watched as the pupils expanded ever wider, knowing that gray darkness was flooding the warrior's vision. Holding his dying nephew's cold hand, Jaguar Hide could sense the life going out of him. He felt Bowfin's heart slow, weaken, skip, and stop. With the shallow breathing at the end, the vile odor was no longer pumped from his punctured gut. Jaguar Hide's skin prickled as the young man's Life Soul slipped out through his open mouth and rose. He could imagine it as it drifted to the door, caressed Yellow Dye where she sat at the opening in the thatch, and slipped out into the darkness above the hut.

"He's dead." Jaguar Hide placed young Bowfin's hand on his still chest. Yellow Dye bit off a sob as she fled through the low doorway into the night, where her son's Life Soul now hovered like a bat.

"Uncle?" Anhinga knelt next to him, staring curiously at Bowfin's vacant eyes. The boy lay naked, his body bathed in firelight. The wound in his belly gaped open under the rib cage. "Can't the Serpent save him? Call his souls back to the body? He has already tried to

suck out the evil the Sun People shot into him, but..."
She pointed at the clotted blood on the boy's side.

Jaguar Hide had watched as the Serpent, the old
medicine Dreamer, had punctured the boy's skin with a
sharp chert flake. Then the white-haired elder had bent
down, using a clay tube to suck at the blood in an effort
to draw the evil from the body. No amount of piercing
and sucking or smoking with medicine herbs had stilled
the fever or the ever-stronger stench rising from the
wound.

"Sometimes, Niece, nothing can be done."

They had come here from the big settlement—a
circular complex of clan houses and seven mounds
called the Panther's Bones—to the western margins of
their territory in response to reports that the Sun People
were raiding again.

They constantly tried to sneak into Swamp Panther
territory and quarry the valuable deposits of sandstone
in the western ridges. Jaguar Hide's arrival at Raccoon
Camp had coincided with young Bowfin being
wounded by the skulking raiders.

"I don't agree, Uncle." She was glaring at him, eyes
hard.

"I meant about Bowfin." He leaned back on his
haunches and studied her. Firelight shot gold through
her long black hair and accented the hollows of her
cheeks. She had a straight nose and perfect mouth. The
past fifteen winters had shaped the little girl he had
once known into a most attractive woman. She was
fully budded now, with high breasts, a slim waist, and
rounded hips leading into long, sleek legs. He understood the fire in her eyes, felt it himself as he looked at
the dead warrior.

17

"It is *our* land. He was *my* brother!" Anhinga whispered passionately, her fist clenched. "Why do they come here?"

"For the stone," he answered simply. "Stealing it is far more exciting...and a great deal cheaper than dealing with us."

Bowfin made a gurgling sound. As the dead man's gut hissed, clots of black blood, white pus, and intestinal juice leaked out. Anhinga clamped her nose with her fingers. Jaguar Hide could see the crystal shine of tears as they crept past her eyelids. The shaking of her shoulders betrayed her an instant before the first sobs broke her lips.

Jaguar Hide ignored the stench. "He was just defending our territory. Remember that, girl. Remember what you see here."

"Bowfin?" Anhinga cried as she turned away.

Jaguar Hide watched the girl's muscles tense as she fought to control grief. She was twisting the knotted fringes of her short skirt, her beautiful face tortured.

He stood slowly, reached down, and pulled her to her feet. "We have tried to keep them away. It would seem as though their gods favor them, for they grow as numerous as the trees. Now they are building their huge earthworks, as if they are to become gods themselves."

Through a grief-tightened throat, she choked out, "They are malignant spirits, Uncle. I would destroy them if I could."

He studied her speculatively. The wound in her souls was raw and bleeding. Pain had mixed with anger, seething, burning, consuming. *My, such passion for a woman just coming into her own.*

"One day," she continued, "I will become our leader, and when I do, I will take war to the Sun People and destroy them."

This brought a crooked smile to Jaguar's old lips. "Do you think I didn't try just that?"

"But this time—"

"You will be defeated, just as I was."

"He was my brother." She pointed at Bowfin's corpse, ignoring the fact that his Dream Soul was still watching her from those wide, glassy eyes. "Uncle, we cannot allow this to happen. Not anymore. This is a disgrace! To Bowfin, to our clan, to you and me. All of us!"

"Yes. It is. But the Sun People cannot be defeated by war."

"Then how?" she demanded. "You tell me, and by the Panther's blood, I will destroy them!"

"Will you, girl?" The amused smile remained on his lips. He fought the urge to laugh aloud as she ducked under the low doorway and stomped off into the night.

Your mother is going to have her hands full controlling you. She was very different than her older brother, Striped Dart. She had never had the relationship with him that she'd had with the personable Bowfin. If any of Yellow Dye's children had to die, too bad it couldn't have been Striped Dart. When he heard about little Bowfin, he would posture, stomp, and curse, and do nothing. The fires of life hadn't hardened him like it had others.

So, what are you going to do, old man? What will become of your people when you die and your nephew takes over?

In the darkness, he glimpsed the midnight-colored crow that circled on silent wings above him.

The clamor gave Mud Puppy his first hint that something was happening. He lay quietly on the cane mat, a small ceramic jar cupped upside down in his hand. The glow from the central hearth illuminated the inside of his house with a reddish hue, the light so dim that the cricket's natural wariness should be lulled. The beast had been chirping under the split-cane floor matting. Rather than tear it up, it was much better to let the fire die down and coax the cricket into stepping out. Then he'd catch it.

Mud Puppy turned his head, listening to the calls on the still night. Excited, yes. Panicked, no. Therefore, whatever it was, he would eventually hear about it. Everything came with time.

That attitude drove his mother to distraction. She was Wing Heart, the Clan Elder, or leader—the most important woman in the world. It wasn't that he wanted to disappoint her, he just didn't act the way she wanted him to. He couldn't. That simple reality made her half-frantic with frustration. He suspected that she loved him in spite of the way he was.

"Just once, can't you be like your brother? White Bird is the kind of man our clan needs! And you, boy, what will you be? Just a thorn in his side? He is going to be a great leader, the best our clan has ever had, and you, you will be like a net sinker tied around his throat. Forever dragging him down."

He wouldn't be, of course. White Bird had his way,

that was all. And yes, if he returned alive from the journey upriver, he would be a great man, a born leader for their clan. Owl knew, Uncle Cloud Heron was just hanging to life, the pain in his bones debilitating no matter how many times he sweated or that the old Serpent and his acolyte, Bobcat, sucked bits of evil out of his body with their copper lancets and stone sucking tubes.

Mud Puppy hunched his fifteen-winters-old body. People said he was skinny, just bones wrapped around an insatiable curiosity. He was short for his age, too. Shaggy black hair tumbled over his eyes as he grasped the ceramic cup in his hand. The cricket began singing its shrill music. How could such a little creature make such a noise? It pierced the ears like a lancet, almost painful.

He barely heard the continuing commotion outside. Someone shouted. Voices called in answer as a party trotted past his house, coming in from one of the outer ridges. "They're back," one of the voices called. "At last, they're back!"

Back? Mud Puppy frowned in the red-tinged gloom. Perhaps the party that had gone down to steal sandstone from the Swamp Panthers? Over the turning of seasons they had become ever more stingy about their precious sandstone. The trouble was that the Sun People depended on the hard sandstone for so much of their manufacturing. When people weren't packing baskets of earth for the mounds, or Singing and celebrating, they were making things. Making plummets, gorgets, celts, and adzes required hard, gritty sandstone. It was used for all kinds of things, even smoothing wood and grinding pigments. Lately, it seemed like every expedition to the Swamp Panthers' country, two days' journey to the south, ended in a fight. Surely, there had to be a better way.

The cricket darted a finger length out from the mat, its body a black blot against the charcoal-stained dirt of the floor.

Mud Puppy waited, still as could be. The gray cup filled his hand, his arm poised. He would have to be fast, like a striking snake, lest his little target escape. Did his muscles have it in themselves? Could he do it?

Wait. Let Cricket relax. He is on his guard now, freshly removed from cover.

Mud Puppy didn't breathe, wondering how long it would take for Cricket to drop his guard. Long moments passed as Mud Puppy closed his ears to the continued calling and laughter outside. He blinked his eyes when Cricket's black body blurred into the shadowed earth and seemed to lose its shape.

At last, the little beast began its high-pitched screeching.

Mud Puppy nerved himself and clapped the cup down over the cricket, the move so violent it was a wonder the fiber-tempered pottery didn't shatter.

"Got you!"

Now, how did he turn the cup over without allowing the cricket to escape? For a moment he puzzled on that, and in the end, rose from his bed and crossed the room to the net bag that held basswood leaves. Reaching in, he removed one of the big leaves and returned to his cup. He took a moment to toss a couple of hickory sticks onto the fire and waited for the flames to cast yellow light over the inside of his mother's house.

He glanced around at the wattle-covered walls and the wood-framed thatch ceiling overhead. Seeing nothing helpful there, he considered the soapstone bowls, the loom with its half-finished cloth, and the stacked pottery, then returned his attention to the cup, upside down on the dirt that separated the cane matting from the fire pit.

He stooped and carefully slid the leaf under the cup. Only when it extended past the other side did he lift both leaf and cup, slowly turn them over, and smile.

"Got you!" The swell of triumph expanded under his heart. "Now, tomorrow, when the sun is bright, I'm going to see how you can make such a loud noise, little fellow."

Feet beat a cadence toward the doorway, and Mud Puppy looked up as Little Needle came huffing and puffing to duck his head into the doorway. Despite being thirteen, Little Needle—of all the children—was Mud Puppy's only good friend. He had a face like the bottom of a pot with a pug nose pinched out of it. His most prominent feature was a set of large dark eyes that had a moony look. "Are your ears plugged, or what?"

"My ears are fine." Mud Puppy held up his leaf-capped cup with pride. "I just caught a cricket!"

"Why do I put up with you?" Little Needle shook his head, a look of disbelief on his round brown face. The black tangle of his unkempt hair had tumbled into his eyes, and he took a swipe at it with a grimy hand. "Your brother's back! He's alive. After all this time...and despite the people who bet he was dead. And you won't believe it, but he's brought *four* canoe loads of Trade. Four! Can you imagine?"

Mud Puppy nodded, a thrill shooting through him. "I know."

"You know?" Little Needle's brow furrowed. "He just got here, fool. You couldn't have known."

"Maybe," Mud Puppy retreated, using one hand to tap his chest. "But I'd have known here if he was dead."

"Uh-huh." Little Needle's frown deepened. "I suppose one of your pets"—he indicated the jar—"came to tell you."

Mud Puppy's expression fell. "I can't say. I promised."

Little Needle studied him thoughtfully. "At times, my friend, I'm almost tempted to believe you. It's scary, some of the things you know. Like Soft Moss being hit by lightning that time. You said it was going to happen."

"You didn't tell anybody, did you?" Mud Puppy felt his souls twisting with sudden anxiety. He hadn't meant to tell Little Needle, but there were times that his souls just cried out to share some of the things Masked Owl told him. He didn't. He wouldn't. Not even to Little Needle, whom he trusted completely. Masked Owl was too precious to him.

"It is the price you must pay for now." Masked Owl's Dream words echoed in his memory. *"Be worthy of me."*

"Well? Are you coming or not?" Little Needle was dancing from foot to foot. "Barbarians came with him! Six of them! They call them Wolf People, but they just look like real people, except different. You know, in their hair and what they wear. But then White Bird and your cousin, Yellow Spider, are dressed like them, too."

Mud Puppy looked around, wondering where to put his cricket. "All right, I'll come."

"How can you be so unconcerned?" Little Needle almost shouted it.

"Because my cricket might escape!"

"Sometimes I think everyone is right, and you're nothing more than an idiot!" With that, Little Needle turned and sprinted off into the darkness.

"He just doesn't understand, does he?" Mud Puppy asked the trapped cricket as he set the cup down and laid a piece of polished slate over the leaf to keep his catch in place. Then he turned and ducked out into the warm spring night.

The Serpent

I watch the boy with my eyes squinted.

This evening, for the first time, I think maybe he's not the half-wit people say he is.

There is a very old story my people tell in their lodges on cold winter's nights—about a bridge guarded by animals. You see, we believe that there is a narrow log bridge that spans a deep canyon on the trail to the Land of the Dead. That bridge is guarded by the animals each person has known in his life. If the person treated those animals well, cared for them, and helped them, then the animals will be happy to see him and will guide him safely across the bridge to where his ancestors wait in the Land of the Dead. But if the person treated the animals badly, if he shouted at them or hurt them, they will chase him across the bridge, tearing at his heels with sharp teeth, or stinging him, or clawing his head with their talons, until he loses his balance and falls into a rushing river of darkness and is lost forever.

As I study the boy, I wonder.

He listens very attentively to everything alive, and

often to things like windblown leaves that I'm fairly certain are dead.

But I could be wrong.

Innocence is the opposite of Truth, isn't it? That's what I've always thought. But perhaps it's just the price, and maybe that price is too high.

The thought makes me smile.

Perhaps if I sought my solace in innocence rather than Truth, I would see what the boy sees.

I vow to watch him more closely.

Chapter Three

The scar tissue that crisscrossed Mud Stalker's mangled right arm ached and itched. That boded no good. Mud Stalker, Speaker for the Snapping Turtle Clan, son of Clan Elder Back Scratch, ran idle fingers over the ridges of hard tissue. He had been but a youth when an alligator clamped itself on his arm and began thrashing the water into bloody froth. He had been insane with pain and panic, half-drowned and vomiting water, when Red Finger had beaten the alligator off with an oar and pulled him from the red-stained water. It had nearly killed him, infection eating at his flesh, fever burning his souls from his body. It had taken several turnings of seasons to recover—and crippled his arm for life.

As the itchy feeling increased, he scowled, thinking it a sign. It was bad enough that White Bird had returned. It was worse that so many people were coming down to the canoe landing to see his late-night arrival. Mud Stalker stood between the beached canoes at the water's edge and watched the people trooping to the landing. They carried cane torches down the slick incline from the high terrace above the lake. The yellow flames bobbed with each step. In the inky night, the light might have been a Dream creature that flowed down the packed silt embankment.

Mud Stalker turned his head, staring out at the silent black waters where the canoes waited. Four of them, solid craft, floated less than a stone's cast from the shore. They reminded him of fingers stretching out of the night, monstrous and black. The canoe's occupants were standing, their feet balanced on the narrow gunwales. Over the babble of excited people, Mud Stalker could hear the grunting and clucking sound of the barbarians' tongues as they talked.

What could have possessed White Bird to bring them down from the north?

"Are you sure we cannot land?" one of the foreigners asked in Trade pidgin.

"Not until we are given permission." That was Yellow Spider, another youth from the Owl Clan. Unlike White Bird's family, Yellow Spider's had declared him dead just after the winter solstice.

Mud Stalker turned his attention to where White Bird stood in the rear of the canoe. Even across the distance, he could see the young man's teeth shining as he smiled, cupped his hands to his mouth, and called, "What news?"

"Things are well," Clay Fat, the Rattlesnake Clan Speaker returned. His round stomach stuck out like a pot, his navel a protruding knob. "We have sent for your mother."

"And my uncle?" White Bird asked cautiously across the water.

Yes, there it was. The dilemma they all faced. Cloud Heron was little more than a breathing corpse. He could die at any moment. Why hadn't he had the grace to do so before this foolish youth floated back from the dead?

"Not so well," Clay Fat replied. "Your return has come at a very opportune moment for your clan."

That, Mud Stalker thought, was just the problem. He turned, aware that his cousin, Red Finger, had walked up. The old man held a flickering cane torch in his bony hand. He raised it high to look out over the black water at the canoes riding so peacefully.

"So, it is true? White Bird is back?" Red Finger kept his voice low, fully aware of the continuing flood of people who were descending to the landing.

Mud Stalker lifted a foot and planted it on the gunwale of a beached canoe. "He is back." He tried to keep his voice from communicating his displeasure. "Back, indeed—and with three upcountry canoes full of barbarians. Not only is he not dead—as we had hoped—but he returns at just the right moment. With canoes packed full of Trade."

"Look at them," Red Finger muttered, as more people crowded the shore and raised their cane torches to stare across the water. In the yellow light they could better see the new arrivals. "If those piled bundles are Trade, and for as low as those canoes ride in the water, he has brought back great wealth."

Yes, if he has, his status will soar. Aloud, Mud Stalker said, "Let us wait and see, Cousin."

"Why, in the name of the Sky Beings, couldn't he be long dead with worms crawling in and out of his skull?" Red Finger growled under his breath, looking around. "Where's Wing Heart? I would have thought she would have been one of the first people down here. Is she missing the opportunity to prance up and down while telling of Owl Clan's Power, courage, and skill?"

"Oh, she'll be here." Mud Stalker wet his lips. "But only when the timing is right. As always, she will want to make a grand entrance."

"Wretched bitch. What I'd give to—"

"Patience, old friend. A great many things may yet go wrong for our young hero."

"White Bird!" The shrill yell carried over the growing babble of voices. Mud Stalker turned in time to see Spring Cypress running down the slope, pushing through the growing throng of people. Having passed fifteen summers, she was a tall girl, thin and lithe. Her dress consisted of a virgin's skirt loosely woven from bass-bark thread. It had been tied in the back with two beaded tassels. Cord fringe that attached to the hem dangled down past her knees. Each had been tipped with a stone bead so that it clattered and swayed with her steps. Born of the Rattlesnake Clan, Spring Cypress was Elder Graywood Snake's granddaughter. The girl had pinned her hair for White Bird long ago. As the seasons passed, and rumors circulated that her young swain had died upriver, she had grown despondent. Now, despite the fact that she carried no torch, she seemed to glow. But that might just have been the reflection of the light on her oiled skin.

"Spring Cypress?" White Bird craned his head, the canoe bobbing at his action. Despite the youth's exceptional balance, a careless move could capsize the boat.

"Yes! It's me! They said you were dead!" She was jumping up and down on charged legs, her immature breasts bouncing in time to the necklace on her chest. The weighted fringes jerked and jangled on her skirt.

"Dead?" White Bird threw his head back and laughed. "Anything but! I'm more full of life now that I've come home."

"What have you brought?" someone called.

"Where have you been?" cried another.

"What took you so long?"

"White Bird, who are these people with you?"

"Yellow Spider? What did they do? Marry you off to one of their grease-smelling hags up there?"

"How was the river? Is the water high?"

A thousand questions came boiling out of the crowd, each person trying to outshout the others.

Mud Stalker struggled to hear the answers. White Bird and Yellow Spider hollered back, but the roar of voices drowned them out. Instead, he turned his attention to the six young barbarians who stood uneasily on their canoes, watching with wide eyes. He couldn't make out much about them, other than their hair was pinned to the backs of their heads in tight buns. They were muscular, naked to the waist, where hide breechcloths had been secured by thick white cords. Someone, probably White Bird and Yellow Spider, had given them grease and taught them how to smear it over their bodies to thwart the plagues of mosquitoes and biting flies that filled the swamps.

"Hides, tool stone, copper, buffalo meat and medicines, a great many things..." White Bird's words carried through a lull in the conversation.

"Here comes Wing Heart!" Red Finger pointed up the hill.

The Owl Clan Elder was picking her way down the

slope, two of her clan's people, Water Petal and Bluefin, bearing torches to light her way. The yellow light reflected from her silver-streaked hair as if it had previously caught the sun's rays and was now releasing them into the night. She wore a bearskin mantle pinned atop the left shoulder with a deer-bone skewer. Her right shoulder and breast were bare. Despite the late hour and the unexpected call, she wore a finely woven cloth kirtle. Spotless and white, it swayed with each step she took. The preceding turning of seasons had been hard on her. Speaker Cloud Heron, her brother, had been slowly failing, his mind and health draining away like upland floodwaters. When White Bird had not returned last fall, she had taken it stoically, calmly stating that her son was detained. But the months had passed, and winter had dragged on, one grim, gray day after another passing as her clan's influence ebbed.

Now, here she came, looking to all the world as if it were just another day and not the salvation of her authority and prestige. The crisis of clan leadership had been delayed yet again, perhaps forever.

"You'd think she planned this from the very beginning," Red Finger hissed irritably. Then he paused. "You don't think she did, do you? Do you think that rascal son of hers has been hiding out in the swamp for months? Did she do this just to keep us off-balance? To make us show our hands?"

"What about these barbarians?" Mud Stalker twitched his lips in their direction. "Did she hide them in the swamps, too? And all the Trade things that I overhead White Bird say he brought? She might be a Powerful old hag, but she and White Bird didn't just conjure Trade and barbarians from the mud and swamp moss. No, Cousin, he went north. Just as he said. We had better plan on how we are going to deal with that."

"He was always a Powerful boy. Had a way about him." Red Finger tapped his chin thoughtfully.

"We must take other steps, Cousin."

Red Finger shot a sidelong glance at him, his eyes shadowed black in the torchlight. "Are you thinking what I think you are?"

"Perhaps. Let us be patient. We are descended from Snapping Turtle, Cousin. Like him, we must be prudent, silent, and crafty. Snapping Turtle always lies where you least expect to find him. He is a master of camouflage and stealth." A pause. "And his bite can snap a man's bones in two."

Red Finger's expression hardened. "We must be very, very careful."

The dark soil underfoot had turned treacherous. Evening mist had fallen, then hundreds of feet had churned it. The last thing Wing Heart would allow herself to do was to slip and take a tumble—not with half the town watching her. All of the terrible months of mixed hope, grief, and despair culminated here, now, at this moment and place: White Bird was home! She must use every sliver of advantage and opportunity.

Moccasin Leaf had been nipping at her heels, ready to slip Half Thorn into the Speaker's position. Just that morning, she had been contemplating whether any hope remained. The question had been: Would it be better to declare her son dead before her brother died, or after? Points could be made for either decision, but in the end it had been her Dream Soul rather than her Life Soul that had won out. She simply couldn't stand to make a public admission of what she had come to believe in private. To do so would be too final, too void of even her thinly frayed hopes.

Then out of the darkness had come the word that White Bird had arrived. She was told that even as the runner spoke, her son was waiting in his canoe at the landing. She could hardly believe that he had brought not just himself and Yellow Spider, but three more canoes full of Trade paddled by barbarians!

She picked her way carefully in the flickering torchlight borne by her cousins. No trace of the rushing ecstasy in her heart betrayed itself on her stern face. She kept the fingers of her left hand tightly knotted in the silky bearskin she'd pinned over her shoulder. Aware that all eyes had turned in her direction, she held her head high. That was it, let them all see. Owl Clan would remain the preeminent clan in Sun Town.

She cast a quick glance around as the land leveled. Of course, Mud Stalker had beaten her here. Snapping Turtle Clan had been poised to move on her. She could practically see him choking on his disappointment as he fingered the scars on his ruined forearm. Too bad the alligator hadn't taken the rest of him along with his stripped fingers and skin.

To the left, amid a knot of his kinspeople, Thunder Tail, Speaker of the Eagle Clan, stood with crossed arms, his face like a mask. She inclined her head politely in his direction, thrilled by the smoldering emotion in his eyes. *You would love to cut my throat, wouldn't you, old lover?*

To the rear, just back from the beached canoes, old

Cane Frog stood. The Frog Clan Elder's left eye gleamed like a white stone in the firelight. The empty socket of her missing right eye made a black hole in her face. She was propped up by her daughter, Three Moss. As always, Three Moss was whispering in the old blind woman's ears, acting as her eyes. Several of the Frog Clan's young hunters had gathered behind her, as if for moral support. Their gazes darted back and forth like a school of shiners in shallow water. The two plotters, Hanging Branch and Takes Food, hovered to one side, whispering to each other. But Frog Clan, for all their bluster and strutting, had never really been in contention for leadership of the Council. Cane Frog hadn't the wits, and given Three Moss's dull head, the future didn't bode well for them either. Frog Clan would only be trouble if they aligned themselves with a rival.

Then she saw Deep Hunter. He stood back from the rest, illuminated by a single torch. His sister, Colored Paint, was the Alligator Clan Elder. Colored Paint had recently named her brother Speaker after the death of their uncle. Deep Hunter had his arms crossed, the thick muscles bunched and shining in the firelight. She met his dark eyes, seeing a hard gleam that didn't match his formal smile. Deep Hunter didn't look happy. No, indeed, she thought he looked like a man who had just suffered a disturbing upset. Throughout this last turning of seasons, Deep Hunter—with Colored Paint's approval—had promised Owl Clan their support. Deep Hunter would do anything to keep Mud Stalker and Alligator Clan in a subservient and obligatory position. Even if it meant supporting Wing Heart and Owl Clan.

Why do I feel that I've been betrayed? She nodded a

greeting to Deep Hunter and bent her lips into a facile smile—just in case she needed to keep the fiction alive.

Eagle Clan's Elder, Stone Talon, perched on her wooden crutches, her gnarly hands gripping the smooth wood of the polished branches that kept her crooked legs from collapsing. Toothless, her face looked like a desiccated gourd. Stone Talon worked her gums and wrinkled her fleshy nose as though smelling something foul. Her faded vision seemed to be wavering, as though searching for something. A group of her young hunters —no doubt the ones who had borne her down to the landing—looked as if it was all they could do to keep from crowding at the water's edge and shouting questions at White Bird.

Deep Hunter strode down to face his sister. Gesturing for emphasis, he asked Colored Paint a question, then turned at the answer to frown out at the water where the canoes floated. Deep Hunter was a brash man, given to impulse. He had no halfway in his souls, but being a hothead and unpredictable made him dangerous in his own right.

Yes, they were all worried. That brought Wing Heart a twist of amusement she wouldn't have felt earlier in the day. Cloud Heron wasn't even dead yet, and they had already buried him? Had the fools considered Owl Clan to be defanged? Without any Power at all? She allowed herself to smile with an oily satisfaction. After a turning of seasons filled with worry and fear, her heart felt as though it might burst. This moment was worth savoring. She let the glory of victory fill her, felt it throbbing in her nerves, pulsing in her veins. She might have been a youth again, charged with the sheer joy of being alive.

People parted for her as she neared the shore. In the halo of torchlight, she walked imperiously between the hulls of beached canoes and out into the murky black water. Slippery, clinging mud oozed between her toes. Water lapped against her ankles like a lover's tongue.

The surface lay smooth and glassy before her, blackness lit by dancing yellow ribbons of light that reflected from the rings thrown by the bobbing canoes. Slim arrows of the night, the craft drifted at the edge of the torchlight: four of them, just as had been reported. She gave a cursory inspection to the barbarians, not that they mattered much, and turned her attention to the tall young man who balanced so perfectly on the stern of the canoe floating off to the right.

What a hero he made! Firelight reflected off the grease that he had smeared over his rippling skin, accenting the swell of his thick muscles. He stood like one of the warriors in the stories about the first days. A foreign-looking breechcloth hung from the leather belt at his slim hips. A bright yellow wolf's face was painted on the front flap. His hair, too, was in a bun pinned up at the side like the barbarians wore theirs. She could see his white teeth as he smiled in her direction.

"Are you well, my son?"

"I am *very* well, Mother."

She didn't react to the satisfaction in his voice. "And you, Yellow Spider? Are you well?"

"I am, Elder. Thank you. And my family?"

"They, too, are well. I shall send a runner immediately. Your mother and your brothers and sisters are out at Turtle Shell Camp. They will rejoice to hear of your arrival." Her voice turned dry. "It seems that they have worked most assiduously to placate your angry and lost ghost."

Across the distance she could see Yellow Spider take a deep breath. "I am sorry for that, Clan Elder. I can only hope that my return, with the Trade we bring, will reimburse the clan for any hardships my funeral might have incurred."

Scattered laughter broke out at that. It brought a smile to her thin lips. She had always liked Yellow Spider and had approved of his offer to accompany White Bird upriver. "I would imagine so, Yellow Spider. We can only wish that all deaths would reward us as well as yours appears to have."

"How is my uncle?" White Bird called.

"My brother, the Speaker, is not well, White Bird. Your absence has caused us some concern. Others worried, but I knew that you would not have prolonged your absence were it not that you were acting in the People's greatest interest."

White Bird, in a demonstration of his supreme balance, bowed low at the waist, the canoe barely rocking. "Indeed, Mother, were there any other way, I would have returned last fall. I apologize for leaving you without my help, but my responsibility to the People must be of more importance than my personal desires."

Well spoken, boy.

"And who are the people you have brought in these loaded canoes?"

White Bird was standing straight now, his canoe having drifted sideways as he looked over the torchlit crowd on the bank. "I would present my companions, they are Wolf People, from the far north. Yellow Spider and I, hearing of remarkable Trade up beyond the confluence of the three great rivers, made the decision to change our plans. Rather than simply barter for a load of Trade in the Blue Heron lands, we risked the way north. Many hostile peoples guard the river between the Blue Heron lands and the land of the Wolf People. By means of craft and guile, Yellow Spider and I passed those wild tribes. By the fall equinox, we had reached the land of the Wolf People. There, Chief Acorn Cup, father of my friend, Hazel Fire"—he pointed to the young barbarian in the stern of the next canoe—"welcomed us into his village. He was a most gracious host. At Acorn Cup's insistence, we stayed the winter. And such a winter...you have never seen snow so deep! Or felt such a biting cold that almost splintered a man's bones!"

Wryly, she thought, *Chief Acorn Cup, good host that he was, no doubt left something warm, willing, and female in your bed to keep icicles from forming on your manhood.*

"Acorn Cup was right in warning us not to travel, so I spared my Trade, passing out a little at a time as the winter passed. And as you can see"—he made a grandiose gesture that rocked his canoe—"we have brought a great many things for the People as a result."

"Then our wait was well worth the time you spent far away." Wing Heart nodded slowly for the benefit of the gathered people.

Addressing the crowd, White Bird raised his voice. "Yellow Spider and I, at great risk to our lives, have brought four canoes piled high with Trade. What we have is a gift from the Owl Clan to the people. We provide these things freely and with an open heart. Owl

Clan asks but two things: We ask that you provide for the needy among the clans first. He who is hunting with a blunt dart must receive the first of the stone points we have brought. He whose children are shivering in the cold must first receive the fine furs until all are warm. Those inflicted by spirits and evils shall partake of the medicine herbs we have brought. We ask that only after the needy are taken care of, will the rest of you take your pick of the remaining Trade."

"And the second thing?" Clay Fat called.

White Bird pointed at the barbarians. "These brave men have risked their lives to help me bring this Trade to the people. Owl Clan asks that you treat them as our honored guests. That you bestow upon them gifts to take back to their distant homeland. We ask that you provide every courtesy to them, as they have provided to us. They come from a different place and have different customs. When we lived in their village, they did not mock us when we made errors in their ways. And, my people, believe me, we made some very silly mistakes! They are not stupid, though through ignorance of our ways they may act like it. We simply ask that you do not mock them because they do not know our customs."

"These things shall be as you wish," Clay Fat cried happily. "Tell your friends that Rattlesnake Clan offers our homes and hospitality to these Wolf People."

Wing Heart lifted her chin slightly, thankful once again that Rattlesnake Clan remained loyal to her.

"What are your orders, Clan Elder?" White Bird called ritually.

"You are to camp on the Turtle's Back. There, you will be attended to. You are to cleanse yourselves before

41

entering the sacred enclosure of Sun Town. You are to divest yourself of evil thoughts, of pettiness, and spite. You are to submit to the Serpent and his attendants when he comes to prepare you. When you are ready, we shall receive you and your Trade."

"It is as you order, Elder." White Bird bowed again, then settled himself easily into the canoe's stern. In what Wing Heart assumed was the language of the barbarians, he said something, and the rest of his companions lowered themselves into their boats. Paddles were collected, and the canoes turned to stroke off into the night, following White Bird's wake.

Wing Heart remained as she was, tall, head up, watching her son paddle away. There, just beyond the glow of the torches, he would land on Turtle's Back, a low island that broke the lake surface. Traditionally, Traders camped there, allowing themselves to be cleansed of any evil taint that they might have picked up, or that might be hovering close to their goods. The People couldn't be too careful. Surrounded by jealous and spiteful peoples, curses and spells constantly flew in their direction—especially from the Swamp Panthers to the south. Despite the Power of their town, malignant evils continued to invade them. No matter that the earthen bands protected their central ground, and that spirits couldn't cross the water boundary of the lake that stretched east of the village, people still came down sick, and wounds festered, even when rapidly and efficiently treated by the Serpent.

After what Wing Heart deemed as a proper amount of time, she turned, slogging out of the mud and onto the crusted shore. Passing between the canoes, she stopped. People began drifting back up the slope, talking animatedly in the light of their torches. Cane Frog's young hunters lifted her and bore her away on their shoulders, while Three Moss, trotting along behind, muttered in low tones.

"Mother?" The voice caught her by surprise.

She glanced down, seeing Mud Puppy standing there, his thatch of hair unkempt, preoccupation behind his large, watery eyes. A cup was in his right hand, a flat piece of slate held over it with his left. "Where have you been?"

"I was catching a cricket."

A cricket? He was catching a cricket? Fifteen summers old, but he might have been ten, given the way he acted most of the time. She shook her head, biting off the harsh comment that leaped to her lips. Not here, someone would overhear, and Power take it, though everyone knew her son to be an idiot, she needn't go out of her way to prove them right.

"White Bird is back?" he asked plaintively.

"Yes, yes, your brother is back. Now, go away. I have things to do. Much must be arranged."

She pushed past him, starting up toward the trail as Clay Fat stepped in beside her. He was a ball of a man, chubby of face, with a wide mouth. His belly preceded him like a canoe's prow. In his four tens of winters he had alternately been an irritant under her skin or a blessing, depending upon the circumstances.

"I see that Mud Puppy actually managed to show up. What happened? No spider dangling from the ceiling to distract him?" Clay Fat smiled. Some of his kinspeople close enough to hear chuckled. Even Wing Heart's torch-bearers smiled as they walked behind her, their burning cane torches held high.

"It was a cricket this time, can you imagine? What is it about that boy? I'd swear, his souls aren't anchored to his scrawny little body. He'd rather hide out in the forest staring into a pool of water for hands of time than learn or do anything useful."

"He has become a very capable stone carver for someone so young," Clay Fat pointed out. "Children his age can't usually sit still to make it through a meal, yet Mud Puppy can finish intricate carvings."

"Carvings will not make him useful when it comes to running a clan." She lifted her arms and let them drop. "As much as I feel cursed by Mud Puppy, White Bird more than makes up for him. Old friend, a weight is lifted from my souls. My son has returned. You cannot know how relieved my heart is."

Clay Fat's smile widened. "I cannot tell you how happy I am that White Bird has returned." He jerked a thumb back at Mud Puppy, who was talking to one of his scrawny friends. "Some people have begun to worry about him. There is talk that he has Dreams. That he sees things. Did you know that the Serpent has been watching him?"

"Mud Puppy? Why would the Serpent be watching him? He's harmless. Witless. And as to his Dreams"—she made a face—"you can tell people to relax. I have more faith in Power than to believe it would be interested in a skinny half-wit like him." She paused, then added pointedly, "He's Thumper's yield, you know."

"Yes. Curious isn't it? He's so different. Matings are such puzzling things."

She raised an eyebrow, shooting him a glance from the corner of her eye.

"Now that White Bird is back," Clay Fat mused,

"Spring Cypress has just passed her first menstruation. She is a young woman now, and I know she favors White Bird."

Wing Heart knew for a fact that Spring Cypress had passed her first menstruation last winter out at Sweet Root Camp—where she would have remained had Clay Fat and Graywood Snake not decided that White Bird was dead. In lieu of that decision they had brought her back to Sun Town to troll her through Frog and Alligator Clans to see what young man snapped at her allure. Gorgeous, nubile thing that she was, and Rattlesnake, having the influence that they did, she had had more than her share of young males swarming after her. Either of those clans would have been more than happy to send one of their sons to her house.

"We shall see," Wing Heart replied casually. Did she dare contemplate another alliance with Rattlesnake Clan? Or, given the potentials of White Bird's exploding popularity, would she be better served marrying the boy to one of the other clans?

"You could do worse, you know," Clay Fat continued. "And, well, until tonight, a great many people were worried."

"As was I," she relented.

"They thought you might name Mud Puppy as Speaker!" Clay Fat laughed, his rotund belly wiggling.

"Mud Puppy as Speaker..." At that moment, she caught sight of old Mud Stalker. He was walking in the shadows off to the side, his ruined right arm cradled in his left.

Beside him, Deep Hunter was talking, his hands moving to emphasize his words. The one person Deep Hunter hated more than Mud Stalker was the Swamp

Panther cutthroat, Jaguar Hide. So, why were they talking now? *What venom are you concocting, old man? How do you intend to inject it into my flesh?*

The thought of it sent a cold shiver down her spine.

When she looked back toward the night-veiled lake, she could see nothing. No fire had yet been built on the Turtle's Back.

Instead, oddly, she noticed Mud Puppy where he stood at the water's edge, a solitary figure, totally absorbed by his cup.

Mud Puppy? Speaker for the clan? I'd lose my souls before I'd allow that to happen.

Chapter Four

T hat night, as Mud Puppy lay deep in sleep, a soft gulf breeze blew up from the south. It carried the tendrils of rising smoke northward, away from the curved lines of houses that dotted the concentric ridges of Sun Town. The darkness lay thick, light from Father Moon and the myriads of stars blotted by the mass of clouds that alternately drizzled rain on the land.

As the Dream slipped its hazy fingers around Mud Puppy's souls, owl wings sailed silently through the falling tendrils of misty rain and over the arched ridges of Sun Town. The great bird circled slowly above a single dwelling on the eastern end of the first ridge.

The oval-shaped house had been built of saplings driven into the ground, woven together with vines, and plastered with clay. Sheaves of grass formed a thick thatch that was bound to the cane roof stringers by wraps of stout cord.

The tight thatch shed the rain, letting it drip just beyond the clay walls to pool in the rich soil.

The door was an oblong hole in the wall covered with a hemp-fabric hanging just thick enough to block most of the chill. Around the top, and along the overhang of thatch, smoke drifted out, carrying with it the odor of hickory and maple.

Inside, a cane-pole bench that served as seating and bedding had been built into the wall circumference. The woman slept fitfully on the western side, her aging body covered with a fine deerskin blanket. The boy, in his bed on the eastern side, lay lost in dreams, his body covered with a worn fabric. He had curled on his right side, the rounded angles of his face visible in the reddish glow cast by the coals in the central hearth. His eyes flicked and wiggled under tightly closed lids.

The Dream knotted itself in Mud Puppy's souls, wrapping around them, spinning and cavorting.

He sat at the top of a high mound, the ground warm under his buttocks and thighs. He reached down and raked the earth into his hands. Holding it to his nose, he sniffed the pungent musk, drawing it into his body and souls. After it became one with him, he pinched the dark, silty soil into shapes with his fingers. The moist earth seemed to flow as though of its own accord, forming at his very thoughts, the image perfectly rendered by his supple brown fingers.

First he sculpted the body, rotund, with a protruding belly. Then he shaped a round head, his thumbs curving up and around the face to reveal a hooked beak between two broadly recessed eyes. With thumb and forefinger he pinched out the ears, pointed and high. Using a fingernail, he circled the large eyes— and when he lifted his hand, they blinked at him, bright yellow with gleaming black pupils.

Along either side of the rotund body, he shaped the wings, outlining the feathers with his nails. From the bottom of the torso, he pulled out the feet, his thumbnail tracing the individual toes and talons.

"You have done well," the mud sculpture told him. "But you have to learn to fly before you can learn to Dance."

Mud Puppy stared at the owl, aware that it was changing, that its beak had turned yellow, feathers softening around the ears, but the face, he realized, looked fake. *A mask! He's wearing a mask!* "You are Masked Owl!"

"Yes, I am." Masked Owl chuckled at that. "And what is a mask, boy?"

"A covering."

"Is it?"

"Of course. Just like at the ceremonies when the deer dancers come in. It's to make them look like deer."

Masked Owl cocked his head. "In so many ways you remind me of Bad Belly."

"Who?"

"A young man I once knew, one carried away by the world. Like you, he saw wonder in everything. It comes of an innocence of the soul. I cannot tell you how precious that is."

"What happened to him?"

"Oh, he became a hero in spite of himself."

"He didn't want to be?"

Owl's head tilted again. "Have you ever been a hero?"

"No." Mud Puppy frowned down at his dirty hands. "But my brother is."

Masked Owl considered this. "Then you do not

know what it costs to be a hero. The price is high, as your brother is about to find out."

"Is he—"

"Why are you called Mud Puppy?"

"I-I had one. A mud puppy, I mean." He looked down at his hands again. As he picked the silt from his fingers, he rolled it into worms. In the sway of the Dream, they began to wiggle and burrow into the rounded top of the mound upon which they sat. Below him, the world seemed to inhale and breathe, the trees, water, soil, and grass alive and vibrant with color.

"What finally happened to your mud puppy?"

"I kept it in a ceramic pot filled with water. I petted it and went out every day and caught it insects."

"And?"

"It changed. It became a beautiful salamander. It went from an ugly brown color to the most incredible reddish orange. Like sunset in the clouds, with black spots all over it. Its eyes were bright yellow, like yours, but smaller."

"That's the Power of Salamander." Masked Owl's haunting yellow eyes bored into Mud Puppy's as if seeing inside to his Life Soul. "People don't understand how magical Salamander is. They ignore him for the most part."

"It's because he's close to the Monsters Below."

"He is, but that's not why people ignore him."

"It's not?"

"No." Masked Owl hesitated, "People usually see the world as a reflection of themselves. Pride, arrogance, and status preoccupy them. Let me ask, would your brother rather have Falcon or Salamander for a Spirit Helper?"

"Falcon," Mud Puppy replied without hesitation.

"And you? Which would you choose?"

Mud Puppy jabbed his fingers into the dirt. "My mother says I'll never have a Spirit Helper. She says that I'm too stupid."

"But if you could have a Spirit Helper?"

Mud Puppy glanced shyly at the owl. "I don't know much about them, but Spirit Helpers pick the people they go to, don't they? So I guess I'd want a Spirit Helper that wanted me. If it was Salamander, that would be all right. Everyone wants Falcon. Maybe it would make Salamander happy if someone wanted him." He paused. "Do Spirit Helpers worry about things like that? About whether people want them or not?"

"Yes, Mud Puppy, they do. And now let me tell you something that most people don't know. Falcon is indeed powerful, and many people want him for a Spirit Helper, but he has a weakness. He is very fragile. His bones are hollow. His body breaks very easily. He can't stand any sort of poison because his system is so delicate it will kill him."

"And Salamander?"

"Ah, Salamander is anything but delicate. He can survive floods, drought, fires, and frost. Not only can he live underwater, but atop the ground, too. His flesh is poisonous to his enemies such as Wolf and Raccoon. Best of all, he stays out of sight most of the time. While the great beasts rip and tear each other's flesh, Salamander lies under the stones and Dreams the Dance."

"The Dance?"

"Ah, yes, the Dance." Masked Owl twirled around,

his wings rising in a splendid arc. "To Dance the One. As I am doing now."

"You are?"

"Indeed."

"Can I learn your Dance? I'm not as stupid as people think I am. I learned the Circle Dance last winter at solstice when we Danced Mother Sun back into the sky."

Masked Owl stopped, and those huge black pupils seemed to expand in the yellow eyes behind the mask. They grew larger and larger, and as they did, Mud Puppy's soul seemed to shrink.

"Would you like to Dance, Mud Puppy?"

"Very much."

He felt rather than saw Masked Owl's smile. "I am glad to hear that." Then came sadness. "But I can't teach you yet."

"You can't?"

"No."

Mud Puppy pursed his lips, a terrible grief that he didn't quite understand lying deep in his breast. Instead, he said, "That's all right."

Masked Owl's eyes swelled again, engulfing the world around them. Like pools of darkness, they ebbed and flowed, pulsing with the rhythm of the universe. "You are a good person, Mud Puppy. It pains me to ask, but will you do some things for me before I teach you the Dance?"

"Yes. If I can. But Mother says I'm not very good at doing important things. I heard her tell Uncle Cloud Heron that I can't even be trusted to carry a cup of water through a rainstorm. You should know that before you ask. And I'm small for my age. Mother says I can't keep my mind on important things. Most of my friends are working hard to become men. They hunt and fish and learn to be warriors."

"Why don't you?"

"I'm not good at those things. I try, but somehow…"

"Yes?"

"I like finding out secrets."

"Secrets?"

Mud Puppy grinned. "Yes, like why Cricket can make such a loud noise. Or how a caterpillar can become a moth in a cocoon. Have you ever looked into a cocoon after the moth leaves? There aren't any caterpillar parts left inside. So, where does a moth come from? And, if you cut a caterpillar open, it's all full of juice. It sure doesn't have a moth hidden in there anywhere. I know. I used a stick and stirred the gooey stuff to find out."

Masked Owl's eyes seemed to shrink, enough that Mud Puppy could see that Masked Owl had thrown his head back. His laughter shook the world and left the clouds trembling. When he stopped, he said, "Mud Puppy, you are a special boy. It has been a long time since I have found such an honest and humble soul."

Mud Puppy winced, turning his attention back to his hands, picked mostly clean of mud now. All of the worms he'd made had burrowed into the ground. "I'm sorry."

"Sorry?"

"Yes. Sorry that I'm all those things. You might want to ask my brother. He's just come back from the north. Everyone is proud of him. If I can't do what you need, he might be able to."

Masked Owl was studying him with those terrible eyes. "What if I said I wanted you?"

"I will do my best," Mud Puppy asserted. "Especially if you will teach me your Dance. Maybe if I do well, and try very hard, I could get a Spirit Helper? Maybe even one that was Powerful like Salamander?" He frowned, then an image of his mother's face formed.

"What's wrong?"

"Would Salamander mind if I didn't tell my mother?"

"Why wouldn't you tell her?"

"She wouldn't like it if she found out that Salamander was my Spirit Helper."

"Why not?"

"She wouldn't understand."

Masked Owl chuckled again. "No, I suppose not. And you, you really wouldn't mind if Salamander was your Spirit Helper?"

"No!" Mud Puppy cried, abashed. "I would be so grateful."

Masked Owl laughed again. "I shall talk to Salamander. I shall also accept your promise of lending me help. You should know, however, that it will be a terrible trial. What I will ask will take both perseverance and cunning. It will mean that you must stay true to your beliefs and never lose faith in yourself, no matter what other people are saying. If you are not clever and committed, it could cost you your life."

Mud Puppy swallowed hard. For the first time fear began to squirm around in his gut. It prickled through him, raising beads of sweat from his skin and making his heart pound.

Masked Owl noted this and nodded. "Ah, good, you understand."

"I will get a Spirit Helper and learn your Dance?"

"If you do not fail me, yes."

"I..." the words couldn't quite form in his throat. *Do I really want to do this? Can I do it? Will I fail? And what if I do? What if I can't do what he asks?*

"Then I will be most disappointed, Mud Puppy." Masked Owl cocked his head. "I do not know if you can do the things I'm asking. Others have failed me in the past. I cannot resist your free will."

Mud Puppy's soul twisted like old fabric as he said, "I will do my best."

"Do you promise on your souls?"

"I do."

"Then, come, let us fly." Masked Owl leaped from the mound top, spiraling in the air. Looking back, he called, "Raise your arms and jump!"

Mud Puppy, his heart trembling in fear, raised his arms and spread his fingers, willing to try, even if Masked Owl laughed when his flailing arms dropped him back to Earth.

It was to his surprise, then, that he rose, carried by the powerful beat of his arms. He flew! His arms flattened into strong -wings that silently caressed the night air. He could see the land, as though in muted daylight, colors oddly drained into a bluish-gray cast.

Among the clouds, he soared and spiraled. Lightning flashed silently around him, flickering from the spotted feathers on his broad wings. Thunder Beings darted and hid among the clouds, showing their faces, only to vanish again, the memory of their grins left behind in the patterns of cloud and wind.

The sound of the birds brought Hazel Fire awake. He blinked, yawned, and sat up, his elkhide robe falling from his shoulders. Fatigue still hung in his muscles, the night's rest hardly a payment on the debt he owed his body for the constant days of ceaseless paddling. But they had made it! He was here, just outside the legendary Sun Town. A place that Traders spoke of with awe-hushed voices. He and his friends were going to see this storied place with their own eyes, the first of their kind to do so. It was the stuff of legends.

The canoes were drawn up on the muddy shore just below his feet. He could see their bundled contents. Everything glistened silver with beads of dew. A drop spattered on his head, and he looked up at the overhanging branches of the sweetgum tree. The star-shaped leaves hung listlessly in the still air.

Droplets, like little diamonds, shimmered on his elkhide as he laid it aside and stood. The effect was magical. A low mist lay over the silver-gray water. It drifted past the trees, curled around the sleeping bodies of his companions, and seemed to slither around the patches of hanging moss that clung to the branches. A fish jumped in the lake, rings widening in lazy circles.

Hazel Fire walked down to the water and relieved himself. For the moment he was limited to looking across the opaque surface of the lake that separated him from the mythical Sun People's town. What little he could see of it was perched atop a gray cliff that rose to the height of four men above the distant shore. Several buildings—tall things with thatched roofs—looked ghostly in the silvered mist. One perched on a mound to the north. Another stood atop a mound to the south, just above where the bluff sloped to a canoe landing. Barely visible, the mist shrouded it again with a closing wall of white. Had it really been there?

Memories came back of their arrival last night, of the procession of torches that had wound down to the canoe landing. Tens of ten at least, so many they had cast a warm yellow light over the landing the likes of which Hazel Fire had never seen. The clamor of the voices had been fit to shake the waters and raise the dead. In that magical moment, the torchlit column of people, like a serpent of light spilling onto the shore, had been dazzling in its spectacle. White Bird and Yellow Spider had called back and forth with the horde for what seemed an eternity, and Hazel Fire had suddenly wished he'd taken more time to learn this odd language. It sounded like turkeys squawking to him. Something impossible to wrap the human tongue around.

"Where are we? Is this real?" Snow Water had asked in awe from his canoe.

"I've never seen so many people," Jackdaw had replied warily.

"Those are only a few of the tens of tens of tens who live in Sun Town," Yellow Spider had assured them from his bobbing canoe.

"Are we going to land?" Gray Fox had asked. "My legs feel like wood."

"For the moment," White Bird had replied, "we will make camp there, on that island. We call it the Turtle's Back. Being surrounded as it is by Morning Lake, it is protected as well as protection from evil spirits and hostile ghosts." He had pointed, and the torchlight had been such that Hazel Fire had seen the black hump of earth like some monster lurking in the calm water.

"Who would have thought?" Hazel Fire wondered aloud to himself as he replayed the events of the night before. Until he died, the sight of all those cane torches burning in the night would be lodged in his head.

"Thought what?" White Bird asked in heavily accented Trade pidgin. His head poked up from the painted buffalo hide he had slept under.

"That I'd really be here." Hazel Fire turned and gestured back at the town, now hidden behind the mist like an eclipsed vision. "Is it really as you said? I mean now that we're here, are we going to be disappointed? Are we going to find out that everything you told us is, well, shall we say, something of a story? A bit of imagination?"

White Bird laughed, a twinkle in his eyes. "No, my friend." The young man threw back his painted hide and stood, stretching. Once again, Hazel Fire admired his muscular body and the character reflected in that handsome face. Something about those shining black eyes made a man instinctively trust White Bird. No wonder Lark had fallen so deeply in love. Despite what Hazel Fire's father, Acorn Cup, might have told White Bird, it had taken all of his Hickory Clan's influence to keep Lark from running off to this magical southern land.

White Bird stepped down to stand beside Hazel Fire. "If anything, Sun Town is grander than I have told you." White Bird placed a reassuring hand on his shoulder. "I've been gone a complete turning of the seasons, my friend. I wager a great deal more has been built in that time. It will almost be as new to me as it will be to you."

"When do I get to see this mythical place? Three days? It will take a whole three days?"

White Bird's smile remained infectious. "If all goes well."

"Why so long?" Hazel Fire raised an eyebrow.

"We have come a long way." White Bird pointed northward with his right hand. "Across many lands. We have been exposed to a great many evils. Spirits can attach themselves to us, or to our Trade. You know this. So before we enter the city's protection we must drive them off, cleanse our souls."

"Cleanse how?" He crossed his arms. "Some magician isn't going to steal my souls, is he?"

White Bird laughed, his white teeth shining. "I sincerely hope not. I'm as fond of my souls as you are of yours. No. I know you, know all of you. We have shared too many trials, Hazel Fire. All of us have done something marvelous. No one has ever brought so much Trade to Sun Town at once, or from so far away. There is Power in that, good friend. Instead of six days, they will cleanse us in three."

"Six? Three? What is the difference?"

"Three." White Bird held up three fingers, touching each fingertip as he talked. "The worlds of Creation: Sky, Earth, and Underworld. Sky is the domain of Father Moon and Mother Sun, the place of sunlight, clouds, and birds. Earth is the surface where we live and the trees grow and the water flows. Third is the Underworld, home of the fish, the roots, moles, and badgers, the place where all things originated. We are born of the underworlds, raised into the light to walk the land, and doomed to forever Dream of flying through the Sky."

"Hmm." Hazel Fire rubbed his chin. "Among my people..."

"Yes, the Magicians can leave their bodies and fly. Here, too, though, we call them the Serpents. You'll meet one soon enough."

"He won't try to steal my Power?" Hazel Fire reached for the small leather pouch that hung from his neck.

"Your umbilical cord is safe." White Bird referred to the dried loop of tissue that all Wolf People carried with them from birth to death. And woe unto he who through flood, fire, or accident lost his. The stories among the Wolf People told of sudden insanity, debilitating illness, and often a wasting death that came within days. It had been a matter of no little awe to Lark that White Bird and Yellow Spider could live, thrive in fact, without one.

"And yours." Hazel Fire pointed to the necklace that draped around White Bird's neck. "I always wondered about those tokens, but thought it rude to ask. I noticed that your necklace never left your neck. Is it magic?"

White Bird reached up, fingering the small stone fetishes hung there. Though some were cubes, others were sections of slate incised with geometric designs, but his fingers went to the little fat-bellied owl carved out of a bloodred stone. "Perhaps it is magic. A protection of sorts. My little brother, Mud Puppy, made this. Can you imagine? He carved each of the pieces, and he was barely past ten and four winters when I saw him last."

"I look forward to meeting him." Hazel Fire saw the sudden reserve in White Bird's eyes. "Is that a problem?"

"Hmm? Oh, no. He's just strange, that's all. A different child. Always has been." The Trader's eyes had focused on something in the distance beyond the fog.

"I suppose, Husband of my sister, that you are normal for your kind? You who braved everything to travel so far north in search of this magical Trade of yours?"

White Bird smiled. "I would like to think I am normal, but no, I suppose I Dream too much."

"I could Dream of that young woman who ran down to wave at you last night." Hazel Fire tried to look unconcerned. "A sister of yours, perhaps? Someone you could introduce me to?"

"Sorry." White Bird had caught his subtle meaning. "She's Rattlesnake Clan. There's a chance I might end up married to her. She won't be Lark, but..."

"She'll be here," Hazel Fire supplied with a shrug. "That is the way of things. Though I wouldn't mind you coming home to be a permanent husband to Lark."

White Bird kept his eyes on the shimmering wall of mist that hid Sun Town. "You don't know how tempting that might be. I have no idea of the situation here. I could tell by my mother's actions last night, by the way she stood, that the clans are at it again."

"And how is that? I would learn what I'm stepping into before it's on my moccasin."

White Bird's preoccupation seemed to vanish. "Oh, you'll be fine. They'll treat you right. It's in the nature of the gifting. You helped to bring the Trade. For that the clans will make you most welcome. Fear not. Just turn your Trade over with a smile, and they will shower you with gifts. Enough to more than fill your canoe before you must head north."

"This giving interests me."

"Giving, Trade if you will, is what binds us together. We are a people of parts and pieces. It goes back to the beginning, to the Creation. It is said that in those times we fought with each other, constantly at war. And then, one day, a magical Masked Owl, one of the Sky Beings from the Creation, came spiraling down to tell us that there was a better way."

Hazel Fire nodded. "Go on."

"We have two moieties." White Bird squatted, using his finger to draw a circle in the charcoal-black mud. This he divided into two sections. "Everything we do is meant to achieve balance. My moiety consists of Owl Clan, Alligator Clan, and Frog Clan. Sky, Earth, and Underworld. We are the night side, that of the north." He divided one-half of the circle into three to denote the clans. "On the other side is the world of day, or the south. The clans are Eagle, Rattlesnake, and Snapping Turtle. Again, Air, Earth and Underworld. Eagles live in the air. Rattlesnakes crawl across the ground and snapping turtles live in the mud underwater." He divided the southern half of the circle into three sections.

"But that's a total of six clans."

"You're right. Six is the number of directions that make up the world. Your people have four sacred directions: north, south, east, and west. My people believe them to be sacred, too, but we add up and down for a total of six directions. In our stories the clans came together here, at the center of the world, from each of the different directions. My people, my clans, my city, all reflect the world. Opposites crossed, night and day, north and south, east and west, up and down. Everything must be brought together to keep Creation intact. We constantly strive to do that, and gifting is how we accomplish such a seemingly hopeless task. The greatest challenge is to hold the world together. Forces, people, are always trying to split it apart. We have to work constantly to bind it back together."

"You told me once that your clan will just give all of these things away to people in other clans." Hazel Fire was frowning. "You won't take anything back from them? Nothing in Trade? No reciprocity?"

"Oh, we'll get our value back," White Bird assured. "We just won't get it in things. Our return comes from the influence our Clan Elder and Speaker have in the Council. We don't collect large amounts of things because that would create envy. People who covet what other people have turn wicked, their souls are the perfect home for evil. But if you give necessary things to the needy, they cannot feel slighted. In turn, when you need, they will provide. We have a very complicated system of give-and-take. It works, it keeps us together, and we keep the Creator happy."

"But I know you were worried when we arrived last night. You and Yellow Spider were unsure about your homecoming."

White Bird nodded absently. "I didn't say that we do not compete with each other. It would have been very different had another clan gained ascendancy. My arrival could have proved, well, shall we say, uncomfortable, for Alligator or Snapping Turtle Clan had they become dominant."

"What about your uncle?" Hazel Fire watched the interplay of emotions on White Bird's handsome face. "You were worried that he might have died while you were gone."

"He wasn't well when I left last spring." White Bird pursed his lips for a moment. "It was a gamble that Yellow Spider and I made. My mother is Clan Elder, her brother, my uncle, is Speaker for the clan when in Council. I told you, Power is passed through the mother in my people. When my uncle dies, my mother, as Elder, has the right to nominate another Speaker. I hope to be that Speaker."

"Then what is the problem? Why can't she just put your name forward?"

White Bird thumped his chest. "I'm young. Not even married."

"You are to Lark. And, if I don't miss my guess, the father of her child."

"On my soul, take no offense from this, but she isn't here, and none of my people recognize her clan. Formally, among the clans, she wouldn't be recognized as a real wife."

Hazel Fire nodded. "No offense is taken. So, let's say you marry that pretty young thing I Dreamed about all night. Marry her and be Speaker."

"Not that easy." White Bird waved a cautionary finger.

"Most men live all of their lives before they are nominated to be Speaker. It's different for a wet-nosed boy like they consider me to be. That's why Yellow Spider and I had to go so far north. That's why we needed so much Trade. That's why I had to risk so much. I had to do something spectacular, Hazel Fire. I may not have gone farther than any of our people have gone before, but I brought more Trade back from that distance than anyone else has."

"For that alone, they should name you Speaker." Hazel Fire made a gesture with his fingers. "But what about your uncle? What if he would have been dead?"

"Mother would have had to nominate another Speaker. I'm the only one left in her lineage. She had no sisters, just brothers. And Cloud Heron is the last of her brothers who is alive."

"What about Cloud Heron's children? Why don't they qualify?"

"You forget, we trace descent through the woman. Uncle Cloud Heron's children belong to his wife. Her name was Laced Fern, and she is a member of the Eagle Clan. So all of Cloud Heron's children belong to the...?" He cocked his head, an eyebrow raised to provoke the answer.

"The children are all Eagle Clan," Hazel Fire supplied. "I understand." He pressed his fingertips together. "Is it so bad for your lineage to lose the Speaker? Couldn't some other clansman serve just as well?"

White Bird shrugged as he dug some of the silty mud from his drawing. Black and slick it stuck to his fingers. "Perhaps. This is difficult to explain, but neither my mother nor I wish to see another take over leadership of the clan. It has been in our lineage for three generations. I am the last. After me, it will go elsewhere because my children will belong to my wife's clan."

"Not the ones from Lark, if you'll recall."

"But Lark is a long way from here."

"Yes, yes, I know, and your people probably consider her to be some kind of wild animal or something."

"I never said that."

"You didn't have to." Hazel Fire laughed. "That's how my people would think of that pretty Spring Cypress if I carried her home, so why wouldn't it be the other way around?" In a more serious voice, he said, "Besides, there's your little brother. What's his name?"

White Bird made a face as he rolled the black silt into a small round ball. "We call him Mud Puppy."

"Like a dog covered with mud?"

"No, a mud puppy is our name for immature brown salamanders. You know, before they are mature, when they still have those star-shaped gills sticking out behind their heads." White Bird rubbed the silt ball between his hands. "Perhaps he'll grow out of this stage he's in, just like a mud puppy grows into a salamander."

"He's how old?"

"Just ten and five winters now." He reached up to finger the fetishes on his necklace. "Mud Puppy as Speaker, now there's a thought for amusement. They would destroy him."

"Destroy?" Hazel Fire cocked his head. "What about all that talk about harmony?"

White Bird gave him a sober look, his dark eyes haunted. In a low voice, he said, "Why do you think we work so hard at it? Prominence of the clans is everything to us. We give things to place people in our debt. Owing something to someone else holds us together like water holds this mud." He lifted the silt ball. "Without gift giving and the obligation it implies, we are nothing.

Barbarians. We need Trade to overcome our real nature. Without it, we would be at each other's throats. I swear, within a generation, we would destroy ourselves."

As he said that, he extended his hand, holding the silt ball between his fingers as he placed it into the water. Hazel Fire watched as the lapping waves melted the ball into goo.

Chapter Five

Mud Puppy sat on a cane mat in the sunlight on the eastern side of his mother's house. Images from the Dream the night before burned through him, replaying between his souls with such clarity that he might have just seen them spun out of the misty morning sunlight. A shiver ran down his bones. He could sense the lingering Power that emanated from Masked Owl. It had been so real!

Frown lines ate into his forehead when he stared down at the cricket. As long as his thumb from knuckle to nail tip, its shell gleamed midnight black in the cup bottom. The antennae were waving in sinuous arcs. But, despite his vigilance, the cricket refused to surrender its secret. Crickets and Sky Beings—they both eluded him.

"What have you got there?" Mother's words caught him by surprise. He looked up, seeing her standing beside him, her arms braced on her hips, face shadowed. The morning sun blazed like white fire in her silvered hair. She had left it down this morning, and it hung over her shoulders. Her white skirt was belted about her hips, leaving her top bare. Mud Puppy could see the line of tattoos, like a chain that circled her sagging breasts and merged to make a double row that ran down the midline of her stomach to surround her navel.

"It's a cricket," he replied in a low voice, wary and unsure. He never knew how she was going to react.

"A cricket?" Wing Heart seemed distracted, her face reflecting no emotion. "What are you doing with it?"

He swallowed hard, knowing better than to lie to her. "I told you about it last night. A cricket is such a small animal. I was trying to see why it makes such a great noise. I've been waiting patiently for cricket to sing, then I will discover his secret. You told me that patience was the footprint of greatness." He hoped that would win him a little goodwill. It pleased her to have him repeat her teachings. "When cricket sings, I'll rip off the bass leaf and see how he makes his noise."

She chewed on the corner of her lip for a moment, then reached out with one hand. "Give it to me."

Reluctantly, he extended the little gray ceramic cup with its bass-leaf cover. She took it, removed the leaf, and stared down into the cup. "A cricket."

"Yes, Mother."

"Do you understand that your brother has returned? Did you see him last night? Are you aware of what he's done?"

"I was at the landing last night. Me and Little Needle—"

"Ah, Little Needle. I'd wager that but for Little

Needle you wouldn't have had the slightest notion that anything was afoot, would you?"

He didn't answer, lowering his gaze to the dark-stained earth at his feet. A bit of red chert gleamed in the sunlight, an old perforator. Someone had broken the tip off and discarded it. It seemed to wink maliciously at him.

"What am I going to do with you?" Mother asked plaintively. "I swear by Mother Sun, I could almost believe that Back Scratch and Mud Stalker knew in advance that you would come of it when they sent Thumper to my bed. I could almost believe that they paid the Serpent to cast a spell on the man's testicles. Thumper's not a dolt, and neither am I, so how did our union produce you?"

Mud Puppy winced, his heart hurting at the tone in her voice. He kept his eyes focused on the bit of gleaming red chert so out of place in the black dirt. Was it trying to talk to him? Was that why it was winking so?

"All you do is waste time." Wing Heart lifted her arms in supplication. "Do you not understand how close we came to disaster? It is not enough that your uncle's Dream Soul has fled? What if he had lost his Life Soul as well? What if White Bird hadn't come back in triumph?" She squatted, lifting his chin with one hand to glare into his eyes. "Do you understand that we are the last in our line to dominate the Council? Do you understand that if we lose that, we are nothing? That we will be just like everyone else?"

"Is that so bad?" he whispered.

"Is that so bad?" she mimicked his voice. "Very well, I'll explain it to you *one...more...time.*" She paused as if searching for the right words. "As you live your life,

Mud Puppy, you will want things. Perhaps it will be a certain woman, though Mother Sun knows, I should be so lucky given your proclivities. When that happens, you must have the position, the prominence among others, and the outstanding *obligation* to be granted that desire. You like to quote my lessons back to me, very well, quote this one: *With obligation comes prestige. With prestige comes authority. With authority comes gratification.*"

He nodded, hating the eye-to-eye contact she maintained. That burning look made his souls squirm around each other.

"Everything we do is based on obligation." Her words were like burning coals. "All that I have achieved, I have achieved through binding others to me through their debt. I didn't achieve my position by studying crickets, or carving little stone figures, but by playing one clan off of the other. By knowing my enemies and making them beholden unto me. That, my misguided son, is the secret to survival. It is by adhering to such a strategy that, in the long run, we will keep Owl Clan in the center of our world."

"I understand." Why did she dominate him like a hawk did a mouse? His ears burned with humiliation. "With obligation comes prestige. With prestige comes authority. With authority comes gratification."

"Very good." She stood then, a frown lining her sun-browned forehead as she studied him. Without a thought, she flipped the cricket from the cup and tossed the empty vessel back to him. "I don't seem to make any impression when I tell you these things." Her eyes drifted to the distance, searching the west. A sudden smile crossed her thin lips. "I want you to know that you have driven me to desperation. I am going to teach you a lesson once and for all."

Mud Puppy swallowed hard. Mother's lessons were never easy.

She narrowed her eyes, a finger on her chin as she thought. "Yes, just as soon as the Serpent can free himself from his duties. It may take a couple of days, but I am going to have him take you up the Bird's Head —and leave you!"

He blinked, trying to understand. No one frightened him like the Serpent did.

She continued, "I want you to spend the night alone up there, Mud Puppy. All by yourself. Just you and the darkness. And if you don't come down changed, I'm going to send you up there again and again until the spirits of the Dead finally get you."

He shot a quick glance westward to where the looming pile of earth rose like a small mountain above the plaza flat. "Can I take Little Needle—"

"Alone!"

"But, if I get afraid—"

"*Alone!* When you get scared—*and I want you trembling to your bones*—you will stay and overcome your fear. No son of mine has the luxury of fear. Do you think your brother was afraid when he went upriver? Do you think he let fear stop him from taking the most dangerous of risks? No. And one day he's going to need you, need your courage and your loyalty to back him." Her voice hardened. *And you will be there for him, or I will haunt you to your dying day."*

She turned, striding purposefully away down the side of the earthen ridge upon which they lived. Her back was straight, her silver-streaked hair swaying with each regal step.

"But I get afraid in the dark," he whispered, turning his eyes to the southwest, past the house where his uncle lay dying, past the line of clan houses and across the plaza. As if embraced by the curve of the raised earth, the tall mound stood, and just below the top, he could make out the little thatched ramada. Terrible things happened up there. Gods came down and whispered things into people's ears. Lightning frequently blasted that high summit. From those heights, it was said that a man could see into the Land of the Dead. Worse, that the Dead could look back and see you. That's why nobody but the most Powerful of hunters and warriors, and old Serpent and his students, ever spent the night up there.

"You'll lose your souls," a tiny voice said.

Mud Puppy looked down at the broken fragment of red chert between his feet. He reached down and plucked it up, watching the sunlight shine off the smooth stone. "Then you'll lose yours, too," he answered, "because I'm taking you with me. Whatever happens to me will happen to you."

The swampland around the Panther's Bones had been inundated for two moons now. Sultry brown waters lapped at the water oak, sweetgum, tupelo, and bald cypress. Long wraiths of hanging moss dangled from the branches. Birds perched amid the lush green leaves, disturbed only rarely as squirrels scrambled from tree to tree in search of ripening fruits. Fish leaped with hollow splashes that barely dented the whirring of the insects and the rising birdsong. Far out in the swamp, a bull alligator roared his desire for a mate.

At the sound, Jaguar Hide turned his head, holding his paddle high. Was it worth turning, going after the big bull? As he considered, his canoe drifted forward, a V-shaped wake disturbing the smooth surface and rocking bits of flotsam and tacky white foam.

"I would rather go home, Uncle," Anhinga said from the bow, her paddle resting on the gunwales. "I have a feeling."

Jaguar Hide cocked his head, asking, "Yes? A feeling? Of what?"

"Of something changing."

He watched the back of her head. She had been silent most of the day, moody since they had departed from the western uplands. Twice he had observed the shaking of her shoulders as sobs possessed her. The grief had been a palpable thing, like a swarm of mosquitoes that shimmered around her.

"Things change, girl. That is the way of the world." He lowered his voice. "But I can see that this is something more. Tell me."

He watched the slight lowering of her head. Dappled sunlight sent shafts of yellow through the green leaves above to speckle her gleaming black hair. "Bowfin's Dream Soul met mine the night he died. He was so anguished to be dead. It was so unfair. I am angry, Uncle. His death has changed my life. I have learned to hate."

Jaguar Hide considered her, noting how her back arched. The set of her head. Gods, she looked just as his sister Yellow Dye had at her age. "Indeed?"

She remained silent, so he extended his paddle, sending the canoe forward as he guided it between the trees. Here and there, they had to duck as low branches blocked the way.

"Whenever I close my eyes I see him lying there, sweat running off of his skin in rivers...his eyes glazed with fear and pain," she whispered. "The smell haunts me, Uncle. It clings to my souls. I can imagine what he felt...how it was to have his guts eaten out like that. It must have burned, like a fire being pulled through his belly on a splintered pole." She shook her head. "He could smell himself. Smell that awful stink coming out of his ripped guts. How did he stand it? Knowing it was his own?"

"Niece, you can stand many things when you have no other choice." Jaguar Hide winced at the pain in her voice. "It is how the Panther made the world. Look around you." He gestured at the brown-water swamp they paddled through. "Everywhere you look, you will see life dancing with death. Does the alligator cast a single tear for the fawn he drags down to death? Does the egret weep for the minnow she spears out of the calm waters? Do you cry at the sight of fish gasping and flopping in the netting of a mud set when it is pulled aboard a canoe? Do these sweetgum trees mourn for the saplings they suffocate with their spreading branches? No, girl. When a hanging spider catches a beautiful butterfly in its web, it eats it with a smile. That is the lesson you should learn. Life is a desperate hunt. As you grin gleefully over your victim's body, remember that tomorrow someone else will be grinning over yours." He hesitated, letting that sink in, then asked: "Do you understand, Anhinga?"

She nodded.

Once again he waited, allowing her time. To his right, a line of yellow-dotted gourd floats indicated that Old Blue Hand had set a gill net.

"It just seems so unfair. This was Bowfin, my little brother. He was just a boy, Uncle. I took care of him. We played together, laughed and cried together. They *murdered* him."

He paddled steadily as she broke down into tears. He had wondered how long it would take for the reality of her brother's death to settle over her souls like a net. Sometimes the young didn't understand. Anhinga had been lucky that life had protected her for the most part. She had never suffered such a rapid and painful loss.

Their relations with the Sun People were always tenuous. Sometimes they traded, but with the most guarded of interactions. Fact was, Jaguar Hide's Panther People had little need for anyone else. The Creator had given his chosen people the finest place in the world to live. Here, in spring, as the floods filled the great river to the east, the waters actually reversed, changed direction, flowing backward into the lakes and watercourses. In the rejuvenated waters, fish thrived. The highlands in the western portion of their territory contained sands, gravels, and their fine panther sandstone: a white, coarse-grained slab that was perfect for smoothing wood and grinding stone. The Creator had made a perfect place for his people. Here they wanted for nothing.

Not at all like what he had done for the Sun People to the north. Perched on their silt ridge, they had no source of stone for cutting, no sandstone for grinding, no sand to temper their pottery. The only riches the

Sun People had been given were fish and plants. So they came here when they needed sandstone, to Jaguar Hide's land, and tried to trade, or more usually, to steal stone. It was when they were caught that young men like Bowfin paid the price.

His heart twisted at the pain and grief in Anhinga's broken sobs. How many times in his life had he heard the wailing and sobbing of relatives grieving for a loved one?

How many lives had been taken from them by a brutal stone-headed dart? If the Creator had meant for the Sun People to have sandstone, he would have given it to them.

I will do something about this. This time, I will find a way to pay them back.

He knotted his souls around the problem as he continued to paddle through the muggy swamp. At their approach, a turtle flipped off a cypress knee, a line of bubbles marking its descent into the murky depths.

Anhinga sniffed hard and straightened. "On my brother's soul," she whispered fiercely, "I will do whatever it takes to make them pay."

"Anything?" he asked casually.

"Anything," she insisted doggedly, picking up her paddle and driving it into the brown swamp water.

An idea was forming in his mind. Something that he hadn't tried. It would take more thought once he had returned home to the Panther's Bones.

The watering of his mouth came as White Bird's brief warning before he bent double and threw up the bitter-tasting brew. Again and again, his stomach pumped, heaving violently as it emptied itself of what remained of a boiled fish breakfast.

The sun burned down on his bare back, its heat adding to the sweat that beaded his flesh. It wasn't enough that he and his companions had spent the night alternately sweating in the small domed lodge and bathing in the brackish waters of the lake, but the Serpent had showed up several hours before dawn and begun brewing his concoctions.

The Serpent had begun by Singing, painting his face, and shaking a gourd rattle as he circled the area. With great care, he laid a fire of red cedar. Then he placed tinder in the center and used twigs to place a hot coal atop it. Bending low, puffing his cheeks and blowing, he coaxed the fire to life.

On this, he placed a soapstone bowl propped with clay balls so the fire could lap around the stone vessel's sides. From his belt pouch, he extracted yaupon leaves and dropped them into the heating bowl. As he did, he called to the four directions: to the east, the south, the west, and north. With a round stone, he crushed the leaves, bruising them to release their color. Using a hickory stick painted crimson, he stirred the leaves as they slowly reddened and curled. When appropriately roasted, he employed a bison-horn dipper to carry water from the lake, and one after another, filled the pot until a yellow froth formed on the boiling liquid. The Serpent stirred it with his red stick, satisfied to see that the roiling liquid had blackened beneath the foam. Reaching into his pouch again, he extracted a section of snakemaster root, and with a white chert knife, shaved slices into the brew. Then, as the steam rose, he began to dance his way around them, thrusting the rattle this way and that.

"Why is he doing that?" Gray Fox asked nervously.

"To announce to any evils that he is coming to drive them off," White Bird explained. "It is hoped that by so stating, the harmful spirits and malicious ghosts will simply leave, making his work easier. This way, he can turn all of his attention to the few stubborn and recalcitrant spirits who remain. It gives him a chance to identify the ones that wish to challenge his Power as a spirit warrior."

"I wouldn't challenge him...alive or dead," Jackdaw muttered in his own language. "Isn't he just the ugliest old man you've ever seen?"

Hazel Fire and the others had laughed at that, and White Bird couldn't find it in himself to disagree. The Serpent had passed more than five tens of winters. His hair had gone white and thin. Now, it waved about his head like a wreath of water grass in a changing current. The old man's face might have been trod upon, so flat was it. The nose looked as if it had been mashed into his features, the sharp brown eyes staring out of thick folds of flesh. Skin hung like dead bark from the Serpent's frame, and through the wrinkles, one could see patterns of snake tattoos that had faded into blue-black smears. He looked more like a walking skeleton, his ribs sticking out, the knobby joints of his knees thicker than his thin thighs.

Not even a finger of time had passed from the moment they had drunk the Serpent's concoction before the first of them had bent double and thrown up.

White Bird's stomach wrenched again. He cramped with the dry heaves.

"We're poisoned!" Hazel Fire cried between gasps. The Wolf Traders were clustered around, some on hands and knees as they wretched and groaned.

"No!" White Bird made a face at the vile taste in his mouth. "Trust me. This is good for us. It's driving any illness or sorcery out of our bodies. I swear, you're not poisoned. It's just..." His stomach knotted, and he doubled up again as his gut tried to turn him inside out.

When the spell passed, he rolled over to seat himself on the damp soil. A shadow blocked the sun as the Serpent bent, mumbling to himself as he inspected the goo White Bird had deposited on the ground. The old man used a blue-painted stick to prod the watery mess.

"I see," the old man muttered. "A chill was headed for your bones, young man. Good thing we got it out."

"How do you know that?" White Bird placed a hand to his aching stomach and gasped for breath.

The Serpent cocked a faded brown eyebrow, the action rearranging the mass of wrinkles. He lifted the blue stick, gaze locked on a thread of silvery mucus that glinted in the sunlight. "You think this is easy? You think just anybody can read what's hidden in vomit? It takes many turnings of seasons to learn these things. And very hard study. The signs of sorcery, not to mention the imbalance of the souls, are difficult even for the trained eye to detect. The spirits alone know what tricks foreign sorcerers would use to kill you."

White Bird blinked, hesitating lest talking lead to another bout of retching. Finally, he said, "What about the others?"

The Serpent had turned and begun to jab his stick into the spattered remains of Jackdaw's breakfast. "This boy was going to have a pain in his leg soon, but it's out now.

"Haw!" The old man jabbed repeatedly at the vomit as if he were tormenting some unseen thing.

Jackdaw leaped back, crying, "What? What's he doing?"

"You're all right," White Bird told him in his own language. "He just saved you from a pain in your leg."

Unsure, Jackdaw backed away as the old man continued to chant and jab. "I'd have been happier with a lame leg. My stomach feels like it's been turned inside out."

"Mine, too," Cat's Paw moaned. Like his friend, he scuttled back as the Serpent turned to the place where he'd thrown up and began jabbing at it and uttering terrible cries.

One by one, he attacked their vomit, and finally raised himself straight, his face lifted to the bright morning sun. "Mother Sun, I have seen the things carried by these people. I have exposed the blackness to your light." He lifted his arms, the stick held high. "Help me now as I purify this place. Burn away the sickness and evil. I brandish your daughter in the cleansing." With that, he swirled about in an elaborate circle. "Take this evil—*and purify* it!" The old shaman dramatically threw the blue stick into the fire, where cedar flames greedily devoured it.

"Why a blue stick?" Cat's Paw asked.

"Blue is the color of the west, of death and failure. It is the color of ending, just as the sky darkens at night after Mother Sun slips away into the world below." He pointed up at the sun. "In the beginning time, just after the Sky Beings came to Earth, they ensured that

Mother Sun would light the world and the creatures that lived here. Fire came from Mother Sun, sent to the Earth in a bolt of lightning. With it, Mother Sun ensured that the Earth could always be cleansed of darkness and disease and sorcery and corruption."

"What now?" Hazel Fire asked warily as he wiped a hand across his mouth.

"We're going to build fires where we threw up. It's all got to be burned." White Bird pointed to the stack of firewood under the thatched shed at the base of the sweetgum tree.

"Is there much more of this?" Snow Water was on all fours, staring hostilely at the old man. "I'm starting to wonder if it's worth it. I might just take my chances canoeing home alone."

"Trust me, it's worth it. One more day," White Bird promised. "And it's easy by comparison."

"It better be." Hazel Fire shook his head. "Or I'm slipping away in the middle of the "night, too."

"It's important that we undergo this," White Bird replied gently. "For the safety of Sun Town. We don't fear the enemies that we know, only the ones we can't see. I ask you to trust me. I told you about the cleansing."

"You did," Cat's Paw admitted. "I just didn't really appreciate what it was going to be like."

"Just wait," Hazel Fire promised, "and see what we do to you next time you come upriver."

White Bird made it halfway to the woodpile before his gut caught him by surprise and sent him into convulsions. Maybe his friends were right about slipping away. But deep in the spot between his souls, he knew the correctness of a proper cleansing.

The Serpent

T rue leaders, it seems to me, are born in betrayal.
My first teacher was a very old woman, a
Clan Elder. When I became the Serpent, she
told me that she believed we are born at the foot of the log
bridge that leads to the Land of the Dead, and that the
instant we slip from our mother's canoe, if we truly
listen, we will hear the animals we have known in our
lives calling to us.

The boy is smiling to himself.

I watch him.

Does he know?

At his tender age, can he possibly understand that a
person has to be shoved off the bridge by the one he trusts
most before he can look up, see no one standing above to
help him, and grasp that being alone is not the curse, it is
the task?

Chapter Six

Wing Heart sat in the afternoon shade of the thatched ramada beside her house. With a facility that came from many seasons of practice, she used her thigh and one hand to spin basswood fibers into cordage. She had stripped the fibers from the tree's bark by first soaking, then pounding it with a stone-headed mallet. That loosened the fibers so that they could be pulled free, then combed, and assembled into the flaxen pile on her right. As she spun the fibers, she looped the finished cord into a coil to her left.

Her house stood at the eastern end of the first northern ridge. From her ramada, she could look out over the wind-patterned waters of Morning Lake. Waves lapped at the bank four body lengths below the sheer drop-off. Three glossy white herons sailed soundlessly southward, their wide wings catching the updraft along the bank before her.

Looking out onto the lake, her view included the

Turtle's Back: a low hump of earth topped by three sweetgum trees and trampled grass. She could make out the Serpent's thin figure as he walked from one young man to another, tapping each of them lightly on the shoulders with an eagle-feather wand.

White Bird sat with his back to the gum tree's trunk. If his posture was any indication, he looked absolutely miserable. It brought a smile to her lips. That was the point, wasn't it? The people didn't want evil spirits from distant places being carried into their midst. By making the host body uncomfortable, those same malicious forces would drift away in search of a more pleasant body to inhabit while they worked their dark and sorcerous deeds.

"Bless you, my son," she said with satisfaction, her gaze lingering on the four long canoes that had been pulled onto the small island's muddy shores. Even from her vantage point she could see the piled packs and reflect on the salvation it meant for her lineage and Owl Clan in general.

She added more fibers from the pile to her right, twisting them into the center of the cord. Fibers had to be added as others were exhausted so that the cordage remained uniform in strength and thickness. The manufacture of cordage was important to her people. Not only did it bind things together like houses, drying racks, and roof thatch, but it was the essential ingredient in their fishnets and small-game snares. From it, they braided strong ropes. On their looms, it became a coarse fabric for burden bags and storage containers. Cordage allowed them to measure out the uniform earthworks that defined the limits of Sun Town and the holdings of the clans. Cordage was always in demand for Trade, as were the fine fabrics they wove and the wooden products they carved. Small loops of cord even provided for days of entertainment as the children played the finger-string game, creating patterns and designs as they plucked the loop back and forth from hand to hand.

She saw Clay Fat as he approached, walking across the open plaza from the line of houses dotting the ridges to the southeast. Rattlesnake Clan had its holdings there. The moment she saw him she knew he was coming to see her. No doubt, the single unifying feeling among the members of Rattlesnake Clan was relief. White Bird had arrived despite their dire predictions. Their political situation, especially their relationship to Owl Clan, had been not only justified but was about to be solidified.

Whereas last week, her very existence might have been suspect—given the lack of attention she had been receiving—her circumstances had changed with White Bird's arrival. One after another she had been entertaining Clan Elders and Speakers. Indeed, the world might have flipped from end to end since her son's flotilla had nosed into Sun Town's placid Morning Lake. Even old Back Scratch, the Snapping Turtle Clan Elder, had been forced to swallow her pride and toddle her creaking bones across the plaza to make pleasant talk. Sweet Root, her daughter, had accompanied her, slinking like the predatory cat she was. One day—and not so far away—Sweet Root would inherit her clan's mantle. Spirits help them all.

Back Scratch kept a lid on most of Mud Stalker's

poison. Sweet Root, however, wouldn't have the sense to keep her brother on a short string. She had always been in awe of him, and after her mother's death, she would be a cunning and willing accomplice, ready and anxious to add her own machinations to those of her bitter, alligator-bitten brother.

As the day had passed Wing Heart had entertained them all. Smiling, gracious, she had played the game with all the skill that her turnings of seasons and innate ability had given her. Calling on her clan she had provided smoked fish and bread made from smilax root. A stone bowl continued to steam by the fire, sweetening the air with the pungent odor of black drink. The foamy tea made from holly leaves was normally reserved for special occasions. Having a pot of it on hand provided that extra bit of elegance to reinforce the notion that Owl Clan remained preeminent.

Wing Heart watched as Clay Fat continued amiably on his way across the plaza. His belly protruded over his loincloth, his knobby navel like the stem on a brown melon. A half-lazy smile traced Clay Fat's thick lips, his expression dreamy, as if he had not a care in the world.

Wing Heart considered him. Clay Fat wasn't an acutely smart man. Rather, he was wedded to stability the way a fisherman enjoyed a deep-keeled canoe. He liked balance and was happiest when he knew exactly what was coming with the next sunrise. The passing of the last six moons—in the shadow of Speaker Cloud Heron's impending death—had been hard on Clay Fat's nerves. The uncertainty over young White Bird's whereabouts upriver—let alone whether or not he was still alive—had been excruciating. Now, with the world set back to rights, he looked much like a fat toad full of bugs.

She owed him. Of them all, he had stood by her, steadfastly believing her promise that her son would return from the north, and that when he did, it would be with a stunning coup that would assure Owl Clan's hegemony.

No, Clay Fat might not be the brightest of the Clan Speakers. Had he been someone other than himself, he would have taken that opportunity to try to propel Rattlesnake Clan into leadership. At least she, or any of the other Clan Elders, would have struck like a hungry snake when she sensed the slightest vulnerability in her rivals.

But is he so dumb? Wing Heart turned the notion over in her mind, trying to see it from Clay Fat's perspective. Was it not better to place Rattlesnake Clan in a perpetual secondary role rather than risk falling into even more pressing debt to the others?

"Greetings, Wing Heart," Clay Fat called, waving as he trooped across the muddy shallows of the borrow pit and climbed the earthen ridge upon which the Owl Clan houses were built. As Clan Elder, Wing Heart had the most prestigious location, on the eastern edge of the berm overlooking Morning Lake. Here, she could greet the sunrise, and best of all, monitor the comings and goings at the Turtle's Back.

"A pleasant day to you, Speaker. How is your Elder, Graywood Snake, today?"

"She is well, Wing Heart. She sends her fondest greetings." He strode up, breath coming in labored gasps. She could see the sweat beginning to bead on his swollen brown skin. "I must say, things are happening. So much talk."

"Talk?" She pointed to the cane mat across from her. "Sit, old friend. Enjoy the shade. Would you like a cup of black drink? As you can see, the bowl is still steaming."

"Bless you, but no. It's too hot," he muttered. "Here we are but a half-moon past spring equinox and it already feels like midsummer." He grunted as he eased himself onto the matting. "Is it me, or are the passing summers getting hotter and hotter?"

"It is you," she told him, her fingers spinning the cord along her thigh. "The summers are no hotter. It's just that your belly gets larger and larger. It holds your heat in like a giant cooking clay."

He laughed at that, slapping a calloused hand against his stomach.

"So, there is talk you say? Anything of interest or are they just scrambling to cover themselves, saying, 'Oh, I knew all along that White Bird would return!'"

He shot her a knowing glance, his dark brown eyes measuring. "Hardly. Envy and venom are whispered behind the hand while smiles and nectar drape public speech. At least that's the way of the leaders' lineages. For those who have no stake in the squabbles among the Council's leaders, interest centers on what lies hidden under those packs in White Bird's canoes. Most people, as you well know, Wing Heart, could care less who holds the ropes to the fish traps so long as they can share in the catch."

"Runners have gone out?"

He nodded, reaching down to finger the end of the cane matting he sat on. "People are beginning to trickle in from the outlying camps. Everyone is expecting a feast and dancing, and an excuse to get together and gossip. For the people who are in need, it is a chance to refit, to replace what is broken or worn-out." He glanced out across the lake, fixing his gaze on the Turtle's Back and the figures that hunched out there in a line next to the sweat lodge. "Is everything all right?"

"My son is going through a nasty cleansing. For a while yesterday, he couldn't stop throwing up. I believe that the Serpent is being particularly thorough this time. He wasn't happy about a three-day cleansing. At White Bird's suggestion, I requested it rather forcefully. It seems that his Wolf companions, as he calls them, are leery about what it will do to the health of their barbarian souls."

"Their souls? Why? Is there something wrong with them?"

"Put it like this: Would you trust some Serpent you didn't know to cleanse your souls? Say, perhaps, some Wolf Serpent whose ways you couldn't differentiate from witchcraft? A strange Serpent from way up north? One who did things you didn't understand? Sang strange songs, made you bare your souls to him?"

"I would be more than a little frightened."

"So are these Wolf Traders," Wing Heart added. "The last thing I need is for them to bolt in the middle of the night and take those loaded canoes with them."

"There's risk in that."

"There's risk in everything."

"What if someone takes sick? What if, after they've been rushed through cleansing, something goes wrong? People will say that you didn't take enough precautions."

"I'll take my chances."

He nodded, that slight smile returning to his lips. "Well, there is already talk."

"Talk? We're back to talk?" Which, of course, was what he'd come to tell her in the first place.

"My cousin, Fork Tail, and his party returned from his trip down south last night. He has several nice pieces of that white Panther sandstone. Not as many as he would have liked to have, but enough to still make the trip profitable. It will allow Rattlesnake Clan a chance to offer something, and at the same time, you have to rid yourself of all those canoe loads of exotics."

"Good for you." She noticed the reserve behind his bland eyes. "But..."

Clay Fat shrugged. "There were complications. He couldn't load his canoe with all the stone he wanted. It seems that some of the Swamp Panthers ambushed him. In the fight that followed, he wounded at least one of them. A youth."

"Kill him?"

"He doesn't know. Apparently, the dart was sticking out of the boy's belly when he ran away. As to how serious it was, Fork Tail couldn't tell."

"These things happen." Wing Heart spliced more fibers into her cord and continued spinning it along her thigh. "If we're lucky, the kid just got nicked. Were others involved?"

"Apparently, a party of youths."

"So there's no chance the boy might have gone off and died before anyone found out?"

Clay Fat gave her a shake of his head for an answer. "You had better circulate the word to Owl Clan that the Swamp Panthers will probably retaliate. My clan is already spreading the word through the lineages to the camps in the south."

"Is that all the bad news you've got?"

"Of course not." His thin lips widened in a smile. "You should know that Mud Stalker is nearly foaming at the mouth. He and Back Scratch were in the process of tightening their grip on leadership in the Council until your son paddled into the middle of their plans. He had come to think you were toothless, and all he needed to worry about was Deep Hunter. Then White Bird floats into Morning Lake with his barbarian friends, and Mud Stalker's world is upside down. It's all that Mud Stalker can do to keep from popping the veins in his head."

"Cane Frog wasn't happy either. She and Deep Hunter would have been overjoyed to wrest control of the Northern Moiety away from me, let alone take a chance on gaining leadership of the Council."

Clay Fat was watching her through his expressionless brown eyes. "Very well, Wing Heart, you've pulled the proverbial hare out of the hollow log yet again. What about the endless tomorrows? You have two sons, the last of your lineage. White Bird has a great future ahead of him, but you can't risk him on another venture like this one. Somewhere, sometime, some barbarian is going to kill him, or his canoe is going to be swamped in a spring flood, or he's going to catch some foreign disease and die. Beyond the protection of our city, the world is a dangerous place. Tens of tens of things could happen. Somewhere out in those distant places, something will eventually get him."

She nodded, aware of just how frightened she had been of exactly that.

"And it's not like you have a lot of choices." Clay Fat tilted his head back to stare up at the thatch overhead. "Mud Puppy is your only other child."

"Would to Mother Sun I had had a daughter out of that mating with Thumper. I could marry her to some daring young man and send him upriver. If he didn't come back, I could marry her again, and again, and again, until one of them got it right and brought me back another four canoes of Trade."

"You wouldn't even need that," he told her. "You would have an heir. A daughter to carry your line on into the future."

"Correct."

After a pause, he added, "You could always name Mud Puppy Speaker. Then it wouldn't matter if White Bird didn't come back." He laughed one of those deep belly laughs.

"You find that funny, do you?"

He straightened his face but the attempt failed in the slightest to mask his amusement. "He's young. He might change. You know, grow out of it."

She arched an eyebrow. "Mud Puppy, grow out of it?"

"Boys do. When they step into the world of men, they can't help but change."

Snakes! He's almost a man now, but you'd never know it. "He thinks differently than any boy I ever knew. I'm at my wit's end. Water Petal has him in the sweat lodge. I've made an appointment to have the Serpent take him up to spend the night atop the Bird's Head. Maybe that will scare some sense into his witless noggin. He's completely hopeless! His brother returns, the most important event in the lineage in how many winters, and he's looking at a cricket in a jar!"

Clay Fat nodded, his head oddly cocked. "In the last few moons, I have come to discover how important leadership of the Council is to you, Wing Heart. Tell me, if it came right down to it, would you declare him Speaker?"

"Perhaps if I'd been hit in the head too hard, or if lightning struck me."

"I've stood with you through the last moons, Wing Heart. Stood with you when many urged me to look elsewhere for obligations. Your clan and mine have made a good alliance through the endless turnings of the seasons."

"What are you getting at?"

"All jesting aside, I need to know something."

"Very well." She had ceased spinning her cord. "What is that thing, old friend?"

"What would you do to retain Owl Clan's hegemony? What would you do to keep your leadership?"

She felt trapped in his wary, brown-eyed stare. The universe might have narrowed to the two of them. "I'd do anything, Clay Fat. I've lived all of my life preparing for the leadership. I *don't* want to give that up. I *won't* give it up."

"Then you'd do anything to keep it?"

She nodded, wondering what this was going to cost her, wondering where it had come from. What did he suspect? Worse, what did he know?

"Anything," she reaffirmed.

He contemplated her in silence, his eyes prying into her souls, as though to see what she really meant. In the end, he sighed, relaxing, his smooth smile returning.

"Then you will understand when I tell you that I...my clan cannot allow Spring Cypress to marry White Bird. Your son will insist. You must refuse."

Mind racing, she asked, "Why?"

Clay Fat's expression had turned bland again. "I almost made a terrible mistake, Wing Heart. But for the return of your son, I could have lost a great deal and found myself and my clan in the same position as Frog Clan is in today. At the bottom, mucking about in the silt for scraps. Obliged to everyone. I will support you and do what I must to maintain your leadership, but I want you to understand that I am going to strengthen the position of my lineage."

"And who were you thinking of?"

"Copperhead."

"Mud Stalker's cousin? He's twice her age." Her mind wrapped around the implications of Rattlesnake Clan brokering an alliance with Snapping Turtle Clan.

"Copperhead is freshly widowed."

"He used to beat Red Gourd when she was his wife. Some people think he killed her."

"That was never proven by her clan." Clay Fat seemed nonplussed.

Her voice dropped. "You'd do that to Spring Cypress?"

The corners of his mouth twitched. "Let's just say there is a compelling reason, shall we?"

"What does Graywood Snake say about this?"

"The Rattlesnake Clan Elder understands and agrees."

She studied him thoughtfully. *So, you, too, had abandoned me. White Bird's return caught you off guard, didn't it? Now I catch you scrambling to reclaim your balance.*

As if he could read her thoughts, he said, "Make this thing easy for me, and I shall give you my obligation for the future." He paused. "Besides, it might not be so bad, having an ear close to Mud Stalker. As you well know, Elder, the future is a very uncertain place."

Chapter Seven

N o son of mine has the luxury of fear. The words echoed around in Mud Puppy's head as he followed the Serpent up the long, steep slope of the Bird's Head. Having almost completed White Bird's cleansing, the old Serpent had finally come for Mud Puppy.

The old man wore a simple fabric breechcloth bound to his waist by a cord. From it hung several small leather sacks that held who knew what kind of magic potions. A patchwork cloak made of muskrat hides draped the old man's shoulders. He might have been a walking skeleton, with thin muscles hanging from his old bones. Mud Puppy couldn't help but notice how the old man's knees and feet seemed so big in comparison with his skinny legs. In all, the Serpent was the most frightening man Mud Puppy had ever known.

His entire body tingled, partly from fear, partly from the ordeal he had endured in the sweat lodge, purifying himself for the coming night's trial. The endless hands of time he had spent alternately roasting and dripping sweat in rivers, versus those few moments when Cousin Water Petal tipped a pot of cool water over his head, had left him feeling oddly weak, though rejuvenated.

"I don't know what your mother's after, boy," Water Petal had told him ominously. "She's been over to the island"—she referred to the Turtle's Back—"talking to the Serpent. Something you did set her off. What was it this time? Did you leave a worm in her water cup? Or did she catch you with your butt up in the air, peeking under leaves when you should have been doing chores?"

"It was my cricket," he had started to explain, but Water Petal had silenced him by pouring another bowl of chilly water over his head. She had just passed two tens of winters, and should have given birth to three or four children by this time. Instead, her abdomen now bulged with her first. Those sharp black eyes of hers intimated that she would rather be anywhere than helping Mud Puppy with his ritual cleansing. A sentiment he shared. But when the Clan Elder ordered, people obeyed, especially those in the lineage.

Despite a deep-seated fear in his belly, he and the Serpent finished the long climb. The Bird's Head, a huge mound of earth, dominated and guarded the western edge of Sun Town. It rose as if to scrape the sky. So high, so huge was it that from the peak Mud Puppy could see the entire world. He could look down on the tops of trees. People looked like mites as they inched along below him.

The old man wheezed, one hand to his chest as the wind whipped his filmy white hair. A faint flush had darkened the wrinkled mass of his platter-flat face, but thoughtful eyes hid deep behind the folds of his skin. His gaze drilled through Mud Puppy like a perforator on a stick.

Mud Puppy fought to still his sudden fear, shamed by the loose gurgle in his bowels. A desire grew in his souls to turn around and run down that long slope on charged legs. Anything to get away from this inspired and terrible place.

His heart began to pound as they topped the highest point. The world spread out before him to the west. The vista made his bare feet curl, toes biting into the crumbly clay soil. They were so high here that when he looked upward, he half expected to see the clouds rubbing against the Sky dome. The feeling gave him the giddy sense of seeing the world as a bird must, everything below him, so far below. He might have been Masked Owl himself.

"In the beginning"—the Serpent raised his hand, pointing at the tree-covered western horizon—"at the Creation, the Sky was cracked off from the Earth. That is a most important event. Do you know why the Great Mystery did that?"

Mud Puppy swallowed hard. Would the Serpent give him that same disgusted look that Mother did? He shook his head in a hesitant no.

"Take a moment and consider," the Serpent told him mildly.

Mud Puppy tried to avoid those hard black eyes. He let his gaze wander, his mind half-locked with the terror of his situation. He had never stood at the top of the Bird's Head. The enormity of the high mound staggered him. How had his people ever managed to build such a mass of earth, basket by basket, one turning of the seasons after another? Could such a miracle really be of human manufacture? Had hands really built this monument to the gods? It had to be the highest point in the world—though the Traders said that other mountains, far to the northwest, were higher.

Along the western base of the great mound, he could see the narrow pond that filled the mighty trench his people had dug into the ground. It glinted silver, like a gleaming worm stretched across the greensward. It was said that monsters lurked under that deep water. Had his people unwittingly opened a door to the Underworld in their effort to erect this huge mountain of earth?

"That's not where the answer lies," the Serpent murmured as if reading his thoughts.

Mud Puppy reached down to pull nervously at the frayed flap of his breechcloth. *It was the clay.* The thought just popped into his head. His people needed the sticky gray clay. No mound of earth the size of the Bird's Head could be raised out of the rich brown silt that covered the ridge. The deeply buried clay was necessary to give the huge earthwork stability. Without it, the silt would soften and flow in the rains, slumping and sagging, until the Bird's Head sank right back into the ground from which it came.

The picture formed in his head: a digging stick being driven down into the hard gray clay and leaving a scar, just one of a number of similar scars in the side of the excavation pit. Like jagged alligator teeth had gnawed the soil away.

"Why did the Great Mystery rip the Sky away from the Earth?" the Serpent's voice reminded.

Mud Puppy raised his head to stare at the glowing

clouds, backlit by the dying sun as they scurried northward. Here, so high above the Earth, the southern wind tugged at him as it rushed up from the gulf, the smell of forest, swamp, damp earth, and spring flowers carried on its warm caress.

"Because the Great Mystery didn't like it that way?" Mud Puppy guessed.

"And why would that be?" The Serpent bent down, his eyes prying away at Mud Puppy's.

"Because a question is always hidden inside another question," Mud Puppy whispered, and instantly winced, afraid that the Serpent would hiss and strike—lash his frightened souls right out of his terrified body.

Instead, the terrible black eyes softened. The old man nodded, which made the wattles on his neck shake. "You are smarter than your brother was when he was your age." The Serpent arched a grizzled eyebrow. "Yes, there is always another question inside a question. But for the moment, I need an answer for this one. And, boy, I do not expect you to give me the answer right now. Indeed, I expect you to think about it, to study it. The answer isn't what you would expect. Certainly not one to be given off the tip of your tongue like an insult or a compliment. Think, boy. Consider it long and hard."

The old man abruptly turned, faced the east, and used one knobby hand to spin Mud Puppy around so that he looked out over Sun Town. The effect took his breath away. In the growing twilight, the arcs of concentric ridges spread out to the left and right in a huge curve. Houses, like warts, might have been marching away along the length of the ridges. The immensity of it —coupled with the perfect symmetry of those nested curves sculpted so artistically onto the plain—left him awed.

As he looked down the long eastern slope the Bird's Head fell away from his toes in a broad ramp that widened as it fanned out like the spread tail feathers of a great hawk. At the base of the tail, the huge clan grounds created a gigantic half oval transected along its midline by the steep bluff running north–south above Morning Lake.

Two large poles, one for the Northern Moiety, one for the Southern Moiety, marked the geometric centers of the offset circles. The six rows of ridges were, in turn, interrupted by breaks that separated the clans. In the north, Mud Puppy's Owl Clan occupied the eastern-most ridges, Alligator Clan lay in the middle, and the Frog Clan's ridges ran right to the base of the Bird's Head on the west. A use-beaten avenue that ran due east–west through the town separated the moieties' plazas north from south. The westernmost ridges on the south belonged to Rattlesnake Clan. Another gap on the southwest separated them from Eagle Clan.

Unique to Eagle Clan's territory, a narrow earthen causeway led straight as a stretched cord for three dart casts beyond the city to the southwest. There, the Dying Sun Mound rose above the plain in a flat-topped oval. Yet another gap separated the Eagle and Snapping Turtle Clans. The latter occupied the far southern course of the ridges.

Two small mounds lay within the plaza area. The Mother Mound was situated at the edge of the eastern drop-off. A two-tiered earthwork, its flattened southern side supported the Women's House: the large menstrual lodge where women resided during their moon-tied cycles. The fact that a woman's cycle was tied to the moon had provoked considerable speculation. The moon, after all, was a masculine being. But then, without male involvement, a woman was incapable of bearing children. In the end, the location of the Mother Mound had been chosen by sighting from the center of Sun Town to the northernmost point where the moon rose on the eastern horizon at the end of its eighteen-and-one-half-turning-of-seasons migration across the sky.

On the south lay the Father Mound, with its gaudily painted wooden-and-thatch Men's House. The rites of war, of the hunt, and Trade were conducted there. Mud Puppy had never seen the inside of the Men's House. Boys weren't allowed. But someday, when he was admitted into manhood, he would. Terrifying stories circulated among boys of his age, tales of the curious ceremonies and bloody initiations that occurred behind those secretive walls. Similar to its maternal opposite to the north, Father Mound had an odd relationship to Mother Sun. When sighting southeast, the Father Mound was in line of sight of the point on the horizon where the sun rose on the shortest day of the writer—another oddity, but one that made sense when placed in context of the People's struggle to achieve unity and harmony. Opposites crossed, brought into balance, that was the central spiritual force that bound the People together.

Mud Puppy could see it in the form and beauty of Sun Town. The disparate moieties, the constantly bickering clans, north and south, east and west, sun and moon. Sun Town unified them all in the form of the great Sky Being: Bird Man. He had sailed down from the Sky World on fiery wings to shape the Earth after the Creation.

From above, Sun Town looked like a huge bird, its wings curved protectively around the clan grounds. The Power of the place seemed to pulse in the evening.

And there, out in the purple water, he could see the Turtle's Back, where his brother should be taking the last of his sweat baths and preparing for the final night of purification.

"Look at what you see, boy," the Serpent told him. "No other place on Earth is like this. We live at the center of the world. The gods and spirits know this, they are reminded each time they look down. It was here, on this spot, that Bird Man first touched the Earth after the Creation."

"It is huge," Mud Puppy said in awe as he looked north across the fields and patches of trees to the distant Star Mound. From here it looked like a bump rising above the tree line. Star Mound provided protection from the terrifying Powers of the North, the way Bird's Head protected the People from the dangers of the West. Winter came rolling out of the north, dark and cold, while in the West, death lurked, and Mother Sun died.

Two smaller mounds had been built, one to the north, the other to the south, on a line that transected the Bird's Head. The conical Spirit Mound three dart casts due north was where the people offered gifts at sunset on the summer solstice. She would need them to sustain her in her southern flight as she perpetually fled Father Moon's infidelity.

The flat mound at the end of the earthen causeway three dart casts to the south was called Dying Sun

Mound. It was there, on the winter solstice, that people implored Mother Sun to begin her journey northward across the Sky.

"From where you now stand, you can look straight south across the Dying Sun Mound." The Serpent pointed at a pole that rose from the shoulder of the Bird's Head. "Each day, at midday, that pole marks Mother Sun's journey across the Sky. On winter solstice, the tip of the shadow falls right here, where your feet now stand, marking the shortest day of the winter." Then the Serpent turned north. "And at night, you look straight north to the Great North Star, around which the Sky World turns." He pointed at a second pole. "By standing here, and bending slightly, you can see that star night after night, season after season. It is because the North, for all of its terrors, is a place of stability, unlike the realm of Mother Sun. She and Father Moon are forever advancing and retreating across the sky, he pursuing, she fleeing. Forever mindful of the time, he betrayed her bed by locking hips with another woman."

"You said the Sky World turns?" Mud Puppy blurted in surprise. His terror had begun to recede, replaced by fascination with the things the Serpent was telling him.

"Indeed it does. If you sit here on a cloudless night, boy, you can watch the stars slowly spin around the North Star. You must be very still and patient and mark the paths of the stars as they circle the heavens. They move so slowly. No one can tell you why. It is only one of the many mysteries." The Serpent smiled wistfully. "But that is not what I have come to teach you today. No, I just tell you this to tease you, to stimulate your curiosity. There are more mysteries, but they are for the future, boy. Instead, I want you to look down at Sun Town and tell me what you see."

Mud Puppy turned back toward the dusk-heavy town. Cooking fires had begun to sparkle on the concentric ridges.

The south wind carried blue tendrils of smoke northward across the ridges and toward Star Mound. Was it imagination, or could he smell the burning hickory and maple from this great height?

"I see Sun Town." The thought struck him again that it resembled a huge bird, its wings outspread. Power rose around him, slipping along his skin with a feathery touch. "I've never seen it from up here before. It's so different."

"Yes, it is. There is a reason for that. You see the One. The unity. That is the miracle of this place, boy. The Power of Sun Town—of the moieties, the clans, and the lineages—is that we are all so many pieces. Just like a body, made of bone, muscle, blood, and organs. Each piece separate under the skin. Sun Town is our body, the whole of the People, living, breathing, *being...* but it is more than that. It is our world. The directions: East, South, West, North, Up and Down. Our mounds rising to the Sky, our borrow pits sinking into the Earth. All the pieces of the world come together here. This place is the reconciliation of the world. What you see around you is the harmony of all the parts of Creation working together."

"You said that we are at the center of the world."

"Ah," the Serpent replied, his old toothless mouth agape, "now you begin to understand. I am an old man, but the wonder I see in your eyes still fills me when I stand up here. All those tens of winters have flowed past like the Father Water, and still I look and marvel at who and what we are. It is here, of all the places on Earth, that the One is knit together."

"The One?"

The old man's eyes had turned dreamy. "The One, the Dance, the terrible disruptive harmony."

Mud Puppy shivered, hearing the words of Masked Owl reverberating from his dreams. *The One! The Dance!* A tingle of excitement ran through him.

The Serpent waved a calloused hand out to encompass the curving lines of houses below them. "They don't see it, don't feel it, don't Dance it in their souls. No, boy, they stand at the center of the world, bathed in a pitch-black brightness, and study the mud between their toes. They scheme, dicker, bargain, and plot to gain prestige or authority—and forget the miracle of who they are."

The venom in the old man's words shocked Mud Puppy. He couldn't help but think of his mother, the Clan Elder, and her constant preoccupation with the demands of keeping clan and lineage preeminent.

"You are different, boy," the Serpent whispered. "No matter what they do to you, remember that. If you ever doubt, climb up here and look down. See with the eyes of your souls and listen to the deafening silence. They will try to take the harmony away from you, to weight your feet down until you cannot follow the Dance."

"I don't understand."

The old man glanced at him, his thin form silhouetted against the scudding charcoal clouds. The wind sent its fingers rippling through the frail white hair and tugged at the old man's sash. Despite the growing darkness, the Serpent's eyes were aglow. "*He* came to me in a Dream. *He* told me your mother would come, that she would give me this chance."

He? He, who? The old man's words made no sense. Fingers of sudden worry stroked at Mud Puppy's souls. He turned his eyes back to the darkening lake and the dimple created by the Turtle's Back. A flickering fire had sprung to life there. "I would have thought you would be out with my brother. It's his last night of purification."

The Serpent muttered something under his breath, sighed, and finally said, "Tell me about how people first came into this world."

Mud Puppy squinted as the wind batted his straight black hair against his forehead. "It was after the Creator split the Sky from the Earth. Everything was water. The Sky Beings looked down from above the dome of the Sky and saw water everywhere. It was Water Beetle who finally flew from the Sky on his wings, dived into the water, and swam to the bottom of the ocean. There, he found mud and brought it up to the surface. Time after time, he dived down and brought up mud. That's why, to this day, Water Beetle's children dive to the depths. They are still making the Earth a bit at a time."

"Yes, that's right. What happened then?"

"The mud was soft and wet and sticky, and the Sky Beings who flew to Earth couldn't land lest they sink into the mud. That was when Bird Man soared across the world, and with each beat of his wings, he pushed the land down or pulled it up. From that, mountains were formed. In the low places, Brother Snake crawled out of the Underworld and slithered down to become the river." Mud Puppy looked out to the east, where he knew the great Father Water flowed beyond the flooded sweetgum swamps.

"And the animals?"

"They were fashioned out of dirt, molded into then-shapes and sizes by the Sky Beings and the Earth Monsters. Wolf was the one who dug into a giant earthen mound and fashioned the dirt he dug out into the shape of First Man and First Woman. He breathed his soul into them and led them out into Mother Sun's light."

"That's right. So tell me, Mud Puppy, having looked down on Sun Town, do you understand why we raise soil into giant mounds?"

"It is to remind us that we are of the Earth."

"What purpose does that serve?"

"I don't know."

"It is to remind us of *what* we are, where we came from. Our bodies come not from the Sky, but from the soil itself. It is our souls that are of the Sky, breathed into us by Wolf just after the Creation. Very well, you have just told me the story of First Man and First Woman. How did the other people come into being?"

Mud Puppy frowned. "They were born of the Hero Twins, the two sons of First Man and First Woman. One, Light Boy, was born of the joining of First Man and First Woman when they lay together. He passed from her womb into air and light. The second twin, Dark Boy, was born of blood and water."

"Very good. Can you tell me how that happened?"

"First Woman had her regular bleeding while she was bathing in the river. The blood draining from her womb mixed with the river water, and the dark twin was conceived. It was Raven who plucked him from the water as he floated past. That's why women are not to enter the water during their bleeding. Instead, they must secret themselves in the Women's House." He pointed at the Mother Mound now barely visible at the eastern edge of the plaza.

"You are here"—the Serpent gestured at the mound top—"to reflect on that story, boy. You are here, at the highest point of the Bird's Head. Symbolic of the place where people were brought out into the light. But your mother wants you to learn another lesson up here."

"She does?"

The Serpent chuckled, the sound like the clattering of cane slats. "Oh, indeed. But I'm not sure if she understands what you are—or the Truth that you will learn here." He filled his lungs, the ribs sticking out on his thin chest as he looked up at the cloud-choked sky. "Remember this, boy: You cannot know the light until you have been blinded by the darkness. Just like this place, opposites crossed. She has never understood that."

"I don't think I do, either."

"Your mother, boy." He knotted a fist of gnarly bone. "She doesn't understand what's coming. She has lost the harmony and never set her feet to the Dance. They are going to destroy her."

"Who is?"

"She is caught between the Twins. Strong, yes, that she is. But the mighty Wing Heart is brittle inside. Her souls hang in the balance." His voice had gone far away, worried by the wind. "The lightning is coming." A pause. Then he clapped his hands together, shouting, *"Bang!"*

Mud Puppy jumped in spite of himself, his heart racing again. The fear that had ebbed with the magic of the place came rushing back to strangle the breath in his lungs.

The Serpent gave Mud Puppy a sad look. The intensity of those dark eyes sent worry pumping through Mud Puppy's veins with each beat of his heart.

"Take this, boy. Eat it." The old man reached into his pouch. When he withdrew his hand, it clutched some shriveled thing.

"What is it?"

"The future, boy." The Serpent extended his hand as if it held something dangerous. "If you're strong enough."

Mud Puppy felt it drop onto his palm, surprised by the lightness. It had the feel of desiccated bark. He lifted it to his nose, smelling must and dust.

"Eat it," the old man said. "*He* told me to give it to you."

"Who?"

"Eat!"

Mud Puppy placed the bit of desiccated plant matter on his tongue. Dry and flaky, it crumbled under his teeth. The taste made him think of rotting logs and leaf mold.

"What did you make me eat?"

The old man smiled sourly. "You ate a tunnel, boy. A hole. Through it, you will pass into other worlds. See other places and talk with other beings. But I must warn you: Do not leave this place. Most of all, do not let loose of your souls. Do you hear me?"

"Let loose of my souls? How can I do that?"

"You will know, boy. *He* told me to make you do this. It was *his* will, not mine."

"Who is he?"

"What did I tell you not to do?"

"Not to leave this place and not to let my souls loose."

"That is correct. I will add one more thing. You must be brave, boy. Braver than you have ever been before. If you are not, if you surrender to fear, *he* will eat you alive. When that happens, you will die here, Mud Puppy."

Mud Puppy blinked, bits of soggy mold still floating around his tongue. "I don't know if I can be brave."

The Serpent pulled his shawl up over his shoulder, hitched it, and pointed to the thatch-covered ramada just down from the summit. "If it rains, you can go there." His sharp eyes searched the scudding clouds that had darkened overhead. "But otherwise, I want you sitting here. At the highest spot. It will be dark tonight. *Very, dark.*"

Chapter Eight

Firelight flickered in yellow phantoms on the inside of the house walls and cast a shadow outline of Speaker Cloud Heron's dead body. It gave the wattle and daub a golden sheen, accenting the cracks that had appeared in fine tracery through the fire-hardened clay. Overhead, the ceiling was a lattice-work of soot-stained cane poles and bundles of thatch. Net bags hung from the larger poles, the contents bathed by the rising smoke. Such was the gift of fire. Not only did it heat, light, cook, and purify, but its smoke preserved and kept roots, dried fish, nuts, and thinly sliced meat from molding in the damp climate of Sun Town.

The dead Speaker lay on the raised bench built against the wall. Poles set in the ground supported the framework that was, in turn, lashed together to bear a split-cane bed. A thick layer of hanging moss rested atop the cane, and a tanned buffalo hide atop the moss. All in all, it made for a comfortable and dry bed just high enough off the floor to stay warm in the winter but low enough that in summer, the haze of smoke kept the hordes of humming mosquitoes at bay and allowed the sleeper some peace in his repose.

Not that Cloud Heron, Speaker of the Owl Clan, would ever need to worry about mosquitoes again.

Wing Heart bit her lip as she studied her brother's body in the firelight. That he had lasted this long was a miracle. Now, after months of watching his muscular body waste into this frail husk of a man, her strained emotions only allowed her a soul-weary sigh. It was over. For that, and for her son's return, she could be grateful.

"How is he?" Water Petal asked as she ducked through the low doorway. Her thick black hair was parted in the middle, indicating her marital status, and hung straight to her collarbones. She wore a brightly striped fabric shawl over her shoulders, its ends fringed. Her kirtle had been tied around her waist with a silky hemp cord, its girth relaxed now that her pregnancy was apparent.

Wing Heart added another piece of hickory to the crackling fire. "The Speaker is dead."

Water Petal exhaled slowly, eyes raised involuntarily, as if she could see his Life Soul floating up in the smoky rafters. "He was a great leader, a man who never flinched in his duty."

"Even in death," Wing Heart whispered. "He waited until my son returned before surrendering his souls. When will we see another like him?"

"When your son assumes the mantle of Speaker," Water Petal said firmly, eyes glittering with resolve. "Who in the other lineages could compare? Name anyone else in the clan—and surely not Half Thorn, no matter what Moccasin Leaf might say about him."

Wing Heart stared absently at her dead brother's face. The flesh had shrunk around it as though sucked down across the bone by the withering souls inside. His empty eyes lay deep in the hollow pits of his skull, the lips drawn back to expose peglike teeth. Sallow skin outlined the bones of his shoulders and chest. This man whom she had shared so much of her life with, whom she had loved with all of her heart...by the Sky Beings, how could Cloud Heron have faded into this wreck of bone and loosely stretched skin?

"Do you wish to be alone, Elder?" Water Petal asked. "To speak with his souls while they are still near?"

Wing Heart vented a weary sigh. "He has heard everything I have to say to him, Cousin. Over and over and over again until I'm sure he's weary of it." *As I am weary of saying it.*

Snakes take it, had she grown so caustic and cynical? She could imagine Cloud Heron in another time, giving her that measuring stare. His brow had risen to a half cock, questioning her as only he could.

Her throat tightened at the sudden, welling emptiness inside.

"Elder?"

"I'd rather have cut off my leg," Wing Heart whispered, barely aware of the tear that burned its way past her tightly clamped eyelids and traced down her cheek.

"I understand, Elder."

"No. You don't, Cousin." She knotted her fists in her lap. "For ten and two winters now, my brother and I led the

Council. For three tens and nine winters, we have lived the same life, breathed each other's air, shared each other's thoughts, and bound our souls together. He was me. I was him. We were one. Like no two people I have ever known."

"That was what made you great."

Wing Heart nodded, hating the grief that rose as relentlessly as the spring floods. Brutal and inevitable, she could feel it pooling around her lungs and heart, lapping at her ribs.

"How shall I continue?" she asked of the air. "Brother, what can I do? How can I do it? Without you, it seems..." Empty. So very empty.

"Your son is ready to step in at your side." Water Petal sounded so sure of herself.

"My son is not my brother." Her fists knotted, crumpling her white kirtle with its pattern of knots. "But he will do." She bit back the urge to sob. "As I have trained him to."

"Elder?" Hesitation was in Water Petal's voice. "Would you like me to care for the Speaker? He must be cleaned, his clothes burned. The corpse must be prepared for the Pyre."

"Not yet."

"As you wish, Elder."

Wing Heart ground the heels of her palms into her eyes, twisting them as if to scrub her traitorous tears from her head. *I thought I had myself under control. I have been so calm, so prepared, and now that he's truly gone, I am broken like an old doll. Why didn't I know this was coming? Why didn't I understand I would hurt so badly? Why didn't you tell me, Brother?*

"Would you like me to make the ritual announcement, Elder?" Water Petal's voice remained so eerily reasonable.

"No, Cousin. Thank you. That is my job."

A long silence passed as Wing Heart sat in numb misery, flashes of memory tormenting her with images of Cloud Heron, of the times they had shared triumph and pain. How did one pack a lifetime of memories, as if into a clay pot, and just tuck them away?

Brother, after a turning of seasons of watching you die, why is it now beginning to hurt?

"Elder, someone should at least let White Bird know that his uncle is dead. He should know before the others. It will give him time to prepare."

"Yes." *Tomorrow, yes, tomorrow, I will be able to think again.* She waited hesitantly, struggling to hear Cloud Heron's response to that, but the clinging silence of grief washed about her.

"And Mud Puppy?" Water Petal asked as she rose and crouched in the doorway.

"What about him?" Wing Heart asked, slightly off guard at the change of subject.

"Should I tell him?" A pause. "He's up on the Bird's Head. The Serpent left him up there at dark."

Wing Heart shook her head, trying to clear the dampness from her eyes. She blinked in the firelight, gaze drawn inexorably to Cloud Heron's death-strained rictus. "No. Forget him. He's a worthless half-wit. It's the future, Water Petal. That's what I have to deal with. The future."

"This is not a good idea," Cooter said from the darkness in the front of the canoe. He stroked his paddle in the rhythmic cadence they had adopted.

Anhinga glared where she sat in the back behind the others. She hadn't anticipated the night being this dark. They canoed northward in an inky blackness that was truly unsettling. On occasion, someone hissed as unseen moss flicked across his face or over his head.

"You would think you had never been out at night," Anhinga managed through clenched jaws. Truth to tell, she was a little unnerved herself. Was it lunacy and madness to strike out like this with her young companions, to sneak north through the swamps in darkness?

"But for the wind, we'd be lost," Spider Fire reminded. Overhead, the south wind continued to roar and twist its way through the backswamp forest. With that at their backs, they couldn't get lost. And it helped to keep the humming hordes of mosquitoes down. They had greased their bodies, but the bloodthirsty insects still swarmed.

"I don't worry about getting lost," Mist Finger muttered. "I do worry about smacking headlong into a tree, capsizing, and drowning out here in the darkness."

"Not me," Right Talon declared uneasily. "It's the stuff we keep sliding under. I don't know when it's hanging moss or when it's a water moccasin dropping down to bite me in the face."

"Thanks," Slit Nose grumbled from his place in front of Anhinga. "That's *just* what I needed to hear! Panther's blood, I'd just about let myself forget about the snakes, and then you let your lips flap."

"Some brave warriors," Anhinga cried. "Should we turn around and go back? Is that what you want? My brother's ghost is wandering about, unavenged because my uncle will do nothing!"

"Out here, in the darkness, where spirits can drift in with the mist and kill us, I'm not inclined to argue," Cooter replied from his position up front. She could barely see his shoulders moving, or did she just imagine them as he stroked with his pointed paddle?

"He was your friend," she reminded hotly. "You were there. You saw it."

"I did," Cooter said. "It was all I could do to escape. There was only the two of us against ten of them, their bodies slick with grease. We caught them levering our sandstone from the side of the hill. When Bowfin shouted at them, they turned...didn't even hesitate, and cast darts at us. Luck must have guided the hand of the first, for his dart sailed true. I still don't know how Bowfin could have missed seeing it. He should have been able to dodge out of the way."

"But he didn't," Anhinga told them. "I was there when he died. No one should die like that, their guts stinking with foreign rot while their blood runs brown in their veins, and fever robs them of their wits."

"I was lucky enough to run." Cooter's vigorous paddling mirrored the anger in his voice. "It was stupid of us to make ourselves known. It would have been better if we'd just sneaked away, called for more warriors."

"That's wrong!" Anhinga felt the anger stir in her breast. "It's *our* land! It's *our* stone! They have no right in our country, treating it as if it were theirs!"

They paddled in silence for a while, accompanied by the sounds of the swamp, splashing fish, the lonely call of the nightjar and the chining of insects. Overhead, the wind continued to slash at the spring-green trees, rustling the leaves and creaking the branches.

Spider Fire finally said, "You're right, it's our territory, given to us by the Creator, but they have been raiding our land since the beginning of time. I will help you end this once and for all."

"Will you?" Mist Finger asked wryly.

She had been glad when Mist Finger volunteered to accompany her. For the past several moons, she had been alternately delighted and annoyed by the way he kept creeping into her thoughts. At odd times of the day, she'd remember his smile, or the way the muscles rippled in his back. The sparkle in his eyes seemed to have fixed itself between her souls.

"Branch!" Cooter sang out. "Duck, everyone."

The canoe rocked as they bent their heads low to drift under a low-hanging branch. Anhinga felt trailing bits of spiderweb dust her face, crackling and tearing as the canoe's momentum carried them past. She reached up and wiped it away, hoping the angry spider wasn't trapped in her hair. The thought of those eight milling legs tangling in her black locks made her scalp tingle.

Slit Nose broke the silence. "That doesn't mean it's acceptable. Anhinga's right. It's got to stop sometime. It might just as well be now."

Mist Finger laughed, the sound musical in the windblown night. "You don't think it's been tried? How many of our ancestors, no matter what the clan, have died fighting with the Sun People? How many stories can you recall? You know, the ones about great-uncle so-and-so, or cousin what's-his-name who was killed in a raid on the Sun People, or who, like Bowfin, was skewered by a dart, or smacked in the head with a war club. Is there any clan, any lineage that you can name that doesn't have a story? In all that time, all those generations going back to the Creation, don't you think that others have tried to teach them a lesson?"

"Does this have a point?" Spider Fire asked.

"Of course," Mist Finger answered easily. "The point is that nothing is going to change. Our war is eternal. No one is going to win."

"Then why are you here?" Anhinga asked, anger festering at the bottom of her throat.

"I'm here for you." Mist Finger's voice carried an unsettling undercurrent. "As are the rest of us. Bowfin was our friend and your kinsman. We would indeed see his ghost given a little peace."

"But you don't think this is going to do any good?" Anhinga tried to stifle her irritation.

"In the long run, no." Mist Finger sounded so sure of himself.

"But you came anyway?"

"Of course." Where did that reasonable tone come from? He might have been discussing the relative merit of fishnets rather than a raid against the Sun People. "Like my companions, Anhinga, I am here for you. As I said."

For me? "I don't understand."

"Then I shall lay it out for you like a string of beads." Humor laced Mist Finger's voice. "Though I doubt my friends will admit to it out loud. We are here to prove ourselves to you. Oh, to be sure, we wouldn't mind killing a couple of Sun People in the process. Bowfin was a good friend. We share your anger over his death. But, most of all, when this is over, each of us wants you to think well of us, to admire our courage and skill."

Her thoughts stumbled. "What are you talking about? Prove yourselves?"

"Shut up, Mist Finger," Spider Fire growled unhappily.

His admonition brought another laugh from Mist Finger, who added, "Anhinga? Are you not planning on marrying soon? And when you do, which of your suitors would you choose? Some simpleminded fisherman who worried more over the set of his gill nets, or one of the five dashing young warriors in this canoe?"

"Be quiet, Mist Finger," Slit Nose muttered.

Anhinga started, considering his words, ever more unsettled by them. "Why are you telling me this?"

Mist Finger calmly replied, "So that my companions here know that they have no chance."

Chuckles and guffaws broke out from the others while Anhinga felt her face redden. Snakes take him, he'd embarrassed her, and in the middle of this most important strike against the Sun People.

"Well," she told him hotly, "if and *when* I marry, it won't be to you, Mist Finger! And for now, it would do all of you good to think about what we're doing. This isn't about courting. It's about revenge."

"Nice work, Mist Finger." Right Talon couldn't keep the gloating out of his voice. "That's one person less the rest of us have to worry about."

The canoe rocked as someone in the darkness ahead of her slapped a paddle on the water, spraying the front of the boat where Mist Finger sat. Laughter followed.

"Stop that!" Anhinga ordered. "You want to know who I'll marry? Very well, I'll marry the man who kills the most Sun People." There, that ought to set them straight.

"Is that a promise?" Slit Nose asked.

"It is. My uncle might be willing to remain at the Panther's Bones and talk about revenge," she told him. "I intend on doing something about it. If I do nothing else in my life, I will see to it that the Sun People finally pay for the wrongs they have committed against us. On that, I give my promise. By the life of my souls, and before Panther Above, I swear I will harm them as they have never been harmed before."

"No matter what?" Right Talon asked.

"No matter what," she insisted hotly. "So there. If you've come to impress me, do it by killing Sun People."

Out in the blackness of the swamp, the hollow hoot of the great horned owl sent a shiver down her soul. It was as if the death bird heard, and had taken her vow.

Chapter Nine

Lightning flashed in the night. The wind continued to gust up from the south. Atop the Bird's Head, Mud Puppy pulled his ragged shawl about his shoulders and huddled in the wind-whipped darkness. He had removed the little red chert flake from his belt pouch and clutched it tightly in his right fist while he rubbed his temples with nervous fingers.

Sick. I feel sick. His stomach had knotted around the bits of mushroom that he had swallowed. Now it cramped and squirmed, while the tickle at the back of his throat tightened and saliva seeped loosely around his tongue.

Please, I don't want to... The urge barely gave him warning as his stomach pumped. Time after time, Mud Puppy's body bucked as he heaved up his meager supper, and then came slime until finally a bitter and painful rasping was all his body could produce.

Coughing, he gasped for breath. When had he fallen onto his side? Cool dirt pressed against his fevered cheek. Hawking, he tried to spit the burning bile from his windpipe. Vomit ate painfully into the back of his nose. Tears dripped in liquid misery from his eyes, coursing across the bridge of his nose and slipping insolently down the side of his face.

Had he ever felt this miserable? When he blinked his eyes, odd streaks of color—smeared yellow, sparkling purple, smudges of blue and green—belied the blackness of the night. His body seemed to pulse, his flesh curiously distant from his stumbling thoughts. Waves, timed to the beat of his heart, rocked him. Yes, floating, as if on undulating darkness. He had felt this way in water. Water. The notion possessed him, and for a moment, he forgot where he lay, so high on the Bird's Head.

"Hold on to your souls," he reminded himself, and when he swallowed, his body turned itself inside out.

What is happening to me? The words scampered around his tortured brain, echoing with an odd hollowness.

"Are you afraid?" The voice startled him.

"Who spoke?"

"I did."

"Where are you?"

"In your hand."

Mud Puppy tried to swallow the bitterness in his throat again and felt his flesh rippling like saturated mud. Raising his hand, he opened it, staring at his palm, nothing more than a smear in the darkness. The flake! That tiny little bit of stone that had winked at him in the sunlight.

"You can talk?"

"Only to those who dare listen."

Mud Puppy blinked his eyes, his body seeming to swell and float. Bits of colored light, like streamers, continued to flicker across his vision. "Do you see them?"

"See what?" the flake asked.

"The lights." Mud Puppy told him in amazement. "Colors, like bits of rainbow broken loose and wavering."

"You're seeing through the mushroom's eyes," the flake said.

"How?"

"The world is a magical place. An old place, one in which so many things have become hidden. The simple has become ever more complex. Creatures come and go along with the land, growing and shrinking, mountains rising and being worn away. Shapes shift. Forms flow."

"How do you know these things?"

"I am old, boy. So old you cannot imagine. Carried across this world from my familiar soil, I am left here, separated from the rest of myself."

"Do you grieve?"

"Do you?"

"Yes."

"Then I do, too."

"I don't understand."

"Neither do I."

Mud Puppy frowned at the thin bit of stone, running his finger over the smooth chert. "What are you?"

"Whatever you make of me. I was alone until you picked me up. As long as you hold me, I shall be whatever you want me to be."

Was it the flake of stone talking? Or the voice of the

mushroom echoing around his souls? Mud Puppy blinked, his souls twining about and floating in his chest. Did it matter? The flake's answer was oddly reassuring: *"I shall be whatever you want me to be."*

The first spatters of rain splashed his skin. The impact of the drops went right through him, as though he were pierced by a cast dart. He forced himself to sit up, dazed, failing to understand as the raindrops thumped and hammered on his head. Each drop sent echoes of its impact through his skull, like rings on a pond. Eternity stretched as he lost himself in the sensations. The water trickling down his cold skin was alive. He could sense its living essence, silver and fluid.

Cold. Have I ever been this cold? Dumbly, he ran his hands down his arms, squishing the water from his skin. He could feel himself, feel the blood being pushed around inside him as he tightened his grip on his arm. His body seemed to glow despite the cold.

A gust of wind pushed at him and relaxed. Wind, a thing of the sky.

I flew! The memory of the Dream floated out of the recesses and re-formed within his souls. Yes, hadn't that been magical? His souls turned hollow with the sensation of dropping, weightless, from a great height. Were those really Owl's wings that had carried him?

"They were indeed," a deep voice told him from the night.

He blinked, lashes wet and cold on his face. "Flake?"

"No." A pause. "Do you remember me? Do you remember the promise you made?"

"Masked Owl?" In the flickering glow of distant lightning, Mud Puppy saw him. The giant owl perched on the grass-thatched ramada. Those huge eyes seemed to gleam in the night.

"Are you seeking the One, Mud Puppy?"

"The One?"

"The One Life. It comes after the Dance."

"Which you will teach me?"

"Someday." Masked Owl agreed. "But first, I want you to talk to your uncle. He is here with a message for you."

"My uncle?" Mud Puppy frowned. "Cloud Heron? Is that whom you mean?"

Lightning flashed again, this time to display Cloud Heron, his body lit by a pale shimmer. To Mud Puppy's surprise, he stood several hands above the earth, floating as though it were the most normal of activities.

"Hello, boy." Cloud Heron cocked his head. His eyes looked as if they'd been painted with charcoal.

"You look well, Uncle," Mud Puppy cried happily. "The illness is gone! I'm so happy! Now, everything is right again. You are well, White Bird is home from the north. Mother won't have to worry so much."

"I'm dead, Mud Puppy. What you see is my Life Soul." The words sounded hollow on the storm. "As we speak, my sister is crying beside my body. I came here, to the Bird's Head, because it is the way."

"What way?"

"To the West, Nephew. You know what lies there?"

Mud Puppy suffered a sudden shiver. "The Land of the Dead."

"That's right. And once my Life Soul crosses the boundary, steps off the mound, it can't come back. Not to this place. Spirits can't cross the rings, boy. They can't walk across water or lines of ash. My Life Soul will be gone forever."

Mud Puppy frowned. "I'll miss you."

"Why?" Cloud Heron demanded. "I never liked you."

"That doesn't matter."

The ghost seemed to waver, shifting when the wind blew through him. "You are right. It doesn't matter now. I never understood who you were, what you were. If I had known, I would have taught you more. Treated you differently."

"Taught me more of what?"

"The things you will need to lead. The world will have to teach you. So many will try to kill you, to destroy you, you must be crafty and cunning. You have so much to learn, and no one to teach you."

"You could teach me, Uncle."

"I don't have time now, Nephew. Perhaps my Dream Soul might, if it is ever so inclined. I can't say how it will decide to treat you." The ghost shifted, twisting in the air. "A canoe is coming. From the south, from the Panthers. Five young men. As many as the fingers on your hand. With them is an angry young woman. They are going to raid Ground Cherry Camp. Can you remember that?"

"Ground Cherry Camp," Mud Puppy repeated.

"They will strike at first light on the third day. She must be allowed to escape."

"Who?"

"She will try to kill you, Mud Puppy. She is very devoted, her soul wounded and angry. Don't trust her." The ghost wavered again. "I don't want to go. So much...undecided. He's going to die."

"Who, who is going to die?"

"So much greatness. Taken before his time. How wrong I was...how very wrong."

"Uncle?"

"Don't fail us, boy..."

Only black wind remained. In the distance to the east, white strobed the clouds as lightning flared and died.

"Uncle?" Mud Puppy tried to stand, wobbling on his feet. His senses spun and tricked him. His small body thumped as it dropped onto the mound's sticky, wet clay.

"He has taken the leap," Masked Owl said, his eyes glowing like coals in the darkness. "His Life Soul has fled. From here it will begin the journey to the West. Do you remember the promise you made to me?"

"That I will help you, yes." Mud Puppy's vision kept swimming, losing sight of the gleaming owl's eyes. "Are you still wearing your mask?"

"Of course."

"Why?"

"Why does anyone wear a mask?"

"To make them look like someone else."

"Sometimes, but not this time."

"Then why?"

"You must find the answer to that, Mud Puppy."

"Everyone is asking things of me."

"It is your destiny. Do you have another question to ask me?"

From the recesses of his head, the question came: "Why did the Creator separate the Earth from the Sky?"

Masked Owl laughed at that. "You must answer

that one on your own, too, boy. But, lest you become totally frustrated, I bear a message for you."

"You do? Is it from Salamander? Would he be my Spirit Helper?" Hope leaped up within him like a fountain of light.

"He is considering it. But, no, the message isn't from him. It is from Cricket."

"Yes?"

"He wanted you to know that he sings with his legs. By rubbing them together. He also said to tell you that there is a lesson in that. The lesson is that you should never judge based upon appearances. A cricket might be a very small creature, but it can still make a great noise. In all the world only thunder has a louder voice than Cricket. Remember that, Mud Puppy."

"I will."

"You had better rest now. Your body needs time to Dance with brother mushroom. Oh, and about your uncle's message, I would give it to the Serpent. He is the one most likely to understand. And, for the time being —outside of myself—he is your single ally."

Masked Owl vanished as if he had been but a fanciful flight of imagination. Blackness, cold, and a terrible sickness remained.

White Bird could have chosen better weather for his homecoming, but instead of bright sunshine, he got a gray drizzle that filtered down in streamers from the cloud-choked skies. Nevertheless, he stood in the rear of his canoe as it slid onto the mucky bank of the landing.

On shore, a throng had gathered amid the clutter of

beached canoes. People stood respectfully behind the Serpent, their brightly dyed clothing creating a speckling of color against the gray, dreary day. In dots and clots, they stretched up the incline above the landing. An expectant excitement ran through them as they talked anxiously with each other. Most were wearing flats of bark on their heads to shed the persistent drizzle.

Yellow Spider leaped out of the bow as White Bird stepped into the calf-deep waters at the stern. Together, they pulled the heavily laden dugout as far as they could onto the bank. The dark silty mud seemed to grip the rounded bottom in a lover's tight embrace. Behind them, the rest of the Wolf Traders landed, dragging their canoes fast against the shore.

White Bird and Yellow Spider straightened, extending their arms to where the Serpent waited several paces beyond them. The old man had a curiously haunted look on his flat, wrinkled face. Water trickled down the faded tattoos on his sagging brown skin. He might have been a standing skeleton, so thin and delicate did he look. Behind him, the crowd went silent. White Bird was aware of their eyes—dark, large, and peering at him in anticipation.

"Great Serpent!" White Bird shouted the ritual words into the misty rain. "We are returned from the north with goods for the People!"

"Are you cleansed?" the Serpent called back.

"We are, Great Serpent. By your Power and skill."

"Are your Dreams pure?"

"They are, Great Serpent! My Dreams have been pleasant this last night. My souls, and those of my companions, have been at peace."

"Do you leave anger and disharmony behind you?"

"We do, Great Serpent."

"Then enter this place and be welcome, White Bird and Yellow Spider of the Owl Clan of the Northern Moiety. And enter this place, you Traders of the Wolf People, and be welcome."

"Is that finally it?" Hazel Fire muttered out of the side of his mouth.

"It is, my friend." Yellow Spider answered in the Trader's tongue. "Now come and be dazzled by the greatest city on Earth."

Together, they started forward, but the first to break free from the crowd was Spring Cypress. She shot down the bank on bare feet, hair streaming behind her in a dark wave. She threw herself into White Bird's arms, hugging him desperately.

"White Bird! I've missed you so!"

He clasped her to him, feeling her round breasts against his chest, enjoying the sensation of her damp skin against his. She was taller and fuller of body than he remembered. After a winter of experience, he could feel the promise in her woman's body. Taut and firm, she conformed to him. Her damp hair smelled of dogwood blossoms. From somewhere hidden in the back of his souls, Lark's face flashed, the image unsettling. He pushed it away and clasped Spring Cypress for a moment longer, then stepped back to look at her.

Snakes, she was beautiful, her heart-shaped face dominated by large dark eyes and a slightly upturned nose. She looked so delicate, and her souls were mirrored in her gaze, and he knew that longing and excitement was for him. For a moment he struggled with the desperate urge to lift her up and twirl her away

133

from the watching crowd. What a shame that once again he had to be the man his mother demanded of him.

"Where is my mother? I would have thought the Clan Elder would be here to greet me. Is she detained?" he asked, matching her smile with his own.

In that instant, Spring Cypress's eyes dropped, her smile fading. "I am sorry, White Bird. Your uncle. Last night."

"Is he...?" He couldn't make himself say the inevitable words.

She nodded. "I just found out. I heard Moccasin Leaf telling the Serpent. Cloud Heron has been sick for so long. It wasn't unexpected."

He closed his eyes, exhaling as he controlled his expression. "I wished to see him one last time." A pang of loss began to grow in his chest. "I had so much to tell him. So many things to ask about."

"What is it?" Yellow Spider asked, disentangling himself from some of his friends. They had charged down the slope ahead of Yellow Spider's sister, Water Petal.

"My uncle," White Bird said. "Last night."

Yellow Spider flinched. "I'm sorry to hear that."

"What happened to him?" Hazel Fire asked, nervous eyes on the crowd that surged down toward them.

"Dead." The word sounded flat in White Bird's throat.

"He's the one you are named after?"

White Bird nodded. Then, he forced himself to meet the oncoming crowd. The Serpent, he noticed, had already turned to leave, plodding up the slope on his stick-thin legs. No doubt he was wanted at Mother's. It was his duty to begin the rituals to strip the body of flesh and cleanse the house site.

"Greetings, White Bird." Gnarly old Mud Stalker strode purposefully down and extended his good left hand. His hard brown eyes took in every nuance of White Bird's expression. "It seems we have a day of joy and sorrow, all mixed together."

How did he take that? *What is his real meaning?* "Indeed, Mud Stalker"—White Bird gave the man a facile smile—"it is always a joy to see you. Or were you thinking of something else?"

"I was referring first to your return, and second to the news about Cloud Heron. He was most adept."

He was...especially when it came to thwarting you and your clan. "He will be mourned by all."

"At least the alligators didn't get you, White Bird."

"Well, we can't always depend on alligators, can we?" He avoided glancing at the man's mangled right arm. "I have brought a great many gifts for your clan, Speaker. I thought of you constantly while I was upcountry."

"I shall look forward to hearing your tales," Mud Stalker said, touching his forehead in deference. "But I am taking up too much of your time, what with the death and all the responsibilities that now fall on your shoulders." He kept his eyes locked on White Bird's. "My deepest sympathies. If I can be of any service, or if I can advise you on any subject, do call on me." He walked on to greet Yellow Spider.

Clay Fat came next, a jolly smile on his face as he clapped White Bird on the back. Rainwater traced rounded paths over his belly and dripped from his knob of a navel. "Glad to have you home, young man. And even happier to see that welcome you gave Spring Cypress." He winked, the action contorting his round face. But behind it, White Bird could sense the man's nervous tension. "I think she's going to be declared a woman soon!"

"Oh?" White Bird asked, wondering what his mother's old friend was hiding behind his bluff and glowing expression.

Clay Fat lowered his voice. "Well, perhaps we could have done so several moons ago, but we were waiting for a special event." A pause. "Have a word with your mother, young man. I can't think of a better match than the two of you."

So, Mother is against a match with Spring Cypress? Why? What has happened since I have been gone? "I will speak to her as soon as I can." He cast his eyes up the slope of the canoe landing, searching for some sign of the Owl Clan Elder.

"I think she's detained. About your uncle, my deepest sympathies, White Bird. He was a great man." Water ran from Clay Fat's bark hat. It sat crooked on his ball-shaped head so that the runoff trickled onto the curve of his greased shoulder. The drips beaded and slid down his brown skin in silver trails.

"As are you, Speaker. You filled my thoughts the entire time I was upriver."

"Better that you had spent your thoughts on Spring Cypress than me. That would have been a great deal more productive—not to mention more pleasant, eh?"

"We will talk more later, Speaker." White Bird clapped him on the back, passing to face Thunder Tail and Stone Talon from the Eagle Clan as they took their place next in line.

"Greetings, young White Bird." Aged Stone Talon offered her hand, birdlike under thin skin. As she balanced on rattly crutches, the top of her head barely reached the middle of his chest. The old woman seemed to have aged ten tens of turnings of seasons since he had seen her last. Her flesh reminded him of turkey wattle, loose and hanging from her bones. Hair that had been black a summer ago had gone as white as the northern snows. Her back had hunched and curled like a crawfish's tail. But she looked up at him with the same predatory eyes that a robin used when it considered plucking an unlucky worm from the ground. "So, the barbarians and the monsters of the North didn't get you?"

"No, Elder, they did not." Instinct told him that no matter how her body had failed, her wits seemed as sharp as a banded-chert blade. The question was, which way would she cut? And which clan would drip blood when she was finished?

Her son, Thunder Tail, the Eagle Clan Speaker, cleared his throat. He wore a necklace made of split bear mandibles that hung like a breastplate. His weathered face reminded White Bird of a rosehip that had been kept in a pot for too many winters. His tattoos had faded through the turning of seasons, darkening and blurring until, like the patterns in his soul, they were hard to decipher. "Are we to call you Speaker, now?"

"Respectfully, I have no idea. I have just arrived."

"Difficult, isn't it?" Stone Talon gave him a toothless smile that rearranged her shriveled face. The thoughts behind her eyes, however, were anything but pleasant. "Having to face all of this when your souls are freshly plunged into grief." She gestured toward the crowd that still awaited him. "Your uncle was a strong leader. Where will you find his like?"

"There is no one like him," White Bird agreed easily. "My clan's loss is indeed grievous, but it wounds us all. My uncle served all the people. Fortunately, Elder, I have four canoes to help lighten the People's sadness. I have set aside some special presents for the two of you. As soon as I find a moment, be sure that I shall bring them to you personally."

"Clever boy, that one," he heard Stone Talon say as they passed on.

"At last!" Three Moss cried from where she waited impatiently. "Come, Mother. Let us greet White Bird." Three Moss led Elder Cane Frog into White Bird's presence. Her hand rested on her mother's bare shoulder.

He reached out, taking the blind Elder's frail hand and clasping it respectfully. "My souls are pleased to see you, Elder. I'm sure your daughter has told you about the Trade we have returned with."

"She has." Cane Frog smacked her lips, as if something distasteful clung to her pink gums. Her sightless right white eye wiggled and quivered, while dirt encrusted the empty orbit of her missing left. "She also told me you brought barbarians with you?"

"I did, Elder." He laughed lightly. "There was no other way to carry so much Trade. It was that, or sink the canoe."

"Never that," Cane Frog agreed. "You know, I lost my oldest brother that way. Tragic. Such a Speaker he would have been for the clan. Best to be safe out on the water. Yes, always safe."

"I agree, Elder."

"Our hearts are wounded by the news of your uncle." Three Moss was looking at him speculatively. Life had been unfair to her. Plain, thickset, and bland of feature, she didn't have that spark of animation in her flat brown eyes. "We are, however, joyous at your safe return. So many had declared you dead. Most had lost hope."

"Hope should never be given up completely," White Bird told her evenly. "In my case, I must apologize for making so many people worry. Events, however, dictated that I go farther than I had planned, and once there, that I dedicate myself to the Trade through the winter. But I assure you I longed for home. In fact, I have some special gifts that I have picked out, just for Elder Cane Frog."

"We are obliged to you," Cane Frog rasped. "Your return was propitious, young White Bird. Indeed, most propitious. But then, luck has always favored your clan, hasn't it? You know, it was just a couple of days ago that we were talking—"

"Mother"—Three Moss took the old woman's arm—"come, we can't monopolize White Bird. Others wish to welcome him home. There is still Yellow Spider to see and the barbarians to welcome."

"Yellow Spider? Who is he?" White Bird heard the old woman ask, as Three Moss led her away.

"Brother to Water Petal, of the Owl Clan," Three Moss was hissing as Speaker Deep Hunter led Elder Colored Paint to White Bird.

Deep Hunter, Speaker for the Alligator Clan, was

watching Cane Frog as Three Moss stopped her in front of Yellow Spider. He had a curious smile on his lips. By the time he turned to White Bird, his expression had grown thoughtful. "So, you are well and healthy. Welcome home, White Bird. After so many declared you dead, it is a joy to know that your souls are safe and returned to those who love and cherish you."

"Thank you for your kind greeting. I regret that I worried so many, Speaker."

"Oh, fear not. It does them good every once in a while to be proven wrong."

"Who, Speaker?"

"The ones who come to think that they know how the world works...and that they are the smart ones. It is always such a shock when they find out that they are not as cunning as they thought. It is healthy to be reminded that people, things, or events can come from unexpected quarters to disrupt everything and throw the simplest of plans into confusion." Deep Hunter's thoughtful black eyes were taking White Bird's measure. His long face always had a sad look, but Deep Hunter was never a known quantity. "Stew, as you no doubt know, is tastier when it is stirred every so often."

"I hear the wisdom in your words, Speaker."

"Do you?"

To change the subject, White Bird reached out to take Colored Paint's hand. "Greetings, Elder. I have brought you some special gifts from upriver. You filled my thoughts throughout the winter. So much so, that it gives my souls great joy to see you again."

"It was cold, your winter up north?" Colored Paint asked, her glinting brown eyes on White Bird.

"Yes, Elder."

"I spent a winter up north, you know. Poison and snakes, but that was a long time ago. How many winters? Three tens? Three tens and three? I can't recall. But cold? I tell you, I thought my bones would crack. You don't know the value of a good hot fire until you've been that cold."

"I agree, Elder."

"We not only come to welcome you," Deep Hunter interrupted, "but to offer our respects over your uncle's death." The enigmatic smile remained on his thin lips as he asked, "There is talk that Owl Clan will have a very young Speaker. Have you given that any thought?"

White Bird kept his expression blank. "I have been in seclusion, Speaker. My first responsibility was to the purification of my souls and body. I have no hint as to what my clan might be considering."

Deep Hunter nodded absently.

What was he hiding? White Bird's souls tingled with warning. It was one thing to deal with Mud Stalker. He had always been an enemy, but what motivated Deep Hunter?

The Speaker smiled easily. "Come and see us when you have a chance. After that winter up north the Elder will have a warm fire for you, and I shall make sure our stew has been adequately stirred. We will have a great many things to talk about."

"Thank you, Speaker. And you, Elder Colored Paint, have a pleasant day."

"Going back to the fire," Colored Paint muttered. "Just talking about it has made my bones shiver. A bit of winter lingers inside me. I think it was because I got so cold upriver that time. Hope it doesn't bother you the way it does me."

"I hope not, too, Elder."

Deep Hunter added: "Give your mother my greeting. Send her my respects concerning your uncle. Tell her that we need to speak. Soon." He led Colored Paint down the line to Yellow Spider.

White Bird glanced uneasily at the growing crowd. He wished he could just press his way through them and sprint up the slope to the plaza. From there he could run full tilt north to his mother's house on the first ridge and learn the news.

Time began to drag as he worked his way through the throng. It seemed that the entirety of Sun Town had poured out to greet him. Everyone was curious as to what he had brought, and just as anxious to see the barbarians and to invite them to visit, eat, and tell their tales of the far north. It took but a suggestion from White Bird to the gathered young men, and they surged to the beach and muscled the muddy damp canoes onto their broad shoulders. He smiled at the clans vying for the honor of carrying the Trade up to Owl Clan's territory.

As they started up the slippery slope, people crowded around Hazel Fire and his companions, shouting questions and invitations.

Not that Traders didn't come from distant places, but these were young warriors, not the professional rivermen with wild tales that were meant to awe their audience into a lucrative Trade.

White Bird did enjoy a moment of satisfaction as the crowd surged up the slope from the landing. He was watching the Wolf Traders, noting their expressions the moment that they stepped out onto the expanse of the great southern plaza. They stopped short, stunned at the sight of the huge curving ridges topped with lines of houses. Even with the drizzle that masked the Bird's Head to the west, they stood stunned, speechless at the majesty of Sun Town's earthworks and the geometric perfection with which it was laid out.

"There is no place like this on Earth!" Gray Fox finally gasped. "Do the gods live here?"

"No," Yellow Spider assured him. "They are in the sky above and under the earth beneath your feet, where they should be. No, my friend, you have just entered the center of the world. We are the Sun People, and there are no others like us anywhere."

White Bird led the procession, striding with the same presence and posture he had seen his uncle adopt for formal occasions. Behind him the crowd lined out, a gaudy procession who marched and clapped their hands, Singing and laughing, the canoes bobbing on a buoyancy of shoulders.

He had forgotten the immensity of Sun Town. In respect, he touched his forehead as he crossed the town's center line, the low beaten path in the grass that delineated the Southern Moiety from the Northern. As he entered Owl Clan territory, his heart seemed fit to burst. A swirl of emotions—joy at success, sadness at the news about his uncle, and pride in his clan—swirled within him like mixing floodwaters.

As he came striding up to the first ridge, he stared through the rain, feeling water trickle down his face to soak his already wet breechcloth. "Greetings, Elder Wing Heart," he called as he stopped short of the borrow ditch below his house. "Your son has returned. He has been cleansed and brings Trade for the People."

As if on cue, his mother stepped out from behind

the hanging, stately, looking every inch the influential Elder that she was. "Welcome home, White Bird. My heart is filled with gladness to see you." She paused. "More so given the sorrow that has filled us after your uncle's death."

"I grieve for the Speaker," he answered, voice ringing.

It was at that moment that the Serpent stepped out behind Wing Heart, his face streaked with charcoal as was appropriate when dealing with the dead. A black face didn't frighten the freshly dead souls.

The crowd had flowed around his party in a semi-circle, watching the greatest of spectacles. He could feel the anticipation, the rising excitement. People hung on every word, wondering if Wing Heart would declare him to be the new Speaker. Or would she wait? Did she have the kind of influence to make such a declaration, knowing full well that her clan would be forced to support her? Would she take that kind of risk, knowing that to have to withdraw it later would amount to a terrible loss of face?

White Bird straightened, his heart hammering with anticipation. Yellow Spider was standing by his side, spine stiff, shoulders back, head proud. The four heavy canoes were lined up behind them, evidence of his ability to provide for the People.

Wing Heart stood as if frozen, staring across the divide created by the borrow pit. In its boggy bottom, cattail and cane had sprouted, the first green shoots of spring. Water lilies were coming back to life, the emerald leaves floating on the black water.

"White Bird," she called out imperiously, "nephew

of Cloud Heron, who was once Speaker of the Owl Clan, I would..."

A muttering ripple ran through the western end of the crowd, people parting as if they were water. White Bird cocked his head at the interruption and the rising babble of excited talk. Unease tightened in his chest, his muscles charged the way they would for combat. He realized he was breathing hard, as if he'd just run for several hands of time.

When the crowed parted, it took White Bird a moment to recognize the boy. He looked like a drowned urchin, black hair plastered to his head. Smears of watery soil blotched his cheeks, shoulders, and scrawny chest. What had originally been a white breechcloth looked gray, stained with clay and ash. But what affected White Bird the most was the look in those large, haunted eyes. Power seemed to radiate from them like heat from a glowing cooking clay.

"Mud Puppy?" the question popped unbidden from White Bird's lips as the boy walked past, that eerie stare locked on a world beyond this one.

The boy didn't hesitate but plodded down and splashed through the water and up the ridge toward Wing Heart.

"Mud Puppy?" she barked angrily. "What are you..."

But Mud Puppy walked past her, stopping instead before the Serpent. In the sudden silence, White Bird couldn't hear what the boy said, just the mumbling of his low speech.

"That is ridiculous!" Wing Heart blurted.

White Bird couldn't stand it. Snakes take the little imp, he'd just ruined everything! Before he could think, he was striding forward, enough aware to round the eastern edge of the borrow pit instead of slogging through the water so that he could stalk up to his mother's house. No, he wouldn't wring his brother's scrawny neck, riot here where the entire world could see, but he'd sure do it as soon as no one was watching.

The Serpent had straightened, his face oddly drawn by a frown. Wing Heart shot a hard hand out to grasp the boy's arm. White Bird could see the muscles in her back tense and knot as she dragged the boy toward the doorway. Her body twisted as she pitched him unceremoniously into the shadowed depths of the house.

"People!" The Serpent raised his hands high. "Word has just come to me that the Swamp Panthers are sending a party to raid us. Five warriors will attack Ground Cherry Camp the day after tomorrow at dawn. Who will go to ward off this threat?"

The announcement stopped White Bird cold. Without looking, he could tell that the crowd hung upon a precipice of indecision. It was instinct that led White Bird to raise his hand, shouting, "I will!" only to wonder what he'd done, and what had happened in this moment that should have been his greatest triumph.

Chapter Ten

A low bank of clouds rolled up from the gulf. They drifted across the dense forests, following the valley of the Father Water northward.

In their inky shadow, Many Colored Crow dived and soared, riding the warm southern winds. On wings of night, he flipped and cavorted. High atop its ridge, Sun Town lay tucked away in sleep.

Many Colored Crow had waited for the last of the figures to leave the Men's House. Had waited for the Dancing and Singing to conclude. He had let the young warriors preparing for battle purify themselves with sweat baths and liberal doses of black drink. He had let the dancers gyrate and pirouette as they wore their totem masks of redheaded woodpecker, bobcat, and snapping turtle. He had allowed the Power to flow into the warriors' muscles and enervate their souls. This night it was to his benefit to allow Masked Owl's vision to come true.

As he spiraled down through the humid air, he located the lone house in Snapping Turtle Clan grounds.

It stood at the easternmost summit of the first ridge, not a dart's cast from the Men's House.

Inside, Mud Stalker had just fallen into a deep sleep, his body lying on a cane-pole bed against the back wall. The Speaker's gray hair was tousled on a raccoon-skin pillow, his body covered with a tailored fox-hide blanket.

Many Colored Crow settled silently on the thatched roof and surveyed the surroundings. He could see the souls glowing in the night. These poor humans who were falling into the lines of Power being drawn by Masked Owl and himself.

For now, however, he had more urgent matters to attend to. The future had to be prepared just so. Perhaps his brother didn't understand what was coming, how so much was going to be decided here.

You never spent enough time looking into the future, Brother. It is a fault which will cost you this time.

Satisfied, Many Colored Crow spread his wings and began to insert himself into Mud Stalker's Dreams.

Anhinga disliked mist. As dawn broke it lay on the swampy land, cottony and thick, tendrils drifting through the trees and rising off the stale water. It obscured the grayish light that filtered through the trees, blurring her surroundings as she led her small party of young warriors up from their beached canoe. The air oppressed, cool, and damp. Moisture beaded on her hair like pearls and left the weapons—the atlatl and darts she clutched in her right hand—clammy in her grip.

She knew this place, had come here once in the

company of her uncle. The Sun People called this Ground Cherry Camp: a clearing where the plants grew in the sandy soil of an abandoned levee a half day's run south of Sun Town. Despite the mist that clung like torn ghosts to every branch and bole, she knew this was the way.

At the landing, several overturned canoes had been propped on sections of rotting log, awaiting their owners' return. A well-beaten path led up through tangled vines that wove an impenetrable web through the mixed sweetgum and oak. Even in the dim light, she could see footprints, still clear from the night before, unfaded by the heavy dew that settled on the green world and beaded on silvered leaves until it dripped stolidly onto the damp ground.

Bobbing mayapple leaves danced as she passed, her bare feet water-streaked as she stepped through the ground cover. Buds were just forming, anticipatory to blooming. Overhead a small beast scampered through the parallel rows of lanceolate leaves on a white ash—then identified itself by a fox squirrel's high-pitched chattering.

Snakes take it, had the squirrel given them away? Anhinga raised a hand, and Spider Fire stopped close behind her. The others, too, froze in place. In silence they waited, ears cocked to the gray dawn, but only the calls of the birds, the soft moaning of insects, and the irregular patter of water dripping from the trees could be heard.

"No voices," Slit Nose whispered from the rear. "Maybe there's no one there?"

"Or they are still asleep," Spider Fire added. "It's early."

"Hush." Anhinga glanced nervously at the encompassing fog that pressed down around them. Was it her imagination, or had it thickened, drawn closer?

A shiver played down her spine. She had never liked thick mist like this. Something about the way it rose from the water, as though alive, played eerily with her imagination. That it flowed around everything in its path bespoke a great Power that she had yet to comprehend. In times like this, when death prowled the land, mist could carry ghosts right around a person. She could imagine wraith hands tracing their way along a living person's body, caressing it, slipping thin fingers into a person's nose, mouth, and ears. How could you tell? How would you know that you had been witched? Any evil could be lurking just there, beyond your vision, waiting for you to step into its lair.

"Let's go," Right Talon muttered as he clutched his darts and atlatl. "If anyone is there, they'll be wide-awake by the time we finally arrive."

Mist Finger gently tapped his wooden dart shafts in agreement, but said nothing. Anhinga shot him a side-long glance, measuring him. After his cavalier words the night they had left, he had been solid, never boastful like the others, and calmly capable when it came to making camp and seeing to the things that needed to be done. During the two days they had been traveling she had found herself admiring him more than once. Smooth muscle rolled under his greased skin. He stood straight, proud. Something in his demeanor made it clear that as he aged, he would become a leader. If only he hadn't been so blunt that night in the canoe.

He just spoke what the others already knew, she reminded herself. Yes, they had come to impress her.

Mist Finger's assertion that first night in the canoe simply lifted the veil, placed all of the young men's actions in complete clarity.

So, are you going to marry any one of them? She had begun to look at them through different eyes. They were no longer childhood friends, no longer the easy companions of hunting and fishing expeditions or harmless teasing. The seriousness with which they dedicated themselves to her, to this raid, bespoke of adulthood as she had never before understood it.

As she considered that, she realized her attention had fixed on Mist Finger. He alone didn't fidget, didn't stare anxiously out at the mist-shrouded trees, but met her uneasy gaze with his clear brown eyes. That look reassured, speaking to her without words. He smiled the way he might if he were reading her souls.

"Are we going?" Slit Nose asked, "or would you rather wait for the mayapples and greenbrier to bloom?"

Anhinga strode forward, breaking eye contact with Mist Finger. A curious tingle had formed at the root of her spine, warming her pelvis. She flipped her hair, worn long and braided in anticipation of the day's coming trials. Her other hand tightened on the darts and atlatl in her hand. After all, this wasn't about handsome young men who made her heart leap. It was about war—about revenge and blood. Within moments, provided that Panther Above favored her, they would be killing enemies.

Taking a long stride, she tried to ignore the mist that sifted through the vines and branches. A sweetgum seedpod rolled under her heel as she marched up the trail. How far was it? She tried to remember.

The trail leveled off, winding through the trees.

The branches overhead disappeared into a gray haze, hanging moss dangling like daggers. The trees themselves might have been ghosts vanishing into the haze. Ghosts?

Why did everything, no matter her momentary revelation about Mist Finger, return to ghosts? Was it because Bowfin's lost souls prowled these selfsame forests? Did her brother's empty eyes even now peer over her shoulder? Was he confused by her oddly timed attraction for Mist Finger when she should be contemplating the death of his killers?

A stab of guilt made her reorder her thoughts. Was this the right decision? Was it the time to strike? Is that what left her filled with unease? When she glanced up, it was to stare straight into the piercing eyes of a huge barred owl. The bird was perched on a branch, half-obscured by the patchy mist. She could see its scaly feet, the black talons gleaming where they encircled the wood. Those night-speckled feathers were grayed by the dew, slick-looking and shimmering. The bird might have been born of the mist itself. The eyes boring into hers did not seem to be of this world.

Attention riveted, she stumbled over a morning glory vine, and her arms windmilled. But for Cooter's quick reaction, she would have fallen.

"Thanks," she whispered.

"You all right?" he asked, voice hushed.

"Fine." She pointed up at the branch. "That owl..." The branch, half-vanished in a gray wreath of mist, vaguely reappeared, empty, the leaves hanging limp. Surely, had the owl flown, they should have been stirred.

Her party had stopped, staring up curiously. She

shook her head. "Nothing," she whispered. "Hurry. Let's get this over with."

Her mind on owls, ghosts, and death, she didn't realize how far they had come. The land opened before she knew it. Thick fog masked the clearing as she led her young men into it. She crouched. Ground Cherry Camp, that was right here, wasn't it? In the clearing?

As she looked around, she could see the characteristic plants rising from the patchy spring grass. The telltale triangular leaves were curled under the weight of the dew, cast in gray by the tiny droplets. The trail they followed continued, winding into the thickening fog.

Turn around and run! The words echoed hollowly between her souls. She could feel it, the wrongness, the sense of impending doom. Had everything gone deathly quiet? Her step faltered. It had been lunacy, bringing these young men here to try and do this thing. Someone would be killed as a result.

But you promised Bowfin. You can't back out now. You are Jaguar Hide's niece. His blood runs in your veins Your heart beats in time with his.

"Anhinga?" Right Talon asked under his breath. She could hear his worry.

"It's all right...we're close," she almost mouthed the words. "Just being careful, that's all."

In swirling mist, she saw a house—just the gray shape like a blinked image that vanished as quickly into the murk. In that instant she realized it was all right, that they had arrived in secrecy, that the Sun People were caught unawares.

She motioned them close. "That is the camp. We charge in, kill all we can, and escape. Keep your wits about you. It's easy to get lost in this fog. If we get separated, meet back at the canoe. If anyone gets cut off, he gets left behind."

They all nodded, eyes wolfish and gleaming as they smiled their anticipation. She could see the fear, the anxiety bundled in their tense bodies. This day's events would be sung about and retold for generations at the fires of her people. Reputations that would carry them for the rest of their lives would be forged here, today. She would be proven worthy of her uncle's pride and respect. Perhaps this was even the first step on the long road to eventual clan leadership.

"Let's go!" She gave Mist Finger a quick intimate smile, seeing his eyes warm as he caught her meaning. She promised herself that if they survived this and made it home, she would be spending time with him. Perhaps that was the Spirit World's attempt at justice. Bowfin's death would be compensated by providing her this perfect young man to love.

As she moved forward in a crouch, her nimble fingers fitted a dart into the nock of her atlatl. She had crafted the spear thrower herself. Made of osage orange imported from the northwest, the hard wood had been carefully shaped to fit her small hand. The length of her forearm, the wood was engraved with the design of a panther that could have been creeping its way around the shaft. A red jasper banner stone hung from the center to provide a counterbalance. The hook in the far end that cradled the cane dart butt had been labouriously carved into the wood itself. The handle she gripped was wrapped with panther sinew. Two loops had been fashioned to insert her fingers into to keep them from slipping.

Her darts were made of straight sections of cane a

little longer than she was tall, each tipped with a sharp stone point flaked from red-orange chert pebbles recovered from the deposits in the hillsides of her homeland. She herself had grooved the cane shafts midway along their lengths. Into them, she had tied split blue heron feathers for fletching to stabilize the long darts in flight. In her hand, she carried five of the deadly darts. Three, she would drive into some enemy's body. Two, she would keep in reserve in case they should have to fight their way out, or should she need them on the way home to kill an alligator or deer for the supper pot.

Her heart had begun to batter her breastbone with an unfamiliar energy. Her whole body felt charged with a bursting intensity. This was the war rush she had heard her elders mention, but never, until this moment, had she experienced it. Nothing she had ever done prepared her for the tingling, the excitement, the heady rush of euphoria, fear, and anticipation.

Panther Above, I am alive! On bunched legs, she charged into the camp, desperate for the sight of the enemy. The mist-shrouded huts were all around her now. It would be but a moment before she found a target. Borne as if by a storm surge, she threw her head back and a scream of ecstasy tore from her throat.

A shape emerged from one of the low doorways, but to her dismay, it ducked away into the mist before she could make her cast. "We are the Swamp Panthers! We are here to kill you! Bowfin! My brother! Come and watch us take our revenge!"

She danced on feathery feet, muscles charged, but only the swirling mist and the gray-thatched huts met her anxious gaze. Behind her, Spider Fire, Cooter, and Slit Nose, slowed, circling, darts nocked and back for the cast. They bent low, peering into the fog, searching for someone, anyone to attack.

"I saw one!" Anhinga declared. "He ducked out and ran before I could kill him."

"This accursed mist"—Right Talon gestured with his free hand—"is the work of..."

She heard the impact: a hissing slap, as it smacked into Right Talon's left side. She blinked, seeing the blood-shiny stone point where a hand's length of dart protruded from Right Talon's right side. On his left, the shaft still vibrated, driven in up to the fletching. The expression on Right Talon's face reflected a wide-eyed disbelieving confusion. The young man's mouth was open, working, but no sound broke his lips despite a mighty contortion of his chest. He sagged to his knees, darts and atlatl clattering to the ground.

Instinctively, Anhinga was in the act of reaching out to him as a second dart hissed and thumped into Slit Nose's body. He had been agape, frozen in disbelief as he watched Right Talon collapse. The scream that ripped from Slit Nose's lungs would haunt Anhinga's nightmares for the rest of her life.

"We are ambushed!" Mist Finger came to his senses first. "Run! Back to the canoe."

His voice broke Anhinga's panicked trance. She turned, pelting back the way they had come. She flinched as something hissed through the air beside her head. Her eyes caught the briefest flicker of something flashing past before it buried itself in the mist.

Cooter, running at her side, grunted, stumbled, and pitched headlong into the charcoal-stained dirt. She saw him hit, saw his body bounce at the impact and slide. He pawed weakly at the damp soil, a long dart implanted in the middle of his back between his shoulder blades.

Screams of rage and ululations of joy broke out on all sides. Shapes emerged from the mist, charging toward her, darts in their hands. *Warriors!* So many of them! Gripped by terror, she opened her hand, letting her darts and atlatl drop into the grass as she sprinted on Mist Finger's heels headlong back down the dark slash of trail up which she had led them brief moments before. She barely heard the sobbing sound her throat made as fear tightened it.

Spider Fire's voice shrieked from behind her, the sound that of wrenching pain. So violent was it that birds broke from the trees, flapping into the gray haze.

Panther, let me live. Help me. Keep me alive. Breath was tearing at her throat as she pumped her arms, flying through the mist-choked forest. The ground dropped away, and she dashed from foot to foot on the wild descent to the canoe landing, feet sliding on the wet dirt as she scrambled for balance and speed.

Mist Finger, too, had thrown away his darts for speed. She was several body lengths behind him as he slewed to a stop, almost toppling as his bare feet slid in the muck. He had started to bend, reaching for the canoe, when a man rose from behind it.

She watched in horror as Mist Finger raised his arm, barely having time to block the blow as a stone-headed axe snapped both bones in his forearm. Mist Finger screeched in agony as the enemy warrior whipped his axe back and forth, each smacking blow breaking through Mist Finger's pitiful attempts at defense. As she watched, Mist Finger was being beaten into a hunched mass of blood and broken bones.

A wild scream, instinctive, broke from her lips as she threw herself at her enemy. Her fingers were out, ready to scratch him apart.

Instead of the hard impact she expected, the man turned. He looked young, no older than she, a smile on his lips. She could see Mist Finger's spattered blood stippling the young warrior's face, hair, and chest. A dancing fire lit the man's dark eyes as he gracefully pivoted on one foot. Carried forward by her momentum, Anhinga couldn't react as he artfully dodged out of her way. As she flew past, his arm swung, the movement blurred. Yellow flashed—lightning in her brain— as her head rocked with a hollow bang that deafened her.

Her loose body hammered the muddy ground. A shrill ringing in her ears and pain, such terrible pain, filled her. Her brain had been dislocated from her body, as though floating behind her swimming vision. Her eyes blinked of their own volition. She was staring into Mist Finger's face—seeing but not comprehending the blood that ran from his gasping mouth or the blank emptiness behind his eyes. That image cast itself on her souls as she fell away...and away...drifting into a soft gray blankness.

Chapter Eleven

T he way the Swamp Panthers' slim canoe lanced into the bank filled White Bird with admiration. The wake came from behind, rippling the smooth brown water as it rushed up onto the grimy black shore. People were shouting and waving as they spilled down the long slope from Sun Town to the canoe landing.

White Bird laid his paddle to one side. Ahead of his feet, the dead warrior lay limp and beginning to bloat. He had been laid in the canoe bottom, facedown, limbs akimbo. Ahead of the corpse, just behind Yellow Spider, lay the girl, her arms and legs trussed as though she were a captured alligator.

White Bird had studied her all the way back from Ground Cherry Camp. She hadn't regained consciousness, and her breathing was labored. The way her head was turned he had been able to see her eyes jerking under the lids, as though she were locked in frantic dreams. Despite the way her face was mashed against the curving side of the canoe, he could see that she was a pretty thing. Thick black hair had been pulled into a braid that now lay curled like a blood-encrusted snake behind her head. The smooth lines of her muscular brown back slimmed into a narrow waist before the full swell of her hips. Her kirtle had been displaced, revealing a rounded curve of buttock above a long and firm thigh. Sleek calves ended in delicate if mud-stained feet. In all, his masculine self had been delightfully distracted by that enticing young body.

And, best of all, she is mine! He had captured her fairly. Not only that, but he had killed an opponent in hand-to-hand combat. Of all of his party, White Bird was the one who had fought toe-to-toe. He glanced happily at the dead warrior lying naked and supine behind the girl's feet. The young warrior's broken arms rested at unnatural angles. A dribble of urine leaked from the limp penis. Bright midday sunlight gleamed on the blackened wounds on his head. The eyes had dried, graying and vacant. A swarm of flies already droned in a wavering column when they weren't crawling across the dead flesh. From where he sat, White Bird could see pale knots of eggs the flies had laid in the dead man's eyes.

White Bird's companions might have killed the others—those who had driven darts into the raiders had been singing ecstatically on the trip and waved their bloody darts when they weren't paddling. He, however, had faced the enemy alone. Power lay in that. His exploits would be talked of among the clans. Pride, like a flood, rose within him as he stepped out of the canoe and helped Yellow Spider pull it onto the shore.

The crowd engulfed him like a wave. People were looking into the canoe, the more adventurous reaching in and prodding the bodies with a foot or hand. The flies rose in an angry buzz.

"Tell us! Tell us!" the cries came. Someone near the rear said, "The boy's vision was true!"

White Bird lifted his hands, stilling the throng. "My people, yes, my brother's vision was true. It was as he said. We found them where he said they would be, at Ground Cherry Camp. This dawn, in a thick mist, we ambushed them. This girl, I have taken on my own."

The other canoes slid onto the beach, warriors laughing as they shipped their paddles and leaped ashore. The victors lifted their bloody darts and shook them as they hooted and pranced in their joy. The trophy corpses were lifted—bloody and leaking fluids— before being borne up the long incline to be displayed on the western side of the Men's House atop the Father Mound.

"White Bird killed one bare-handed and took the girl! He took two!" the story circulated from lip to lip, eyes drifting his way.

Aware of their sudden awe, White Bird acted with the humility expected of a warrior, saying, "I was lucky. That's all. Someone had to cover their escape route. It was the others who laid the trap and broke their attack."

"But it was White Bird's planning," Yellow Spider insisted. He and Eats Wood, a man from Snapping Turtle Clan, reached down to lift the girl from the canoe bottom. "Because of his cunning, not one of us was even injured!"

"Carry her correctly," White Bird reminded, fully aware that Eats Wood—who already had an unsavory reputation when it came to young girls—held the captive in such a way that his hand was cupped suggestively around one of her breasts. "You be careful, Eats Wood! Hear? The Snakes alone know, I hit her hard enough to drive the souls loose from her body. I don't want her dead."

"We know how you want her!" old Red Finger barked wryly. "And for that, she doesn't need any souls!"

A round of laughter came in response. White Bird waved it down. "Yes, yes, but let's just get these corpses up to the Men's House, shall we? On the way, please, thank these warriors who have demonstrated their courage and skill. They have placed their lives at risk for your safety. While these were young and inexperienced raiders, they might just as well have been more cunning and dangerous. So, treat my companions with the respect they deserve. We are all obligated." In appreciation of the moment, he faced his fellow warriors and touched his forehead in respect. To his surprise, so did the rest of the gathered people.

Water Petal dropped into step beside him as he started up the slope. She wore her kirtle loose around her pregnant belly and a fabric shawl over one shoulder. Behind him, Yellow Spider and Eats Wood bore the unconscious girl. The dead warrior was dragged unceremoniously by his feet. His broken arms and battered head left marks on the damp soil.

"How is Mother?" White Bird kept his voice low, casting a glance to read Water Petal's expression.

Her round face betrayed her concern. "She is grieving, Cousin. All through the last winter, she knew that your uncle was failing. The two of them were a team. They built Owl Clan's prestige and indebted the other clans to ours. He might have been dying, but as long as he was alive, she could act as if it were the two of them working in unison. She could go at night, and even though fever was eating him, she could talk her ideas over with him, share her fears as she had since she was a young girl and he a starry-eyed youth." She shook her head. "But now...I don't know. It's as if part of her souls died with him."

"When will the funeral be?"

"Since you have returned, we will burn his house as soon as you have finished your obligations at the Men's House. Bobcat, the Serpent's apprentice, has cleaned Cloud Heron's bones. Your safe arrival, and in such triumph, will do more than anything to relieve your mother."

He nodded at that. "What about Mud Puppy? Has he...I mean, he came out of that odd trance, didn't he?"

Water Petal's frustration showed in her expression. "He has spent most of his time gone, much to your mother's despair. He has been shadowing the Serpent like a hawk, but when the Elder asked, the Serpent said the boy's constant company was agreeable."

He lowered his voice, fully aware of Eats Wood behind him. "Did you hear the talk at the landing?"

In an equally guarded voice, Water Petal said, "I did. But, White Bird, it was as he said, wasn't it? There were five—and the girl?"

He nodded, bothered as he had been since the beginning of this madness. "It was just an accident that I didn't kill her." He glanced back. "But let me tell you, she was a scrappy one. Fit to take me down with her bare hands."

"So, now that you have a wildcat, what will you do with her?"

"Keep her as a slave." He took a deep breath. "A Speaker should have someone to serve him, to cook and keep his house until a suitable marriage can be arranged." He shrugged. "Besides, Spring Cypress can make use of her."

"If she's as scrappy as you say, she'll run."

White Bird nodded. "Before I let her loose, I'll cut the tendons behind her ankles. It will slow her down to an awkward walk, but she doesn't need to run in order to cook, or clean, or..."

"Or accept your hard manhood?" With that, Water Petal laughed. "Under all that blood and mud, she looked comely, what I could see of her."

He remembered the rage in her eyes, the terrible desperation as she flew at him, arms outstretched. "Let's say she will be a challenge for me." The knowledge that she hated him would delight him every time he shared her bed.

"Swamp Panther, isn't she?" Water Petal asked.

"Yes." A pause. "How did Mud Puppy know they were coming?"

"Your mother and I have been talking. I think we have an explanation. Some of Clay Fat's cousins killed a boy while they were down digging Panther sandstone. It was probably just a lucky guess on Mud Puppy's part. Of course they would want revenge. Snakes! I should have figured that out on my own."

"By why just these youngsters?" White Bird wondered, idly aware that they were but a few winters younger than he himself. "Jaguar Hide isn't this clumsy."

"No. Keep that in mind, Cousin." Water Petal shot him a warning look. "Tell me, are you keeping her alive just because you want her as a slave? Or do you take Mud Puppy's warning seriously?"

"It was just as he said, Cousin. It might have been a lucky guess, but it was just as he said. There were five young warriors and the girl." It had been luck—not Mud Puppy's prophecy—that he'd managed to smack her unconscious. Since then his interest in her had been enflamed by the charms suggested by her very alluring body.

He concluded, saying, "As to the future of Mud Puppy's vision, we'll see."

"I suppose," Water Petal said into his silence. "Well, when you wear her out, or find yourself married to a willing wife with an appetite of her own, your interest will slacken—as male members always do after they've inserted their seed." She patted her pregnant stomach. "Then you can dispose of her as you will."

He laughed. "How did you come to be such an expert? You're but three winters older than I."

"I've been married for nearly two of those winters," she replied tartly. "My husband, like you, is a young man. Believe me, I have learned about appetites and desire." She lowered her voice, "But your mother may not remember when she was young, filled with a craving for a man's flesh inside her canoe. So we'll share this secret—just the two of us."

He nodded as they crested the rise. The Men's House loomed to the left. The large thatched building dominated the western side of the irregularly flattened mound. Above the centerline atop the roof, carved wooden effigies of Snapping Turtle, Eagle, and Rattlesnake stood against the afternoon sky. The totems of war glared out at the world with painted eyes, beaks, fangs, and talons raised to remind the world that Sun Town's warriors and hunters were to be feared.

Lifting a hand, he placed it on Water Petal's shoulder. "Thank you."

She gave him a knowing glance, a faint smile hiding behind her full lips. "Remember, Cousin, I am here for you. Now, as well as in the future."

He recognized the wariness in his breast for what it was: the realization that the world would never remain as it was today. He met her gaze and nodded, not in commitment, but in acknowledgment. Would she be the one he wanted for Clan Elder after Wing Heart was gone? Could they forge that kind of relationship? The same sort his mother had had with his uncle?

"Where do you want her?" Yellow Spider interrupted his thoughts as they approached the Men's House.

"Lay the dead ones out in a line there." White Bird pointed to the shoulder of the mound. "As to the girl, tie her to the sunset post. Just the way you would a captured alligator."

Yellow Spider nodded as he and Eats Wood carried the girl over. Though she still hung limply in their arms, White Bird was certain that he saw her eyes flicker. Snakes, could she be awake? If so, she must have the self-control of a piece of stone. A blow to the head like that should have been agonizing, and the pain of her hanging head would have felt as if her skull were exploding.

"Tie her carefully!" White Bird added. "I think she is a tricky one. I can't take the time right now to cut her tendons—and I don't want her in a position to wiggle herself free when no one is watching."

"I'll cut her tendons for you," Eats Wood chimed in. He had his hand on her bared breast again, and White Bird could see the girl's brown nipple pinched between his calloused fingers.

"No!" White Bird barked, angered by the man's familiarity with the captive. "I want to do it. She's mine, property of Owl Clan. Thank you for your service in bearing her here. I am obliged."

Eats Wood gave him a sour nod, released his hold on her, and allowed her torso to drop soddenly to the ground. The girl's head bounced on the packed silt. White Bird was sure he caught the painful wince before she could hide it. No matter, with Yellow Spider doing the binding, she wasn't going anywhere. For his part, he had the ceremonies and war cleansing to attend to in the Men's House. Even as he turned toward the large thatched building, he could smell the pungent odor of black drink wafting from within.

Mother Sun painted the evening sky with a marvelous display of red-orange, a fire spun through the clouds. The western horizon—glowing like a liquid blaze—outlined the high peak of the Bird's Head in a purple silhouette. So, too, did the marvelous sunset cast the curving ranks of house-topped ridges in perfect profile. The effect could be likened to a series of peg teeth on a giant jaw fixed to snap shut and crunch Wing Heart's very bones.

She sat under the worn ramada on the southern side of Cloud Heron's ominously dark house and watched Thunder Tail, the Speaker of the Eagle Clan, striding away, his long frame like a dancing shadow in the elongated dusk.

"Perhaps it is time to renew our obligations to Owl Clan," he had said. *"We have a long and mutually beneficial history, your clan and mine. With the death of an old Speaker, perhaps it is time for Eagle Clan to marry one of its young women to a new Speaker."*

"I suppose that you have someone special in mind?" she had asked. His somber expression had belied nothing as he fingered the bear claws hanging from his necklace. Always a canny player was Thunder Tail.

"I would have you consider young Green Beetle. She is just a woman, strong, with a smile that would melt your young man's heart."

To that she had offered some platitude concerning Green Beetle's charms but remained noncommittal.

Thunder Tail had watched her carefully, searching for some reaction as he added, *"As Speaker for Eagle Clan, I can tell you that we are happy to extend this offer. Elder Stone Talon was most impressed by your young man and his quick wit. He is well-spoken and astute. Our Elder enjoyed the gifts of carved stone that he presented to us from upriver. He has prevailed at countering the Swamp Panthers' raid. Our Elder has asked if you would be amenable to considering both Green Beetle and our support for your young man's rapid confirmation to the Council."*

"How could you ensure this?" she had asked in an offhand manner. *"Snapping Turtle Clan might object."*

He had smiled warily. *"I think I can assure you that Frog Clan would side with us. I assume that you still have Clay Fat's ear, and the Elder, Graywood Snake, would back you. That leaves Snapping Turtle Clan alone to complain. Together, we have a five-to-one vote in the Council."*

There it was. Everything she could have wanted. Her influence and authority were ensured through the foreseeable future. Cloud Heron, may the spirits embrace his souls, would have approved.

Just the thought of him brought a spear of grief to her heart. She couldn't help but glance back at her brother's silent and brooding house. Had it really been six moons ago when she had used her influence to move her brother into the dwelling next door to her own? His wife, Laced Fern, had indicated that she could no longer keep a husband who didn't provide for her children. Not that any great love had been lost between the two of them. Cloud Heron had done his duty, siring four children for her clan. The alignment had been politically dictated at the time. Laced Fern had been Cloud Heron's second wife, a woman ten and four turning of seasons his junior.

Cloud Heron's illness had robbed him of his manhood. Laced Fern, given her age, couldn't be blamed for wanting a younger man, one who could still plant his seed in her womb and contribute his support to Eagle Clan through his hunting and fishing skills. That was, after all, what men were for.

And now Eagle Clan, once ready to strip her of her position and cast her away like a broken clay pot, wished to renew their alliance.

Wing Heart rubbed her shins, her hands sliding on the nightshade-scented bear grease she had spread over herself to thwart the humming cloud of mosquitoes. She glanced off across the large plaza to where people still crowded around the Men's House. The Swamp

Panthers' corpses had provided great entertainment during the day. Bit by bit, they had been cut apart, burned, kicked, urinated upon, and otherwise abused. The camp dogs had gorged themselves on the bits of human flesh that had been scattered far and wide. While their horrified ghosts couldn't cross the mounds, or lines of ash, they could still see what befell their abandoned bodies from the trees just west of the Bird's Head. It was hoped that they would be so appalled that they would return home to haunt the dreams of the living Swamp Panthers. During nightmares they would tell their kinsmen never to repeat such a foolish thing as attempting to raid the Sun People.

But did it ever happen that way? Wing Heart sighed, raising her eyes to stare at the fading light in the clouds. They had darkened now, purpling into a bruised color. As if it were the sunset of her own life, she had grown cynical.

She knew the Swamp Panthers, had even traded with their leader, Jaguar Hide. In all of her years, she had never heard of an enemy war party being turned back because of pleading ghosts.

Warfare was a thing that people did. That was all. Over the years, she had come to the conclusion that abusing the dead was done for the surviving victors' self-satisfaction. It gave them a way to savor the triumph, prolonging the time until they had to return to the ordinary and await the news someday in the inevitable future that some kinsperson of their own was being cut apart and defecated upon in the enemy's village.

"Lost in thought?" a low voice asked from the shadows behind her.

She turned and recognized Mud Stalker as he stepped out from behind her house. "I would have thought you would have been in the middle of the festivities." She indicated the Men's House. "One of your young warriors killed an enemy this morning."

Mud Stalker walked over and lowered himself beside her, his mangled arm cradled in his left hand. "I think such doings are more for the young."

Did he mean that, or was it a way of building a rapport with her? "Were we ever that young?"

He gave her a curious appraisal, the lines of his face deepened by the shadows. "Once. I think." He chuckled. "I have been told that your brother is taken care of." He glanced over his shoulder at the silent house. "I assume the final rites are to be soon?"

She nodded. "As soon as my son is finished with his responsibilities to the People."

Mud Stalker lifted his good hand to chew on his thumbnail. Who was this new, companionable Mud Stalker? What was he after?

"He will be a great Speaker." Mud Stalker's attention was fixed across the distance.

"Thank you. I am proud of him myself."

"I salute you, Wing Heart. It is a great coup, a victory well worth savoring, much more rewarding than what our clanspeople are doing over there."

"I thank you again, Speaker."

He turned hard black eyes on her. His expression, never anything to contemplate with any pleasure, now appeared strained and slightly bitter. "Let us be blunt. We are old adversaries, you and I. Just this once, can we speak as two people without the dodging and darting?"

The old wariness warmed her insides. "Can we?"

He laughed again, sounding genuinely amused. "I'm not sure, but let us try. I have a question."

"I may or may not have an answer."

"This son of yours, Mud Puppy? Did he really have a vision?"

That caught her by surprise. "The boy has always been peculiar. Half of the time I'd be forever grateful just to marry him off—even if it was to someplace like Yellow Mud Camp. He's young, Speaker, and I don't know if he's going to end up as a great Serpent ten winters from now, or as a half-wit."

"And the vision?"

"I can only say that he was right about Ground Cherry Camp, and the Serpent believed him."

"But you don't? Interesting."

"I didn't say that."

"You didn't have to." He continued to stare at the crowd gathered around the Men's House. "What a curious fate Power has made for you. One son is almost a god—smart, clever, and daring. Look at him over there. People are already calling him Owl Clan's new Speaker. Even his rivals admire him. Those who should resent him are delighted to share their time with him. Two days ago, even though he should have been locked away in the Men's House in preparation for the attack, he still managed time to bring me a piece of copper." He reached into his belt pouch and held up a flat disk of the metal. "Told me he remembered that I had that necklace of copper beads and that this would make the perfect pendant for it." He turned it in the fading light so that she could see the turtle image engraved in the burnished metal. "It is indeed perfect."

"My son takes his duties to the People very seriously. It is the pleasure of my lineage and clan to make you happy."

Mud Stalker took a deep breath, replacing the heavy copper pendant into his belt pouch. "Thunder Tail was here earlier. I saw him walk away after a long talk with you."

"He was." *Spying on me, are you, old enemy?* "He brought Elder Stone Talon's regards. Apparently, her joints are bothering her."

"I heard that Thunder Tail mentioned a potential marriage."

She fought to keep the shadow of a smile from the corners of her mouth. Now she knew where this was going. "He mentioned one of his nieces, a girl named Green Beetle. I've seen her. She was just made a woman two moons ago. She's comely, a bit busty for my tastes, but that just makes milk for babies. I've seen her coming in from the river a time or two. She's the one who likes diving for clams. Most of those pearls that Eagle Clan has been passing around were found by her."

Mud Stalker was silent for the moment, calculating the investment Thunder Tail was making in the offer. Green Beetle, more commonly called Pearl Girl, had been the topic of considerable speculation. Not only was she Stone Talon's first granddaughter, but pretty and charming to boot.

"But I think my son is interested in Spring Cypress," Wing Heart added with a slightly wistful tone. "I may have to look in that direction. We have obligations to Clay Fat and Rattlesnake Clan. If Clay Fat were to ask for White Bird, I'm not sure but that I wouldn't have to give him."

She let that dangle. Snakes, it would break the boy's heart if she promised him to someone besides Spring Cypress. But here, for the moment, she could set a trap.

Mud Stalker tripped it when he said, "Clay Fat and old Graywood Snake can be reasoned with."

"They can?"

"I might have a little influence. You have obligations to Rattlesnake Clan, but they have obligations of their own. ...Assuming that White Bird and the girl wouldn't do something so silly as to elope—"

"Never! At least, White Bird wouldn't. As to the girl? Well, whatever lengths she might be tempted to try wouldn't matter. It takes two to elope."

"Indeed." He ran his fingers along the scar tissue that ridged his ruined arm. "Thumper gave you a good child when he was your husband."

"Is that a fact?" she countered crossly. "Did you know that the night of his brother's return, Mud Puppy was engrossed with a cricket?"

"Some would say that was Power speaking through the boy. Rumor has it that he had a great vision up on the Bird's Head in the middle of that storm and that Ground Cherry Camp was only part of it. Even the Serpent is overjoyed to have the boy following him around." Mud Stalker made a tsking sound. "I think the boy's eccentricities are something else."

Like half-wittedness? Is that what you are banking on, that my second son is an idiot?

Mud Stalker slapped his knee with his good hand. "What if I could persuade Clay Fat to look elsewhere for a husband for Spring Cypress?"

"Why should I want that?" *How much is he going to offer?*

Mud Stalker's eyes followed the first of the fireflies that rose over the grass in the plaza. The dancing yellow lights made magic in the gathering gloom as they hovered and whirled. "I might be willing to consider Pine Drop and Night Rain."

"Pine Drop and...*both of them*."

"It's not the first time a man has had two sisters for wives." He sounded so casual about it. "A great deal of prestige could come to a young man who was thought of so highly as to have a clan offer two of its daughters."

She turned the notion over in her mind. Agreeing would cause a major realignment of influence among the clans. It would be a solid bonding with Snapping Turtle Clan, a reciprocal agreement that changed the entire political landscape. "Pine Drop is freshly widowed, isn't she? She was married to that Alligator Clan boy."

"Blue Feather. He died of some lingering illness two moons ago. Nothing she or the Serpent did seemed to shake the evil from the man. It is my belief that White Bird would make her smile again."

"And Night Rain is..."

"Her little sister. Sweet Root's youngest."

"Yes, I remember. She was just declared a woman. I saw her in the Women's House last moon. She's a doe-eyed thing in her virgin's dress."

"Both are hard workers. They would make a solid household for a man. It's not like taking two wives from different clans or lineages. They wouldn't be jealous or spiteful of each other. These are sisters. They already like each other. They wouldn't distract White Bird into tearing his hair out."

With forced aplomb, she said, "I appreciate your

kind offer, Mud Stalker. In spite of our past, it intrigues me."

"Let me ask: What if I added nectar to the suggestion?" He was stroking his throat now with the studied indifference of a man who held all the right gaming pieces. "What if I told you I would not only support White Bird for Speaker within the Council, but I would argue, no, insist, that Mud Puppy be confirmed in White Bird's place should anything ever happen to his brother."

It was said so casually, almost in an offhand manner. With difficulty, she kept her voice even. "Why would you do that?"

Mud Stalker's head lowered, irritating her that she couldn't see his eyes. "Sometimes, Wing Heart, the best way to win is not to fight. Sometimes, a smart person finally realizes that to win tomorrow, he must lose today. For years I have tried to break Owl Clan. This is no secret between us."

"No," she responded flatly. "It isn't."

"The night the warriors prepared to counter the Swamp Panther attack, I had a Dream. A very Powerful and persuasive Dream. Bird Man appeared and told me how the fight would end. He told me that I would know the truth of his words. Very well, I have seen the return of White Bird, seen his Power in Trade and war. He will be Speaker—and a very capable one. Perhaps the most capable of all the Speakers in memory."

"Bird Man told you to make this offer? In a Dream?"

"He did."

"I will still be the Owl Clan Elder."

"Indeed you will," Mud Stalker said grimly. "But you and I both know that it will not be forever."

She finally chuckled, reading his meaning beyond the words. "When I am dead and gone and another is Elder, my son will still be Speaker."

"And he will be Snapping Turtle Clan's friend." Mud Stalker smacked his gums. "To ensure that, I will make you yet another offer. Snapping Turtle Clan will offer to marry Pine Drop and Night Rain to your second son should anything happen to the first."

"They'd go to Mud Puppy?"

"Indeed. If anything should happen to White Bird, Mud Puppy shall inherit his wives." Mud Stalker gave her a challenging grin that the darkness couldn't hide. "Tell me, Clan Elder, can anyone else offer so much? Back Scratch, Red Finger, Sweet Root, Falling Drop, and I have discussed this. My lineage is committed to making this alliance. Your son shall be Speaker. And your second son after him. With their support you shall be the leader of the Council."

"Forgive me, but I still have trouble understanding why."

He chuckled dryly. "Because in six days the world has turned itself upside down. We can't help but believe that the spirits are on Owl Clan's side. Who are we to fight the spirits? For the future of my clan, I will even allow you to maintain leadership of the Council."

She felt like howling in triumph, but not yet. *He knows me too well.* She couldn't help but narrow her eyes against the darkness. "We shall consider, old enemy. First, I have a funeral to conduct. And then, after I dissect this offer you have made, I shall give you my decision."

He inclined his head before standing. "That is fine. In the meantime, as a gesture of our goodwill, we would like to provide a feast in honor of your dead brother. He served the People well."

"We would be obliged."

Mud Stalker waved it off. "It is simply a gift, a gesture of our goodwill."

As he walked away into the night, she couldn't help but wonder: *What kind of trap have you laid for me, old enemy?*

The Serpent

The Truth is in the error.

That's the problem.

It is the deep-throated rumble of buffalo calling to each other in the wintertime. The flash of the firefly on pitch-black nights. It is the far-off call of the blue heron on her way to the sunset.

Don't you see?

Meaning is not in words, but in between them.

Do you think the buffalo hears Truth when she is calling out to another buffalo? Or when someone answers her? No. She hears Truth in the space between.

When she is listening.

Just listening.

Chapter Twelve

Anhinga clenched her teeth, desperate to keep the vomit that burned the back of her throat from passing her clamped lips. Should they see that, it would shame her, as if she were not already more than shamed. Enough of the accursed Sun People had come by to kick her and urinate on her that she could no longer feign unconsciousness. She had surrendered that fiction the first time one of them touched a smoldering stick to her naked side.

She glared around her like a trapped raccoon, snarling and hissing her hatred as her tormentors heaped physical and symbolic abuse upon her. Her legs and arms had been wrapped in tightly bound cords. Even her ability to flop like a beached fish had been curtailed by the rope that tied her to an upright log set into the dark earth. Her skin stung where they had seared it with hot brands. The odors of urine and feces plugged her nose. Most of it had dried. She didn't need their waste spattered upon her to be shamed or broken.

They could do nothing to her that she hadn't done to herself.

By craning her neck, she could see the remains of her companions. Blood-and-offal-stained earth marked the spot where the bodies had been dismembered. She had watched with horror as little boys gleefully pulled the intestines out of a long slit cut into Mist Finger's abdomen. The horror had been so great that she couldn't help but weep as a young man used a bloody strip of flesh flayed from Cooter's leg to beat her. She'd flinched, more from the feel of Cooter's cold black blood than from the pain.

Her souls numb, she blinked and watched the last of the dancing men. Their bodies flickered in the firelight, greased and shining yellow and black as the flames licked up from a central fire pit. Night had fallen cool and moist. Her skin prickled with gooseflesh.

A great shout broke the silence as the men leaped and raised their arms to the night. Then they stood frozen, watching the door where her assailant stepped out into the open. She could see the young man, naked, his muscular body bathed in firelight. The wash of fresh blood might have been painted on the skin of his chest. Her staggering thoughts couldn't quite place it—then she remembered where she had seen the like before: He had been freshly tattooed, the designs pricked into his skin with a copper needle.

Her gut heaved, and bile rushed into her mouth. Tattooed: the realization stuck in her head. A victorious warrior celebrating some great accomplishment underwent tattooing to mark the occasion. In this case, her captor was being marked for his actions in capturing her alive and killing Mist Finger face-to-face.

If only I could die! She tensed against the binding cords, finding no looseness. Die, she would, but not yet. Soon though, when they had taken the time to sever the thick tendons that ran behind her heels and finally untied her, then she would take the first opportunity to scavenge a sharp piece of stone and open her veins.

The young men were hooting and dancing, slapping the blood-smeared young man on the back as he passed through their ranks.

"Thank you, my friends," he called out in a fine baritone. "Together we have done great things. We have shared black drink, undertaken the ceremonies to cleanse ourselves of the taint of war, and paid our enemies our highest compliments."

They laughed at that. In the darkness, Anhinga spat the bile from her mouth.

"The middle of the night has come." The young man pointed to the north, a bronzed god in the firelight. "The stars have nearly circled the heavens. Go home, my friends, and sleep. Tomorrow, I am told, my uncle's house will be burned and his Dream Soul set free to find the ghosts of friends long dead."

"And Snapping Turtle Clan will provide a huge feast," the burly warrior on one side called as he shook his fist. Anhinga remembered him—the slimy weasel that had groped her as he carried her up from the canoes. Her nipple, the least of her hurts, was still sore from when he had pinched it.

"Until tomorrow," the war leader cried.

"Tomorrow!" the rest shouted in unison. As they broke up and dispersed into the darkness, she could hear them chanting, "White Bird, White Bird, White Bird" over and over again.

The blood-streaked White Bird watched them go, a smile on his face as he stood illuminated in yellow firelight. Only when the last of them had stepped out of sight did his expression fall and his shoulders slump. He made a face as he reached up, prodding carefully at the drying blood on his chest. Where the tattoo had been pricked into his skin must have felt like fire.

Walking like an old man, he stopped long enough to stare down at her and say, "Tomorrow...I'll cut you then." She almost sighed as he walked past and into the darkness.

Left alone, she finally allowed herself to weep. Tears of rage and grief came welling from the hollow between her souls. One by one, she saw the faces of her friends: Cooter, Slit Nose, Right Talon, Spider Fire, and finally, Mist Finger.

Mist Finger's eyes were sparkling as he looked into hers. If she but glanced over to where his body had been laid, she could still see the bloody arch of his ribs. His hollowed-out pelvis was a dark mound in the shadows. Two of the hungry brown dogs were growling, chewing on the edges of his hipbones as they tugged against each other. In another life, far away in the world of imagination, she would be holding him, sharing her body with him, planning a life with him as her husband.

Sobs choked in her raw throat. All she had left was death.

"Are you all right?" a voice asked softly from the darkness behind her.

She started, fear leaving her shaking as she blinked at the tears that clung to her damp lashes. She jumped at the feel of fingers on her calves, trembling as they moved down to her ankles.

"He didn't cut you," the soft voice continued. "Good. It would be harder if you had been maimed."

"Who...who are you?" She struggled to keep her teeth from chattering.

"He said you have to live. He said you have to go back."

"Who...who said?"

"He did."

She felt the vibrations as something sawed at the ropes binding her. "What are you doing?" Fear leaped up like a thing alive to sing along her nerves and muscles.

"I'm cutting you free."

Hope like a flame tingled within her.

"He said you had to live. To be free."

"Who? White Bird?"

"No. I can't tell you." It sounded like a boy's voice, and she flopped her head over, staring at the dark form that hunched above her. From the corner of her vision she could just make out his skinny body as he crouched over his work. The sawing was more vigorous, and she could feel cords parting.

"Can you walk?" he asked.

"Yes." But could she? She hadn't been able to feel her arms or legs for hours. And the headache, Snakes! That alone might double her over when she stood up.

"You stink," he said vehemently.

"When they weren't urinating or defecating on me, they were pelting me with my friends' guts." How could she say that so matter-of-factly?

"You shouldn't have come here."

"It's your people who shouldn't come to my lands. As long as you come to take our stone and kill us, we will come to kill you!" The last cord around her middle parted, and her arms fell like severed meat to slap onto the ground. Her horror grew when she couldn't move them. *Tell me I'm not paralyzed!*

Had it been the blow to the head? She had heard tales of warriors hit hard on the skull who hadn't been able to move afterward. But then the painful prickling began as circulation ate its way into her upper arms.

She gasped as her legs came free and rolled loosely apart. They, too, might have been wood for all she could feel.

"There," the boy said. "You can go now."

"I can't," she hissed, fear trying to strangle her. "My legs...I need a while. Time for them to come alive again."

At this, the dark form above her seemed to hesitate. She wiggled sideways enough to see him as he peered owlishly into the dark. The dying fire barely cast a red glow onto his round face. She could see his profile, a stub of nose, thin cheeks, and thatch of black hair. More than a boy, he was less than a man. As he stared around the movements were furtive, frightened.

"Why are you doing this? Are you one of my people? A lost relative taken as a slave? Do you want me to take you home, is that it?"

"No. I'm Owl Clan."

She shook her head, face contorting as blood pouring into her arms began to ache and pulsate. She tried to remain still, the slightest movement shooting fire along her limbs.

"No one can know I did this," the boy continued. "They wouldn't understand. I'm already in enough trouble."

She couldn't stifle a gasp as he reached down and began massaging her leg. "No! That hurts!"

"But it will be gone sooner." He sounded so sure of himself. "We don't have time. He told me to be fast."

"Who?" she gritted through clenched teeth, as his hands ran waves of agony through her legs. She might have been floating on a flood of biting ants.

"He said you had to live," was the simple answer.

Whining, she managed to pull her arms up and blasted her souls numb when she bent her knee. Movement was coming back. No, she wasn't paralyzed. Blessed Panther, she had to get up:

An eternity passed before she could prop herself on all fours, and one arm around the boy's neck, stagger to her feet.

"Come on," he hissed, as they wobbled off into the darkness. "It's this way."

"What is?"

"The canoe landing. But maybe you could be so kind as to take one of the Snapping Turtle Clan's boats? They don't like us anyway."

"Sure, boy. Anything you want. I owe you."

Mud Puppy stood with his feet sunk in the black mud of the canoe landing and looked out into the darkness. The dugout canoe faded into the night, a dark streak on midnight waters. He could hear the faint gurgle of water as she stroked, droplets tinkling as she raised the paddle.

It didn't make any sense. Why let her go? What could Masked Owl have in mind? She hated them, and he had felt it rising off of her like the stench of waste she had been coated with.

A shiver ran down his back as he turned and trudged wearily up the incline above the canoe landing. White Bird would never forgive him if he found out. And Red Finger would slit his throat if he ever learned that Mud Puppy had fingered his canoe for the Panther woman to steal.

"What is going on?" Hazel Fire asked, as he and Yellow Spider joined the growing crowd. They stood on the far northeastern corner of the plaza. At their feet, the marshy borrow pit separated them from the first ridge. Atop that, Wing Heart and White Bird watched as the Serpent chanted and reached into a small clay bowl of black drink. This he cast from his fingertips onto the walls of the second house in the line that stretched ever westward in the long arc of the Northern Moiety.

"That is the house where Speaker Cloud Heron lived."

Yellow Spider's expression betrayed his inner feelings: sorrow, grief, and a curious sort of expectation.

"Ah, yes." Gray Fox came to stand beside them. "He was White Bird's uncle, yes? The one who died just after our arrival?"

"He was my cousin," Yellow Spider replied. "In many ways he was my teacher as well as White Bird's. Snakes, I could tell you some stories. Once, when I was much younger, he caught me handling his atlatl. It was his most sacred possession. He was subtle, our Speaker, and instead of beating me to within a hairbreadth of my life he made me eat raw fish guts for a whole moon."

"You *did* that?" Hazel Fire asked incredulously.

"Everyone knew that I had done something terrible. The Speaker never told people what. And you can wager that I never did, either. But it was so humiliating and vile that I never broke one of his rules again."

"I'd have sneaked something cooked when no one was looking," Gray Fox muttered uneasily.

"I wouldn't," Yellow Spider declared. "Trust me, the Speaker would have known. He would have seen it reflected from my souls."

"He was part sorcerer then?" Hazel Fire asked, his eyes focused on the house. Perhaps he thought some smoky spirit was going to rise from the door and cast enchantments around and about.

"No." Yellow Spider rubbed his calloused palms together. "He knew people, that's all. Knew their souls. When my punishment was over, he treated me as if nothing had ever happened between us. He never even mentioned the event again, and he was most enthusiastic when White Bird suggested that I might go upriver with him."

"Was he much like White Bird?" Gray Fox was watching the increasing numbers of people who walked toward them across the plaza.

"They were much the same," Yellow Spider admitted. "Like White Bird, the Speaker was smart, friendly, and forever thinking two or three steps ahead. Seeing them together, you could almost think them twins. That is why so many people are coming to honor his passing. Even the other clans respected the Speaker. He had a way about him."

"And what is the Serpent doing?" Hazel Fire pointed to where he was still casting droplets of black drink from his fingertips.

"That is to feed the soul of the house and the Speaker's Dream Soul. By doing so, it reminds them both that while the site must be cleansed by fire, the People bear them nothing but goodwill. Think of it like this: When people live inside a house, they become part of that place. The light is bad, this being sunset, but you can look into the doorway. There, see on the pile of wood? Those are the Speaker's bones. His Dream Soul is hovering there, attached to them."

Hazel Fire swallowed hard, stepping back as if to distance himself from the dead spirit.

"No, don't fear," Yellow Spider said with a chuckle as he reached back and pulled the Wolf Trader forward. "The Speaker was a good and wise man. A person's soul doesn't change just because of death. At least, not unless something terrible was done to kill him. Only then does a soul turn vengeful, just as the living would."

"Why burn his bones?" Gray Fox's brow had lined with worry as he stared uneasily at the low doorway. "Why not bury them as my people do?"

"Fire cleanses," Yellow Spider reminded. "Any evils or bad thoughts that might have gathered at this place will be destroyed or driven off." He pointed to the gaps that separated the sections of concentric ridges. "When the fire starts, any evil that is trapped here can escape out through the gaps. If you walked to the outer ring, you would see that the line of ash has been parted to let any malevolent spirits out. They will flee toward the setting sun, drawn inexorably to the west."

"What happened to his flesh?" Hazel Fire shifted uncomfortably. "Those bones look pretty well cleaned off. He didn't die that long ago. Not long enough to have decomposed like that."

"The Serpent's apprentice, Bobcat, stripped the meat from his bones," Yellow Spider said. "That has to be done soon after death, before the flesh has a chance to draw evil to it. You know what happens to a body after death. Corruption is drawn to it just like ants to fruit nectar. Corruption and the forces that lead to festering are ravenous, forever driven by a fierce and consuming hunger. Since we can't drive them away, it's better simply to take the flesh and carry it outside of Sun Town. Each clan has a place where it leaves corruption and rot. Those locations we mark and no one, unless they, too, are filled with evil, would go there." Yellow Spider shrugged. "Who knows? Maybe as the years pass, we'll concentrate so much evil outside the powerful rings of Sun Town that the world will be a better place. Even as far away as your own villages."

"And your Speaker's Dream Soul?" Hazel Fire asked.

"Because of the black drink and the Serpent's requests to his soul, it will stay here, within the safe confines of Sun Town."

"You mean you try to keep his ghost here?" Gray Fox was looking increasingly nervous.

Yellow Spider cocked a disbelieving eyebrow. "Why wouldn't we? Just because the Speaker is dead doesn't mean he isn't still part of the clan. Part of what our earth works do is keep the spirits of our dead within. This way, they can whisper to our Dream Souls at night when we're sleeping."

"I'll never let myself Dream again while I'm sleeping here." Gray Fox touched his breast as if for reassurance.

"I think they speak their own language," Hazel Fire muttered. "At least no ghost has talked to me in my dreams in any language but my own."

Yellow Spider turned his attention to Wing Heart as she stepped to the house, calling, "Brother, hear me. We are cleansing this place now. Thank you for all that you have done for our lineage, our clan, and our people. Stay with us, help us, fight for us from the Land of the Dead. Whisper your wise counsel when we are in need, and intercede on our behalf with the forces of light and darkness. Be well, my brother, for we shall meet your Dream Soul when our earthly bodies fail us."

She turned and walked to a low-smoking fire before reaching out to take a smoldering stick. White Bird stepped forward, his face a mask against the pain in his freshly tattooed chest. He placed his hand around his mother's where she grasped the smoldering stick. Together, they touched it to a corner of the thatch. White Bird had to lean forward, blowing the glowing end until the thatch caught, and the first flickers of fire began climbing the dry grass.

"I see things inside," Gray Fox said as the fire illuminated the interior of the house. "A man's atlatl, a bundle of darts, and isn't that a pile of folded clothing?"

Yellow Spider whispered, "Goodbye, Speaker. I will see you soon." Then, after a pause, he said in a louder voice, "Those are the Speaker's personal belongings. He cannot take them to the Land of the Dead in their present form. They, too, must be transformed into their spirit selves in order for him to use them in the afterlife."

As they watched, the Serpent cavorted and shook his turtle shell rattle. His reedy voice rose and fell as he Sang in words Yellow Spider couldn't understand. The flames spread through the roofing. Thick white smoke curled through the tightly bound shocks of grass before being whipped up into the sunset sky.

Chapter Thirteen

White Bird stepped back, an arm raised to protect himself from the violent heat radiating from his uncle's house. There, just within the doorway, he could see his uncle's bones laid in a careful bundle on the rick of hickory and maple wood. In the midst of the bonfire, the skull charred and blackened, grease sizzling as the rounded bone split, steamed, and oozed. The long bones had been tied in a tight bundle that now spilled down into the crackling logs. One by one, they popped as the marrow began to boil inside.

White Bird backed up another step to where his mother stood, arms at her sides, a grim expression on her drawn face. He flinched at the heat, amazed that she could stand it, and struggled with the desire to step back even farther to where the crowd had gathered on the other side of the borrow ditch.

"Farewell, Brother," she said in a voice mostly drowned by the fire's roar. Clay began to flake off the walls as the cane-and-pole substructure began to burn.

A wreath of black rose in a pillar, bearing the smoke of a dead life to the Sky World. Mother Sun sank below the horizon beyond the Bird's Head, the sky uncharacteristically blue and cloudless.

White Bird might have been able to stand it, but the dull smarting on his chest where the Serpent had tattooed the red pattern of dots became unbearable. The design marked him as a blooded warrior and a leader worthy of respect. He unwillingly took his mother's hand and half dragged her back.

The look she shot him was nearly as frightening as the searing heat. Grief lay behind her eyes, grief so powerful it sucked at his souls. And then, as if he truly saw her for the first time, he cataloged her face: Threads of white streaked her hair where she'd pulled it back and pinned it into a severe bun. Deep wrinkles hatched her hollow cheeks, and her mouth had thinned. When had her angular nose gone to extra flesh? He had never noticed that the smooth skin of her forehead had hardened and lined. Her throat, once so fine, now wattled and bagged like an elderly man's scrotum.

She's so old! He stood stunned, trying to fathom what it all meant. The popping of his uncle's bones, his mother's old age, the pain of his new tattoos. As of that morning the world might have been dislocated, shifted somehow as it floated on the endless seas. From this day onward nothing would ever be the same. His life might have ended and begun anew.

Even the mysterious nighttime escape of his captive seemed somehow of lesser import—though he'd vowed to find the culprit who had sawed her ropes in two. Protestations aside, he was sure it had something to do with Snapping Turtle Clan, and perhaps Eats Wood and his preoccupation with sticking his penis into anything female.

"Are you all right?" he asked as he leaned close to his mother's ear.

For several heartbeats she stared blankly at the fire, then his words seemed to penetrate. She swallowed hard, the loose flesh at her throat working. "Yes. Part of me is in there with him. I am burning, White Bird. My souls are becoming ashes."

"He was a great Speaker for our clan," White Bird replied as he turned his attention back to the flame-engulfed structure. "I am honored to bear his legacy."

"Honored enough to take the responsibilities of the clan over your own desires?"

"Of course." He pointed at the blackened bones now half-hidden in an inky veil of smoke. "He taught me that. My first duty is to my clan."

"Even if it means giving up your own desires for the good of all? Surrendering the needs of your lineage for those of the whole?" Her voice sounded far away, oddly brittle.

"Yes." Must they have this conversation now?

"What would you give up to be Speaker?"

At the serious tone in her voice, he studied her from the corner of his eye, aware that they were surrounded by a huge throng of people. Tens of tens of tens had come to watch the cleansing of Speaker Cloud Heron's house, belongings, and remains. For the moment, he and his mother were the center of all attention.

"Whatever I have to," he said in a low voice.

"Spring Cypress?"

The question shocked him. "Why? I love her. She

loves me. We want to be together. Why do you think I—"

"For the clan." Her low voice had all the flexibility of a stone bowl. "Or did you mislead me?"

"No, I..."

"The clan places its demands above those of its Speaker."

"Yes, but I don't understand what that has to do with my marrying Spring Cypress. Rattlesnake Clan has been our ally for so many years that—"

"Things change, boy. Clay Fat has his own plans for Spring Cypress...but that is not your concern. Tell me now, would you marry Spring Cypress, or be Speaker of the Owl Clan? I must know. Time is short, and if you are not interested in serving, I must quickly find another."

He tried to keep from gaping, aware that the Wolf Traders were standing across the borrow ditch with Yellow Spider, several arm's lengths to his left. They kept glancing back and forth between the fire and White Bird. He could see them talking in low tones, trying to understand what they were seeing.

"Mother, I went north—"

"You are talking to your Clan Elder. Whatever your mother wishes is not germane to this conversation. How do you answer your Clan Elder? Will you be Speaker?"

"I would, yes, but to—"

"Even if it means giving up your own desires for those of your clan? Yes, or no?"

"I've planned on marrying Spring Cypress since I was a boy! We've always understood that she and I—"

Her implacable gaze had fixed on the burning house as the thatched roof slumped, sagged, and collapsed. Smoke, sparks, and glowing ash whirled about within the still-standing walls to rise in a curling vortex. Inside the open doorway, the inferno obscured the splintered and scalloped bones on the pyre.

"Yes," he muttered, feeling a hollow anger begin to strangle his grief. "As you have known all along."

"No matter the cost?"

"No matter the cost." His heart might have been stone when he added, "Even if it means I cannot have Spring Cypress." How odd? At that moment he could barely remember what Lark's face looked like. Had he left her so long ago? It seemed like a lifetime.

His mother nodded, reaching out to retake his hand and turning him to face the crowd. Raising his hand high over his head, she cried, "People of the Sun, Speaker Cloud Heron is dead. His remains have been cleansed. His Dream Soul will reside with us here forever. As required by our laws, his house and his belongings, the remains of his body, are being cleansed before your eyes. It is in this moment that I, as Elder of the Owl Clan, do raise this young man's hand. Greet White Bird, nephew of Cloud Heron, son of Wing Heart, fathered by Black Lightning of the Eagle Clan. As Clan Elder I place this young man before you for your inspection."

White Bird battled the wheeling sense of confusion, conquered it, and stood tall and straight before them. He wondered what they were seeing. A muscular young man, his chest a painful mass of fresh scabs. A man too young for such a responsibility. This was madness. A Speaker needed to be older, tempered and wise as his uncle had been.

"Hurrah for White Bird!" The shout carried over

the crowd. To his surprise, the caller was none other than Mud Stalker.

While he was still reeling from the sight, Spring Cypress caught his attention by bouncing on charged legs. Her whole face beamed with joy and excitement as she clapped her hands for him.

Beside her, Clay Fat's subdued gaze had fixed on the young girl, his look anything but reassured.

What is going on here? White Bird wondered, face neutral against the tight agony in his mutilated chest. Not all of it came from the wounds left by his tattooing, as his mother continued to thrust his hand up toward the deep purple sky. The cheering of the crowd before him did little to ameliorate the heat burning into his back.

From the corner of his eye he noticed Mud Puppy, standing off to one side, his slight form illuminated by the ghastly yellow firelight. A haunted look, one of terror, reflected from his large brown eyes. He was shaking his head, and even across the distance, White Bird could read his lips. They were repeating, "Don't do it!" over and over.

Anhinga let the canoe drift, carried forward by its own momentum. She banked the pointed paddle across the gunwales as the craft curved slightly to the left—a flaw in its shaping during construction. Paddling it, she had constantly had to correct for that peculiarity. Now, however, she was so exhausted that she didn't have enough energy to feel frustrated.

Around her, the swamp pulsed with life: the

humming of insects, the piping song of the birds rising and falling in scattered melodies, fish sloshing as they broke the surface for slamming bugs. Heat lay on the water, burned down through gaps in the trees by the relentless sun. Sweat beaded on her aching body.

For a long moment she stared at nothing, blind to the brown water with its bits of yellow-stained foam. Dark sticks from a forgotten forest floor bobbed gently, and the flotsam of bark and leaves lay in dappled shadows. The trees, so rich and green in the light might have been shades cast by another world. She did not see or feel the patches of triangular hanging moss that draped the branches and traced over her skin as she floated past. The dark shape of a water moccasin gliding away from her course didn't register in her stunned mind.

Again and again she relived the nightmare images. All she could see was that last instant when Mist Finger collapsed under the battering of the Sun warrior's stone-headed war club. Heartbeats later that scene faded into fragments of images as she watched her friends being torn apart before the Men's House. The vibrant red of bloody flesh, the odd gray of the intestines, the dark brown of the livers as they were cut loose from under the protective arch of human rib cages, painted her souls.

One instance in particular stood out. She flinched as she watched a blood-streaked warrior toss Cooter's shining liver high. It had risen, flopping loosely, to hang at midpoint and then dive steeply. At impact it had literally exploded into a paste, bits and pieces spattering hither and yon. Who would have thought a man's liver was so delicate?

She stared, sightless to this world, hearing the

humming of the mosquitoes and flies as they hovered about her. Even the sweat trickling down her face seemed so far away, intruding from a different world than her own.

Blinking her dry eyes she glanced down and took inventory of herself. They had stripped her naked, of course. Clothing left wounded souls with a final if ever so small place of refuge. They had denied her even that. Blister-covered welts itched and oozed where they had used burning sticks to elicit her screams. A black bruise marked her left breast, where the one called Eats Wood had viciously pinched her nipple. Despite the bath she had taken at first light, she felt dirty, filth-smeared in a way that no amount of scrubbing could ever cleanse. If she reached up, she could feel the swollen lump that stuck out of the left side of her head. That was where the flat of White Bird's stone axe had brought her down. Broken and scabbed skin overlay deeper bruises on her wrists and legs where they had bound her.

In defiance she flexed her feet against the gouged wood on the canoe bottom, thankful that White Bird hadn't had the time to cut the tendons in her heels. Despite her other wounds, she could still walk, still run, instead of hobbling like an old woman on loose-hinged ankles.

Those were the wounds to her body. Try as she might, she could not even catch a glimpse of the wounds to her souls.

As she had paddled through the morning, dream images had flashed in her head: she and Mist Finger in love, their marriage, their first child—his smile as he stared up from moss bedding. She had imagined Mist Finger, grinning at the sight of her as he walked up to their house at the Panther's Bones. Gone, vanished like the morning mist that gave way to a burning midday sun.

Other memories of her and the dead sifted through her disjointed thoughts. She had grown up with them. Like the vines surrounding a tree, she had woven bits and pieces of their lives into her own. Cooter had brought her the first fish he had ever caught. How old had he been? Five summers?

She remembered the accident when Slit Nose had been running full tilt across Water Lily Camp, and fallen to slice his nose open on a discarded stone flake. The scar had never fully healed—and now never would. Until she died she would remember the way one of the Sun People propped his severed head onto the flames of that crackling bonfire. How it had sizzled as his face was blackened and burned, the scarred nose curling into ash while the eyeballs popped like overinflated bladders.

Spider Fire had always been a wit and a tease. Sharp of tongue, a bit irreverent, his puns had often left her incapacitated with laughter. Not more than two winters past, she had held him as he mourned his big brother's untimely death. In a freakish accident, a wind-lashed tree had fallen on him. It was to her that Spider Fire had come for comfort. Then, yesterday, she had seen his muscles carved away and fed to camp dogs until only the blood-streaked bones remained.

Right Talon had been the sober one, the youth of whom no one had expected great things. Instead, he had been carried away by dreams that would never come true. One day he was going to be a great Trader, the next he would become a most holy Serpent. Later that same afternoon he had been sure that a warrior's fame lay ahead of him. Dreams. All Dreams. They had died, locked away behind his sightless eyes, unable to escape past the tongue protruding from his gaping mouth. She could see his disbelieving face, wet and witless as a Sun warrior urinated on it.

The bumping of the canoe jarred her back to the present. She blinked at the swelling knot of pain that grief placed under her tongue. No tears remained to leak past her raw eyes. The canoe had fetched up alongside the trunk of a sweetgum tree. Patterns of green mottled the gray bark where wrist-thick vines twisted their way up into the canopy. A lizard skittered upward, disturbed by her arrival.

Where am I going? How am I ever going to live? The answers eluded her. When she glanced down, no less than a dozen mosquitoes dotted her arms. Their abdomens were dark and swollen, their back legs lifted as they drank deeply of her blood.

She would have to face the families of the dead. How did she explain what had happened to them? How did she put the terror she had observed into words?

One by one she watched the mosquitoes rise and fly off, their blood-swollen bodies heavy on the hot, still air. As they went others landed on airy feet, probing with their spiky snouts until they tapped her veins. Let them. She no longer needed her blood.

She no longer needed anything.

Chapter Fourteen

Mud Puppy crouched on the grass and fingered the tasseled ends of the fabric breechcloth his mother had made for him. The knotted hemp fibers rolled roughly under his fingers as he watched the proceedings beneath the roofed Council House ramada. He was but one of the large crowd that had gathered around the circular ramada to watch this historic session. Tens of tens of people ringed the open-sided enclosure, all watching with excitement as a new Speaker was voted on.

The packed crowd reassured Mud Puppy, provided him with the anonymity he desperately desired. Unlike the others who had come to watch, he felt an increasing sense of despair. This was going to doom them all. He couldn't say why he knew that, where it came from. Something that was spun out of forgotten Dreams lay just beyond his ability to grasp.

The Council was a reflection of Sun Town in miniature. Under the northeast portion sat Owl Clan, then Alligator Clan to the north, with Frog Clan in the northwest. In the southwest was Rattlesnake Clan. Eagle Clan sat in the south, and Snapping Turtle Clan in the southeast portion.

The ritual entryway in the east and the exit on the west were left open. A crackling fire burned in a pit at the center of the ring.

Mud Puppy watched with a heavy heart. Masked Owl had come to him in a Dream the night before, telling him exactly how it would come about. But what was the rest? The part that eluded his memory?

Mud Stalker stood by the fire in the center of the Council, his mangled arm covered by a white fabric with an artistic rendering of a snapping turtle woven into the warp and weft. His head was back, expression thoughtful, as he stated, "It has been a long time since such a young man has walked among us. Do we need any more proof of White Bird's abilities? Have we not all seen the wealth that has spread among us from the north over the last couple of days? Do we need to remind ourselves that this young man killed one of the Swamp People's raiders, and took another alive? Have we not heard his thoughtful words, spoken as if from the lips of his departed uncle?" Mud Stalker smiled when he met White Bird's eyes. "It is, therefore, my pleasure, as Speaker of Snapping Turtle Clan, to cast the majority vote in accepting White Bird to this Council."

He stepped forward, offering his left hand to White Bird, saying, "We have often been adversaries, White Bird. Now, with this gesture, I welcome you as my friend, and offer my clan's and this Council's most sincere support."

Don't do this thing, Brother! The words boomed

through Mud Puppy's head, but he couldn't make himself stand, couldn't make himself shout them out for the world to hear. Instead, he seemed as impotent as a cooking clay, watching with a kind of mute horror.

White Bird sealed his fate as he rose to take Mud Stalker's hand in both of his, and said, "I thank you, Speaker. I am honored and will do my best to serve my people and this Council."

Since Mud Stalker held the floor, White Bird reseated himself next to Wing Heart.

Across the distance, Mud Puppy could see his mother's expression—a look of satisfaction that seemed to radiate from the center of her souls. But when he looked deeply into her eyes he saw an unfamiliar bitterness, like a clay pot stressed beyond its limits.

It is short-lived, Mother. Enjoy this day while it lasts. You are lost...we are lost.

Mud Stalker raised his good arm high. "Not only does Snapping Turtle Clan vote to accept this new Speaker to the Council, but it is with pleasure that we announce to all that he is promised to marry two sisters from my own lineage."

Mud Puppy watched the various expressions, curious that only Thunder Tail and Stone Talon appeared surprised.

"They play a devious game," Masked Owl's voice echoed in Mud Puppy's head. *"Like a snake swallowing its own tail, it shall consume them in the end."*

"Tomorrow, White Bird shall be joined with Pine Drop and Night Rain." Mud Stalker raised his good hand, palm up in a gesture of satisfaction. "And in further demonstration of the faith that Snapping Turtle

Clan has in Owl Clan's leadership, we make this marriage in perpetuity."

That brought looks of astonishment to everyone's faces except Wing Heart's. Even Clay Fat appeared to be stunned.

"You what?" Cane Frog cried, blinking her one white eye.

"Should anything happen to White Bird," Mud Stalker continued, "the sisters shall go to White Bird's brother. An uninterrupted alliance between our clans."

"You mean...they would go to Mud Puppy?" Clay Fat cried incredulously.

"No!" Mud Puppy lurched to his feet. In the sudden silence, he was aware of all eyes turning his direction, seeking him out.

In a blind panic, he turned on his heel, almost bowling Little Needle over in his horrified flight. Careening off people, he broke free and sprinted toward the Bird's Head and the dark safety of the summit.

It was all going wrong. This night would lead to a future he wanted to refuse with all of his heart. "Please, Masked Owl? Make it go away! Leave it the way it was. *Please?"*

White Bird stretched, blinking himself awake. Morning light cast a blue shaft through the doorway to illuminate the inside of his mother's house. The central fire still smoldered, smoke rising to collect in a dusky haze that filled the low roof just above his bed. From the angle of the sun entering the door, he knew it was still early. He should have been dead tired. It couldn't have been two hands of time past since he'd crawled into bed, his stomach bloated from the feasts he'd attended. After the breaking of the Council, he and his mother had made the rounds, walking from clan ground to clan ground, shaking· hands, eating what was offered, and accepting gifts and accolades wherever they passed.

The worst jolt had come when he finally faced Spring Cypress. The broken look in her eyes had wounded his souls as had nothing he had ever experienced.

"You want this?" she had asked in a quavering voice, her eyes searching his, desperate for any hint of negation.

"I must."

She surprised him with the rapidity in which she pivoted on a heel and raced off into the night. That momentary glimpse of the betrayal she had felt stung the space between his souls.

How do I ever make it up to her? The question rolled around the inside of his head as he studied the smoke-filled rafters. *What are the clans up to?* Even in the glow of his success he could feel the net cast about him, unseen hands ready to draw it tight. His mother's role was apparent enough. Her single purpose in life was to be the Clan Elder. From the time he had been a small boy he had understood that she would do anything, sacrifice anything, to maintain that position. And were she ever to be stripped of that duty? What then?

He shuddered at the thought, then glanced over to where she slept under a thin deerskin robe. Even in the softly filtered morning light her lined face betrayed its age. Her mouth hung open, and he could see missing molars in the back. Deep wrinkles surrounded her sagging breast, and loose skin had folded around her armpits. Tyrant that she was when awake, in sleep she looked pitifully vulnerable.

She couldn't stand it if she weren't Clan Elder. Relieve her of the tide, and she would destroy herself rather than accept a lesser role.

For the moment, he was unsure what to think about that. It all had been placed on his shoulders—all of her dreams and aspirations—as he had always known it would be.

Am I good enough? Strong enough? Can I meet all these expectations?

"We need to talk." The soft voice caught him by surprise. Startled, he could just make out Mud Puppy's form where it sat in the half darkness behind the shaft of morning light.

"Mud Puppy?"

"Not here."

"But I—"

"Come." Mud Puppy stood, allowing the thin fabric blanket to fall from his skinny shoulders. Without another glance at White Bird, he stepped into the shaft of sunlight and ducked out into the morning.

Swinging his legs over the bed poles, White Bird got to his feet, checked to make sure his breechcloth was hanging straight, and ducked out into the cool dawn. Mud Puppy stood awkwardly several steps from the door, his vacant gaze fixed on the blackened ring of ash that marked Uncle Cloud Heron's house site. Fragments of gray-white bone could still be seen among the smoldering ashes, a reminder that their uncle's Dream Soul was still present, watching.

"What is it? What did you want?" White Bird asked, irritably unnerved by Mud Puppy's manner.

"What are you going to do with that sack of goosefoot seeds you brought from the north?"

The question caught him by surprise. "Plant them. Why?"

"I would ask you the same question, Brother." Mud Puppy slid his haunted eyes toward White Bird. Fear glistened behind the glassy brown depths.

Shaking off misgivings the way he would cold rain water, White Bird stiffened his back. "To grow them, my silly young brother. When I was up in the north I discovered that the Wolf People grow goosefoot. They do it on purpose, not just nurturing stands of the plants the way we do, but they actually plant the best seeds to grow. They take special care of these fields, keeping out the grasshoppers and birds. The end result is that they have made bigger seeds, Brother. The advantage to these bigger seeds is a larger harvest per plant. Unlike leaving Sun Town to travel around to different places... uh, Ground Cherry Camp, for example, we can grow these bigger and better plants here, right around Sun Town. If we choose nothing but the best plants to replant, over the years we will have larger and larger harvests. Do you see what I'm after? We won't have to worry so much, or travel so far in the poor years, or when the flood isn't as beneficent as it is this spring. By storing what's left over, bellies won't be so thin during the hard times."

If anything, the haunted look had deepened in Mud Puppy's eyes. "Don't do this thing."

"What do you mean, don't?" White Bird crossed his arms.

"Don't plant the seeds. Make a feast for everyone instead." Mud Puppy's voice sounded as if from far away. "If you feed them to the People, it will be all right."

"What? What will be all right? You're sounding like you've been hit in the head! You expect me to give up on the seeds? Of all the things I brought from the north, Brother, they are the most important! Why do you think I haven't given any away? Why do you think I've ignored them? It's to show people. I'm going to plant them within the next couple of days. When I harvest them from the earth right there"—he pointed at the rich black soil near the bottom of the borrow pit—"I am going to make everyone understand."

"Please don't."

White Bird shook his head. "I swear, you're half-witted. What's wrong with you? Stop being a child. You are ready to become a man, but you act more like a boy than that pesky Little Needle—and he's winters younger than you are."

"Why can't you let this idea go?"

"Because it is better for the People, better for our clan. When they understand, everyone will look up to us."

"He'll kill you." Mud Puppy's voice had dropped to a whisper, his eyes shifting back to the burned house.

"Who? You can't mean Mud Stalker? He's come over to our side, Brother. We've beaten him. Forced him to make an incredible deal to gain our patronage. He is *obligating* Snapping Turtle Clan to us. Don't you understand what that means? We're the preeminent clan in all the world!"

"If you defy his warning, he'll kill you."

White Bird narrowed his eyes. "Who?"

"Masked Owl."

"Oh, Snakes take us! How can you be so stupid and still be my brother? Today I am marrying Pine Drop and her sister, Night Rain. Name another man of my age to make such a match."

"If you do this, I will be stuck with them. I don't know if I can turn them. They are controlled by their uncle."

"You?" The tone in the boy's voice left him half-hysterical. "You only inherit them if I die!"

"You will," Mud Puppy replied woodenly, "if you don't destroy those seeds."

"Back to the seeds again." White Bird slapped his hands angrily against his legs. "Just why are you so insistent? Do you think they're poisoned, is that what this is about? They're just *seeds!*"

Mud Puppy stared miserably at the few fingers of blue smoke still rising from Uncle Cloud Heron's. "They are the future," he whispered.

"Which is why I'm planting them." A thought crossed White Bird's souls. "Wait a minute. Who put you up to this? Yellow Spider? One of the Wolf Traders? They are the only ones who know the importance of the seeds." He fit the pieces together. "No, they wouldn't have an objection, but if they had told someone else, someone in the other clans who would do anything to keep us from gaining even more influence and position." That could be anyone. He grasped Mud Puppy by the shoulder, spinning him so that he could stare into those large, haunted eyes. "Who, Mud Puppy? Tell me, or I'll whip you to within an inch of your life."

Mud Puppy swallowed hard, his eyes like glistening pools. *"He* did."

"He? He who?"

"Masked Owl. In a Dream."

White Bird shook the boy again, feeling his thin bones slipping under his skin. "Masked Owl...in a Dream. You're telling me that because you had a nightmare, I am supposed to give up my seeds? Surrender the future of my people and clan?"

Mud Puppy nodded miserably, flinching at the pain caused by White Bird's strong grip.

Snakes! The fool believes it! "It was a dream, Mud Puppy." He shoved him away. "Go on. Get away from here. I have important things to see to. I'm getting married today. I have new obligations. I'm Speaker now. I can't take up my time with your foolishness." With those words he strode off, needing to relieve himself before he put the rest of his day in order.

The glance he cast back over his shoulder revealed Mud Puppy, fingers absently prodding his shoulder where White Bird had shaken him. His haunted eyes were fixed on the smoking house remains again, and he had his head cocked, as if listening to someone he could barely hear.

Nonsense, all of it.

So, what am I going to do with you? "Mud Puppy you are going to be a burden in my life until the day they burn my bones!"

Chapter Fifteen

A gentle shower fell as Mud Puppy and Little Needle stood in the crowd and watched White Bird move his possessions into the snug mud-walled house he would share with his new wives. The dwelling lay three houses down on the third ridge in Snapping Turtle's Clan grounds. Unlike the others, it was new: the thatch still tawny, the walls freshly daubed with mud. A darker ring of charcoal-stained soil could be seen where Pine Drop's old house had been burned after her husband, Blue Feather's, death.

The two sisters, Pine Drop and Night Rain, looked like each other. Both were attractive, round-faced, with delicate noses, long glistening black hair, and uneasy white-toothed smiles. As a widow, Pine Drop had dressed in a matron's kirtle. She wore all of her finery, layers of beaded necklaces and colored feathers. In contrast, Night Rain wore a virgin's skirt with knotted fringes. She didn't have as many necklaces, but as Elder Back Scratch's granddaughter, she was still opulently turned out for the occasion. Their skin had been lightly slathered with a rose-scented bear grease. White magnolia flowers were pinned in their hair, and garlands of redbud had been placed around their necks.

Something about the Snapping Turtle Clan Speaker reminded Mud Puppy of a raccoon fishing in a shallow puddle full of crawfish. That smug assurance cast an uneasy shadow on his thoughts. Elder Back Scratch, looking incredibly ancient and frail, stood to one side, eyes gleaming with anticipation. But for what? Mud Puppy could swear that a glint of triumph lay behind Sweet Root's eyes as she watched White Bird take his place before her daughters.

In front of them, Wing Heart held herself erect, her absent eyes on her son as he strode confidently forward. Mud Puppy kept shooting glances at her. Something about his mother worried him. Her posture, the tone of her muscles, that downcast expression, sent unease creeping along his bones.

The women ceremonially greeted White Bird at the doorway of their house. The traditional offerings of baked fish, sweet honeysuckle, and dried wild squash were borne before them on wooden platters. Neither of them looked happy as White Bird lowered his fabric bag of possessions and took the wooden platter in his muscular brown hands. Unlike the women he was calm, in possession of the moment, aware of the gathered crowd and the importance of the event.

"Two wives?" Little Needle asked. "Who has ever heard of such a thing for someone as young as White Bird? You must be very proud."

"He has taken the path," Mud Puppy said sadly. "I cannot call him back."

"You sound as if he's dying instead of becoming the most glorious Speaker in memory," Little Needle muttered. "What's wrong with you? Ever since you went up on the Bird's Head, you've been flighty—like a duck hit too many times in the head. All you do is flap and quack."

"Am I your friend?" Mud Puppy asked suddenly.

"Of course, you silly fool." Little Needle crossed his arms. "But I don't know why. Even though you're older than I am, people still make fun of me for spending time with you."

"I am going to need friends."

"Stop being morose. You'd think you were swimming with rocks around your neck rather than becoming the second most powerful man in your clan. If anything happens to him, those are going to be your wives! I've heard that you will be voted into the Council. It's unheard of. You should be Dreaming about the future, about what to do if anything ever happens to White Bird."

Mud Puppy bit his lip as his brother received the offerings of food and turned, facing the watching people. He raised the wooden plate that bore his first meal as a married man. "By accepting this meal I tie my life with that of Pine Drop and Night Rain, daughters of Sweet Root, who is the daughter of the great Clan Elder, Back Scratch. My clan is now their clan, their clan is now mine. I accept these women as my wives, to share with equally, to comfort and care for."

Pine Drop and Night Rain, hands held demurely before them, cried out in unison, "We accept this man, White Bird, of the Owl Clan, as our husband. In doing this, we bind ourselves to him and to his clan. Let it be known among all people that we are married."

"Let it be known!" Mud Stalker called from where he stood to one side.

"Let it be known!" Wing Heart absently shouted from the other.

"Let it be known!" the gathered people shouted, smiling and slapping each other on the back.

Escape! The sudden desperate urge seized Mud Puppy. He turned and slipped away through the gathered ranks. Ducking behind a house, he made his way down the long curving ridge until the line of houses hid him from view. Cutting across to the steep bank, he let himself down to the water and looked north. From the canoe landing, he could see a slim boat putting out onto the lake. Despite the distance, he recognized that lonely occupant: Spring Cypress. She didn't look happy.

But then, perhaps she, too, could guess what was about to happen.

Jaguar Hide squinted as the morning sunlight burned white atop the mist rising from the still water. He paddled slowly through the boles of trees and out into open water. Across the rippling brown surface he could see a patch of greenery—an ancient and abandoned levee that protruded from the brackish waters. This was the place that old Long Mad, while fishing, had caught a glimpse of the girl. Here amid the vines and water oaks his people had periodically camped or stopped just long enough to attend to any activities that required dry land.

With relief he passed into the shadow of the trees again and aimed the bow of his dugout canoe toward the shallow bank. As it slid onto the sandy ground, he stepped out and looked around before replacing his paddle with his atlatl and darts. A thousand birds called in the trees, and the faint hum of insects laced the air. The gleaming scales of a small snake shone as the reptile whisked itself into the safety of thicker vegetation. A dragonfly darted past his ear. Muscadine grape hung like thick brown strands of web.

He stepped through the lush matting of spring growth and sniffed. Ever so faint, he caught the whiff of smoke. On silent feet he wound his way through the moss-patterned boles of trees, ducking vines, spiderwebs, and hanging moss until he found her. She lay in a clearing that consisted of little more than crushed grass, strawberry and chickweed. Her fire pit—a rude hole in the ground—still smoldered. Wood too wet to burn traced lazy spirals of blue smoke into the air.

Though she was asleep, faint whimpering broke her cracked lips. His gaze traveled down her naked body, reading the welts and bruises through the stippling of insect bites. Scabs crisscrossed her skin and her hair was matted with filth.

Are you there, Niece? Or have your souls left this poor body in search of a more pleasant, place to live? His heart went hollow, and an empty heaviness sucked at his souls. Blessed Panther, what had she gotten herself into?

He sighed, hunkering down on his knees to probe at the fire. Little help lay there. The wood she'd managed to find had no doubt been soaked through and through. He found chewed frog bones, probably the only food she'd managed to scrounge. A paddle lay beside her, the workmanship unfamiliar to him, though he suspected it was something she'd stumbled across on her errant adventure.

He seated himself and waited, arms across his knees. Perhaps a hand of time passed before she stirred, shifted, and cried out. Whatever nightmare had been winding through her dreams startled her awake. Her eyes flickered and batted, unfocused, before she moaned and twisted on the flattened leaves of her bed.

When she did open her eyes for good they locked on his. He saw her incomprehension, and then fear, shame, and self-loathing reflected as they came tumbling out of her souls. A strangled sob choked in her throat, and she scrambled into a sitting position.

"Old Long Mad thought he saw you out here," Jaguar Hide said amiably. "People have been worried. I have been worried. Your idiot brother, Striped Dart, of course, can't seem to fathom what the trouble might be, for obviously you've just run off to explore the delights that a canoe load of strong young men could introduce you to. Or so he seems to think."

She just stared at him as if he was a corpse freshly risen from the dead.

"Myself," he continued unhurriedly, "I've come to the conclusion that you and your companions fared poorly on your raid against the Sun People. The gods and spirits that oversee war are capricious beasts at best. Snakes, don't I of all people know that?" He cocked his head, pausing. "War is such a chancy thing. When I was young I had a great deal of good fortune at war. Some would like us to believe that the gods, Sky Beings, and Earth Beings grant us success or *blind the enemy's eyes* or some such rot."

He chuckled at the notion, hand tracing an easy gesture in the air. "Me, I can tell you that it is just happenstance. Like casting gaming pieces. Sometimes one pattern comes up, sometimes another. I no longer believe in the intervention of spirits, Dreams, or sacrifice." He paused. "In all my years I have come to the conclusion that other ways of harming the enemy must be embraced. Something that doesn't entail chance events."

Her jaw trembled as she hugged her naked flesh and curled in on herself.

"Whatever happened," he continued, "I assume that you blame yourself. I can tell you not to, but you will do as your souls demand. Like your body, they, too, are wounded and need time to heal."

Her glazed eyes were fixed on some terrible vision hidden deep inside her.

"From the bruises on your wrists and ankles I see they captured you. You've taken a bad beating." He couldn't see blood or other evidence that she'd been raped. "How in the name of the Sky Beings did you manage to escape?"

Her frightened eyes widened, and her voice seemed locked in her throat. He could see her lungs working, as though her breath couldn't catch up with her heart.

"It is all right," he told her softly and opened his arms. "Come over here. Let me hold you. Together, you and I, we will make this right."

Everything depended on how strong she was, whether she was a survivor or a broken captive. For long moments he waited, his eyes willing strength into her.

His arms had grown heavy before she made the slightest movement.

She might have been an old woman, so slowly did she begin. When the tangled flotsam of her emotions finally let loose, she rushed him. He folded her into his arms, and she burst into tears. While sobs knotted her body, he held her, humming gently as he rocked her back and forth.

Mud Puppy was acutely aware of the giant barred owl that watched him with moist brown eyes. The huge bird perched on a branch three arm's lengths above where Mud Puppy's canoe floated on limpid brown water. The flooded backswamp steamed in the hot afternoon, columns of insects wavering as they drifted aimlessly in the still air. The faint hum of their wings echoed over the smooth surface.

Despite the owl, Mud Puppy lay stretched the length of his canoe, chin resting on the bow. He kept his attention focused on the alligator who floated no more than an arm's length away. The big bull had caught Mud Puppy's attention by roaring earlier. After paddling as close as he dared, Mud Puppy had let the canoe drift toward the bull.

Two eyes, like glistening golden brown stones, stared across the glassy surface with pupils in vertical black slits. The nostrils protruded in a rounded hump. Regular lines of scutes made dimples in the water where the big beast's back lay submerged. The bull was old, his muzzle scarred. Mud Puppy guessed that he had to measure twice the length of a tall man. Some would say he was being foolish to drift his canoe so close to a swamp giant like this. Perhaps, but so long as he didn't move, didn't allow his scent to taint the water, he would be all right.

Hello, big fellow. He projected the words with his mind, unwilling to break the spell by speaking. He stared into the single slitted eye facing him. The soul behind that alien eye spoke of eternal patience and age. That same eye might have watched the Creation and absorbed all of the changes that had befallen the Earth since. It was said that Alligator knew of secret things: of poisons and medicines, of ways to breathe underwater, and the workings of debilitating illness and miraculous cures. The greatest secret that Alligator possessed was the knowledge of passages and tunnels that led into the Underworld. Alligator was the messenger. People had seen him slip up to grab people, thrashing them in the water before diving, carrying them down into the murky black depths. All that remained was a trail of bubbles that finally ceased to pop on the opaque surface. They left silence behind.

The bodies were never seen again, but often the souls of those Alligator had taken spoke to the Serpents when they entered trances and traveled to the Underworld. That was how people learned of Alligator's secrets.

As Mud Puppy watched, he noticed minnows flicking along the line of the alligator's jaw. The little fish were nibbling at the scales, tails wiggling as they appeared, then vanished into the murky water. The sight amazed him. A lesson lay in that. Delicate little fish, dancing back and forth, safe in the presence of the most terrifying of beasts. How could they, of all creatures, pass with immunity?

Because they are small, unnoticed, and unimportant. He considered that as he stared into the impenetrable eye. What was he supposed to learn? How did he use a lesson like that?

"Mud Puppy?" an accented voice called, breaking his concentration.

"Shush!" Mud Puppy carefully lifted his chin high enough to answer. "Stay where you are."

The alligator seemed not to have heard. No change of expression could be seen in that black slit of an eye. Not a ripple moved in the still water. Alligator remained oblivious, the little fish playing around his head. Was he Dreaming? Floating and Dreaming, seeing things of Power and magic and joy?

Mud Puppy himself had lain in the warm water, his body buoyed while sunshine beat down in radiant warmth. For him, too, it had been dreamlike, sharing a oneness with the swamp around him. Sound had been dulled, turned inside of him. The faint beating of his heart, his slow breathing, and the water stroking his skin, had left him in a shallow state of bliss. Was that how Alligator lived, his world muted by the pressing warmth of the water?

"Snakes! That's the biggest alligator I've ever seen! What are you doing? Trying to get killed?" the accented voice cried from somewhere behind Mud Puppy.

"Stay back," Mud Puppy replied carefully. "Come no closer. We were just talking, he and I." Reluctantly Mud Puppy gathered himself, inching upward and back. As his silhouette began to emerge over the gunwales, Mud Puppy said, "Go away, Grandfather. I mean you no harm."

With a flip of his tail, the big alligator eased ahead, a faint V drifting back from his nose and eyes. Water rippled along the protruding scutes in his back.

"I don't believe it." The accented voice sounded stunned.

Mud Puppy turned to see Hazel Fire and Two Wolves, the Traders, watching from one of their sturdy canoes. Both had darts nocked in atlatls, ready to cast. Each had a bright expression of wonder in his eyes as their canoe drifted slowly to one side. Mud Puppy looked back in time to see the big alligator drift into a duckweed-filled cove and come to rest, eternally one with the swamp.

"What are you doing out here?" he asked when he looked back. They were still perched, their darts held at the ready.

"We went fishing." Hazel Fire lowered his atlatl and dart, swallowing hard. "We've been out here for hours, just going around in circles. How do you find your way in this mess?" He indicated the endless trees rising from the still water.

"My people just know." Mud Puppy shrugged and pointed. "That way is home."

"That alligator"—Two Wolves indicated the great reptile with his darts—"you talked to him? You speak his language?"

"He was Dreaming," Mud Puppy said. "Seeing between the worlds." Movement caught his eye as a broad-banded water snake slipped from a tupelo root and swam in gentle undulations to a foam-caked pile of flotsam. There it lay quietly, in wait for whatever might chance by. "He was teaching me things." Why he said that, he wasn't sure, but the words might have been a bee sting given the way they jolted the Wolf Traders. Both of the young men looked as if they had been stabbed by an unseen hand.

For a long moment, an uneasy silence passed, and Mud Puppy couldn't force himself to look at them. In the end, he asked quietly. "Please don't tell people I said that."

"We won't," Hazel Fire agreed, and a crooked smile crossed his lips. "If you won't tell anybody we're lost out here."

"It is done." Mud Puppy dipped his paddle and coasted his canoe toward theirs. "To seal our deal, I have something for you." He reached into his small belt pouch and drew out a red jasper carving he had made, the image of a small potbellied owl with a tilted head. "I just finished this. He's a friend of mine. I call him Masked Owl." Mud Puppy reached across and dropped the fetish into Hazel Fire's open hand.

The Trader lifted the little owl, studying it with a practiced eye. "You are very good at carving, Mud Puppy. Look at this! Such fine detail. What is this around the owl's eyes?"

"That's a mask."

"I see." Hazel Fire glanced suspiciously at Mud Puppy, then back at the alligator where it hid in the duckweed. "Along with alligators, do you talk with Masked Owls?"

Mud Puppy considered the question. Did he dare trust these outsiders? Men from a place he could barely conceive of?

"Do not worry," Two Wolves said, reading his

unease. "Your brother is our kinsman. Among our people, that binds us. What you tell us, remains among the three of us, and *only* among us." He indicated the gleaming stone owl in Hazel Fire's hand. "Our trust is even bound by a gift. There is Power in that."

"Masked Owl comes to me in my Dreams. He is helping me to find a Spirit Helper. There is a chance that Salamander might come to me."

"Salamander?" Two Wolves asked curiously, but there was no derision behind his question.

"He has special Powers, including the ability to make himself unseen."

Hazel Fire resettled himself in his canoe, laying his atlatl and darts to the side. "Why do I have the suspicion that your brother isn't the only outstanding member of your family?"

"What are you talking about?" Two Wolves asked his friend.

"Mud Puppy, here"—he indicated with a casual hand—"is more than I think most people understand. It was his vision that sent us south to meet the Swamp Panther raiders. Now we find him talking to an alligator and making Power alliances." He held up the Masked Owl charm to emphasize his point. "Yet his own people do not take him seriously."

The talk, along with Hazel Fire's intense scrutiny, made Mud Puppy's gut feel like ants were crawling around his insides.

"Two brothers," Two Wolves mused, "two different strengths. But we are outsiders."

"And perhaps less blinded by our prejudices," Hazel Fire agreed, raising the little carved owl. "Mud

Puppy, consider us your friends, no, more than that, your kin."

A sudden idea slipped into Mud Puppy's souls. "Will you do something for me?"

"If it is within our ability, Mud Puppy." Hazel Fire studied the little red owl thoughtfully.

"Tell my brother that he must not plant his seeds."

A wry smile crossed Two Wolves's lips. "I think, married as he is to two new women, he is already planting his seed, young kinsman."

"I don't mean that. I mean the goosefoot seeds he brought down from the north. Tell him not to plant those seeds."

Hazel Fire cocked his head. "Why? He has told us his plan for them. We, ourselves, plant the seeds. Among my people it provides another source of food for the winter. Ask your brother, he ate enough of it last winter to know the advantages."

"It's not me." Mud Puppy hesitated, cringing. Did he dare share this secret?

"If it is not you, then who, Mud Puppy?" Hazel Fire's expression sharpened. "White Bird is a relative through marriage, a member of my family, stranger though he might be. We have shared many things over the last year. His child lives in my sister. If there is some threat to White Bird, I would know of it."

"It came from a Dream," he hedged. "Someone in the Dream told me that my brother would be killed if he planted those seeds. That it is not a thing for my people. Power doesn't want it to happen here."

"Want what to happen here?" Two Wolves looked confused.

"People to grow their own plants." Mud Puppy

made a helpless gesture. "I tried to tell White Bird. He thinks I'm being a silly child and won't listen. He has turned blind. His ability to see is overcome by his new status and all the attention people are heaping upon him. He thinks he cannot be defeated."

"Defeated by whom?" Two Wolves asked. "If there is a threat, we will protect him. He has earned our loyalty through his service to us, our clans, and our people, let alone to yours."

"By Power," Mud Puppy said miserably. "Masked Owl has told me that he mustn't plant those seeds. If he does, he will change the world. Masked Owl doesn't want that to happen. He wants us to stay..." Mud Puppy clamped his mouth, miserably aware that he'd just said too much.

Hazel Fire's thoughtful eyes had narrowed, his face pensive.

"All this came out of a Dream?" Two Wolves asked incredulously. "Why should White Bird believe your Dream, and not his own?"

Mud Puppy felt a sinking in his chest. He must have been sun-touched to have confided in these strangers from the far north.

"Wait," Hazel Fire's low voice intruded. Then he spoke in the Wolf People's tongue, the alien words hammering on Mud Puppy's ears like hail. Whatever it was, it must have been so demeaning they didn't dare talk in a language he would understand.

"Forget I said anything." Mud Puppy picked up his paddle, refusing to meet their eyes. "I shall tell no one that you were lost. The Masked Owl seals that bargain." He turned his canoe. "Come, it is this way home."

"I said, wait." Hazel Fire lifted a hand, those foreign eyes pensive. "You really believe this, don't you?"

Mud Puppy said nothing, but his eyes must have betrayed him, for Hazel Fire said, "We believe you, Mud Puppy." He gestured toward the alligator. "It takes a special person to talk to the likes of him. Your brother has been away from you for over a year. Perhaps he does not understand the changes in his little brother."

"Changes?" Mud Puppy was puzzled.

Hazel Fire smiled. "It took me a while to understand that my little sister had become a woman. It wasn't until I saw your brother's child growing in her womb that I knew. Two Wolves and I, we will speak to your brother. I don't know that we can change his mind, but we are willing to try."

Mud Puppy nodded, a sudden feeling of relief building in his belly. "I thank you. For this, I shall always be in your debt."

"Then we are brothers," Hazel Fire added. "May our bonds strengthen over time despite the distance that will separate us."

"May it be so," Mud Puppy agreed. "Come, let us go. There may not be much time."

Watch For Book Two:
The Masked Owl

New York Times bestselling authors W. Michael Gear and Kathleen O'Neal Gear weave a spellbinding tale of power, betrayal, and survival in Ancient America.

In a world where every alliance is a double-edged sword, the Owl Clan's future hangs by a thread. What should have been a moment of triumph for White Bird and Owl Clan turns to tragedy, forcing young Mud Puppy—mocked as the city's fool —into a role he never expected. Transformed into Salamander and thrust into the center of power, he must navigate a web of deceit spun by the cunning Mud Stalker, the Speaker of Snapping Turtle Clan.

Rushed through his brother's death rites, Salamander marries Pine Drop and Night Rain, his brother's widows, and steps into the Owl Clan Speaker's role. His own mother's descent into madness further weakens their grip on power. Meanwhile, a new threat emerges. Jaguar Hide, the war chief of the Swamp Panther people, seeks peace, offering riches and a marriage pact to strengthen Owl Clan's hand. But his niece, Anhinga, has no intention of peace—only revenge. Coiling like a serpent within Owl Clan, she waits for the perfect moment to strike.

As spirits manipulate from the shadows and enemies gather like storm clouds, Salamander must decide who to trust— before everything crumbles around him.

Will Salamander rise to save Owl Clan, or will the web of betrayal destroy them all?

AVAILABLE DECEMBER 2024

About W. Michael Gear

W. Michael Gear is a *New York Times, USA Today,* and international bestselling author of sixty novels. With close to eighteen million copies of his books in print worldwide, his work has been translated into twenty-nine languages.

Gear has been inducted into the Western Writers Hall of Fame and the Colorado Authors' Hall of Fame —as well as won the Owen Wister Award, the Golden Spur Award, and the International Book Award for both Science Fiction and Action Suspense Fiction. He is also the recipient of the Frank Waters Award for lifetime contributions to Western writing.

Gear's work, inspired by anthropology and archaeology, is multilayered and has been called compelling, insidiously realistic, and masterful. Currently, he lives in northwestern Wyoming with his award-winning wife and co-author, Kathleen O'Neal Gear, and a charming sheltie named, Jake.

About Kathleen O'Neal Gear

Kathleen O'Neal Gear is a *New York Times* bestselling author of fifty-seven books and a national award-winning archaeologist. The U.S. Department of the Interior has awarded her two Special Achievement awards for outstanding management of America's cultural resources.

In 2015 the United States Congress honored her with a Certificate of Special Congressional Recognition, and the California State Legislature passed Joint Member Resolution #117 saying, "The contributions of Kathleen O'Neal Gear to the fields of history, archaeology, and writing have been invaluable..."

In 2021 she received the Owen Wister Award for lifetime contributions to western literature, and in 2023 received the Frank Waters Award for "a body of work representing excellence in writing and storytelling that embodies the spirit of the American West."

Bibliography

Alden, Peter. 1999. *National Audubon Society Field Guild to the Southeastern States*. Alfred A. Knopf. New York, New York.

Amos, William H., and Stephen H. Amos. 1985. *The Audubon Society Nature Guides Atlantic & Gulf Coasts*. Alfred A. Knopf. New York, New York.

Brecher, K. S., and W. G. Haag. 1980. "The Poverty Point Octagon: World's Largest Prehistoric Solstice Marker?" *Bulletin of the American Astronomical Society*. 12:886.

Brian, Jeffrey P. 1988. *Tunica Archaeology*. Papers of the Peabody Museum of Archaeology and Ethnology No. 78. Harvard University Press. Cambridge, Massachusetts.

Brown, Calvin S. 1992. *Archaeology of Mississippi*. Reprint of 1926 edition. University Press of Mississippi. Jackson, Mississippi.

Bruseth J. E. 1980. "Intrasite Structure at the Clairborne Site." *Louisiana Archaeology*. 6:283-318.

Byrd, Kathleen M. 1991. *The Poverty Point Culture: Local Manifestations, Subsistence Practices, and Trade Networks*. Geoscience and Man 29. Louisiana State University Press. Baton Rouge, Louisiana.

Coffey, Timothy. 1993. *The History and Folklore of North American Wild-flowers*. Facts on File. New York, New York.

Connaway, John M., Samuel O. McGahey, and Clarence Webb. 1977. *Teoc Creek, a Poverty Point Site in Carroll County, Mississippi*. Archaeological Report No. 3. Mississippi Department of Archives and History. Jackson, Mississippi.

Duncan, Wilbur H. and Marion B. Duncan. 1988. *Trees of the Southeastern United States*. University of Georgia Press. Athens, Georgia.

Fagan, Brian M. 2000. *Ancient North America*, 3rd ed. Thames and Hudson. New York, New York.

Foster, Steven, and James A. Duke. 1990. *Eastern/Central Medicinal Plants*. Peterson Field Guides. Houghton Mifflin Company. Boston, Massachusetts.

Fritz, Gayle J. 1997. "A Three-Thousand-Year-Old Cache of Crop Seeds from Marble Bluff, Arkansas." In *People, Plants, and Land-*

scapes: Studies in Paleoethnobotany, edited by Kristen J. Gremillion, pp. 42-62. University of Alabama Press. Tuscaloosa, Alabama.

Gibson, John L. 1980. "Speculations on the Origin and Development of Poverty Point Culture." *Louisiana Archaeology.* 6: 319-348.

--. 1987. "The Poverty Point Earthworks Reconsidered." *Mississippi Archaeology.* 22(2): 14—31.

--. 1991. "Catahoula—An Amphibious Poverty Point Manifestation in Eastern Louisiana." In *The Poverty Point Culture: Local Manifestations, Subsistence Practices, and Trade Networks,* edited by Kathleen M. Byrd, pp. 61-88. Geoscience and Man No. 29. Louisiana State University Press. Baton Rouge, Louisiana.

--. 1996. "Religion of the Rings: Poverty Point Iconography and Ceremonialism." In *Mounds, Embankments, and Ceremonialism in the Midsouth,* edited by R. C. Main-fort and R. Wailing, pp. 1-6. Arkansas Archaeological Survey Research Series No. 46. Arkansas Archaeological Survey. Fayetteville, Arkansas.

--. 1998. "Broken Circles, Owl Monsters, and Black Earth Midden: Separating Sacred and Secular at Poverty Point." In *Ancient Earthen Enclosures of the Eastern Woodlands,* edited by R. C. Mainfort and L. P. Sullivan. University Press of Florida. Gainesville, Florida.

--. 1999. *Poverty Point: A Terminal Archaic Culture in the Lower Mississippi Valley.* 2nd ed. Anthropological Study 7. Department of Culture, Recreation, and Tourism. Louisiana Archaeological Survey and Antiquities Commission. Baton Rouge, Louisiana.

--. 2000. *The Ancient Mounds of Poverty Point: Place of Rings.* University Press of Florida. Gainesville, Florida.

Gibson, J. L., and J. W. Saunders. 1993. "The Death of the South Sixth Ridge at Poverty Point: What Can We Still Do?" *SAA Bulletin.* 11(5): 7-9.

Haag, W. G. 1990. "Excavations at the Poverty Point Site: 1972-1975." *Louisiana Archaeology.* 13:1-36.

Hillman, M. M. 1990. "1985 Test Excavations of the *Dock* Area of Poverty Point." *Louisiana Archaeology.* 13:1-33.

Hirth, K. G. 1978 "Interregional Trade and the Formation of Prehistoric Gateway Communities." *American Antiquity.* 43(1):35-45.

Hudson, Charles. 1976. *The Southeastern Indians.* University of Tennessee Press. Knoxville, Tennessee.

--. 1979. *Black Drink: A Native American Tea.* University of Georgia Press. Athens, Georgia.

Jackson, H. E.. 1991. "Bottomland Resources and Exploitation Strategies During the Poverty Point Period: Implications of the Archaeological Record from the J. W. Copes Site." In *The Poverty Point Culture: Local Manifestations, Subsistence Practices, and Trade Networks*, edited by Kathleen M. Byrd, pp. 131-158. Geoscience and Man 29. Louisiana State University Press. Baton Rouge, Louisiana.

--. 1991. "The Trade Fair in Hunter-Gatherer Interactions: The Role of Intersocietal Trade in the Evolution of Poverty Point Culture." In *Between Bands and States*, edited by S. A. Greg, pp. 265-286. Occasional Papers 9. Center for Archaeological Investigations, Southern Illinois University at Carbondale. Carbondale, Illinois.

Kidder, Tristram. 2002. "Mapping Poverty Point." *American Antiquity*. 67: 89-101.

Lazarus, W. C. 1958. "A Poverty Point Complex in Florida." *Florida Anthropologist*. 6(l):23-32.

Mainfort, Robert C, and L. P. Sullivan. 1998 *Ancient Earthen Enclosures of the Eastern Woodlands*. University Press of Florida. Gainesville, Florida.

McEwan, Bonnie G. 2000. *Indians of the Greater Southeast*. University Press of Florida. Gainesville, Florida.

Morgan, William N. 1999. *Precolumbian Architecture in Eastern North America*. University Press of Florida. Gainesville, Florida.

Neuman, R. W., and N. W. Hawkins. 1987. *Louisiana Prehistory*. Department of Culture, Recreation, and Tourism. Louisiana Archaeological Survey and Antiquities Commission. Anthropological Study 6, 2nd ed., revised. Baton Rouge, Louisiana.

Pearson, James L. 2002. *Shamanism and the Ancient Mind*. Altamira Press. Walnut Creek, California.

Penman, John T. 1980. *Archaeological Survey in Mississippi, 1974—1975*. Archaeological Report No. 2. Mississippi Department of Archives and History. Jackson, Mississippi.

Purrington, R. D. 1983. "Superimposed Solar Alignments at Poverty Point." *American Antiquity*. 48:157-161.

Purrington, R. D., and C. A. Child, Jr. 1989. "Poverty Point Revisited: Further Consideration of Astronomical Alignments." *Journal of the History of Astronomy*. 13: 49-60.

Sassaman, Kenneth E. 1993. *Early Pottery in the Southeast*. University of Alabama Press. Tuscaloosa, Alabama.

Schlotz, Sandra C. 1975. *Prehistoric Plies: A Structural and Comparative Analysis of Cordage, Netting, Basketry, and Fabric from*

Bibliography

Ozark Bluff Shelters. Arkansas Archaeological Survey No. 6. Arkansas Archaeological Survey. Fayette Ville, Arkansas.

Smith, Brent W. 1974. "A Preliminary Identification of Faunal Remains from the Clairborne Site." *Mississippi Archaeology.* 9: 1-7.

--. 1976. "The Late Archaic-Poverty Point Steatite Trade Network in the Lower Mississippi Valley." *Louisiana Archaeological Society Newsletter.* 3:6-10.

--. 1981. "The Late Archaic-Poverty Point Steatite Trade Network in the Lower Mississippi Valley: Some Preliminary Observations." *Florida Anthropologist.* 34: 120-125.

Smith, Bruce D. 1992. *Rivers of Change: Essays on Early Agriculture in Eastern North America.* Smithsonian Institution Press. Washington, DC.

Swanton, John R. 1979. *The Indians of the Southeastern United States.* Reprint of the 1946 Bureau of American Ethnography Bulletin No. 137. Smithsonian Institution Press. Washington, DC.

--. 1998. *Indian Tribes of the Lower Mississippi Valley and Adjacent Coast of the Gulf of Mexico.* Dover reprint of 1911 edition. Dover Publications. Mineola, New York.

--. 2001. *Source Material for the Social and Ceremonial Life of the Choctaw Indians.* University of Alabama Press. Tuscaloosa, Alabama.

Thomas, Cyrus. 1985. *Report on the Mound Expeditions of the Bureau of Ethnography.* Reprint of the 1894 Bureau of American Ethnography No. 12. Smithsonian Institution Press. Washington, DC.

Thomas, Prentice M., and L. J. Campbell. 1978. *The Peripheries of Poverty Point.* New World Research Report of Investigation No. 12. New World Research. Pollack, Louisiana.

Tiamat, Uni M. 1994. *Herbal Abortion Handbook.* Sage-femme! Press. Peoria, Illinois.

Vogel, Virgil H.. 1970. *American Indian Medicine.* University of Oklahoma Press. Norman, Oklahoma.

Webb, Clarence H. 1968. "The Extent and Content of Poverty Point Culture." *American Antiquity.* 33:297-321.

Webb, Clarence H., and J. L. Gibson. 1982. "Studies of the Microflint Industry at the Poverty Point Site." In *Traces of Prehistory: Papers in Honor of William G. Haag,* edited by F. H. West and R. W. Neuman, pp. 85-101. Geoscience and Man 22. School of Geoscience. Louisiana State University Press. Baton Rouge, Louisiana.

--. 1970. "Intrasite Distribution of Artifacts at the Poverty Point Site, with Special Reference to Women's and Men's Activities." *Southeastern Archaeological Conference Bulletin.* 12:21-34.

--. 1982. *The Poverty Point Culture.* Geoscience and Man 17. 2nd ed., revised. Geoscience Publications, Department of Geography and Anthropology. Louisiana State University Press. Baton Rouge, Louisiana.

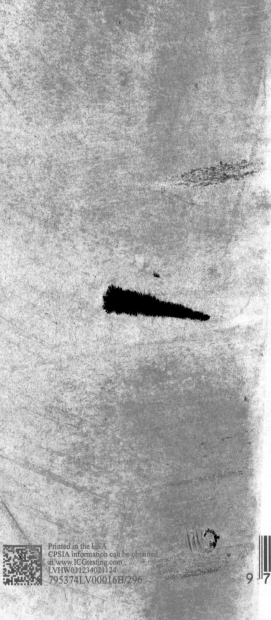

Printed in the USA
CPSIA information can be obtained
at www.ICGtesting.com
LVHW031234021124
795374LV00016B/296